KEY TO THE KINGDOM

Compiled & Edited by
Ben Thomas & D Kershaw

Also available and coming soon from Black Hare Press

DARK DRABBLES ANTHOLOGIES

WORLDS
ANGELS
MONSTERS
BEYOND
UNRAVEL
APOCALYPSE
LOVE
HATE
OCEANS
ANCIENTS

BHP WRITERS' GROUP SPECIAL EDITIONS

STORMING AREA 51
EERIE CHRISTMAS
BAD ROMANCE
TWENTY TWENTY

OTHER VOLUMES

DEEP SPACE
WHAT IF?
KEY TO THE KINGDOM
DEEP SEA
BEYOND THE REALM

Twitter: @BlackHarePress
Facebook: BlackHarePress
Website: www.BlackHarePress.com

Cover design by Dawn Burdett
Formatting by Ben Thomas

Of gold that was beaten, briefly he spake then:
"Hold thou, O Earth, now heroes no more may,
The earnings of earlmen. Lo! erst in thy bosom
Worthy men won them; war-death hath ravished,
Perilous life-bale, all my warriors,
Liegemen belovèd, who this life have forsaken,
Who hall-pleasures saw. No sword-bearer have I,
And no one to burnish the gold-plated vessel,
The high-valued beaker: my heroes are vanished.
The hardy helmet behung with gilding
Shall be reaved of its riches: the ring-cleansers slumber
Who were charged to have ready visors-for-battle,
And the burnie that bided in battle-encounter
O'er breaking of war-shields the bite of the edges
Moulds with the hero. The ring-twisted armor,
Its lord being lifeless, no longer may journey
Hanging by heroes; harp-joy is vanished,
The rapture of glee-wood, no excellent falcon
Swoops through the building, no swift-footed charger
Grindeth the gravel. A grievous destruction
No few of the world-folk widely hath scattered!"
So, woful of spirit one after all
Lamented mournfully, moaning in sadness
By day and by night, till death with its billows
Dashed on his spirit. Then the ancient dusk-scather
Found the great treasure standing all open,
He who flaming and fiery flies to the barrows,
Naked war-dragon, nightly escapeth
Encompassed with fire; men under heaven
Widely beheld him. 'Tis said that he looks for
The hoard in the earth, where old he is guarding
The heathenish treasure; he'll be nowise the better.
So three-hundred winters the waster of peoples
Held upon earth that excellent hoard-hall,
Till the forementioned earlman angered him bitterly:
The beat-plated beaker he bare to his chieftain
And fullest remission for all his remissness

Begged of his liegelord. Then the hoard was discovered,
The treasure was taken, his petition was granted
The lorn-mooded liegeman. His lord regarded
The old-work of earth-folk—'twas the earliest occasion.
When the dragon awoke, the strife was renewed there;
He snuffed 'long the stone then, stout-hearted found he
The footprint of foeman; too far had he gone
With cunning craftiness close to the head of
The fire-spewing dragon. So undoomed he may 'scape from
Anguish and exile with ease who possesseth
The favor of Heaven. The hoard-warden eagerly
Searched o'er the ground then, would meet with the person
That caused him sorrow while in slumber reclining:
Gleaming and wild he oft went round the cavern,
All of it outward; not any of earthmen
Was seen in that desert. Yet he joyed in the battle,
Rejoiced in the conflict: oft he turned to the barrow,
Sought for the gem-cup; this he soon perceived then
That some man or other had discovered the gold,
The famous folk-treasure. Not fain did the hoard-ward
Wait until evening; then the ward of the barrow
Was angry in spirit, the loathèd one wished to
Pay for the dear-valued drink-cup with fire.
Then the day was done as the dragon would have it,
He no longer would wait on the wall, but departed
Fire-impelled, flaming. Fearful the start was
To earls in the land, as it early thereafter
To their giver-of-gold was grievously ended.

Beowulf: An Anglo-Saxon Epic Poem

TABLE OF CONTENTS

CHILD OF WAR

By G. Allen Wilbanks

Since the day he was discovered as a foundling at the door of the blacksmith's shop, Burden was content to spend his life labouring at the forge in obscurity, but an invading army changed his plans; not only driving him from the only home he had ever known, but sending him directly toward the truth of who he really was.

Burden swept out the ash and debris from the forge, preparing it for another day of hard use. When the lighter waste had been cleared out, he set to work scraping and breaking away the slag that had accumulated and hardened on the brick. Master Josa would be greatly displeased if he could not properly

11

heat the forge due to Burden's failure to keep it clean. It was tedious work, although Burden did not mind the chore. He found the repetitive nature soothing and reassuring, as well as deriving pleasure from seeing noticeable improvement as a result of his labours.

Darkness still claimed the morning hour, the sun not ready to begin its daily crawl through the sky for another hour or so, but Master Josa began working very early, which meant Burden must be moving earlier still. A single lantern burned in the blacksmith's shop, and with nothing more than starlight coming in through the windows, gloom and shadow swallowed most of the room. Others might have found it difficult or impossible to work in the almost total lightlessness. Not Burden. He enjoyed the dark, and he moved with practiced ease and familiarity within his surroundings.

When the forge had been cleaned to Master Josa's standards, Burden next stocked it with coke. He dug a small depression in the middle of the hard, black fuel and laid paper, sticks, and small wooden logs which would be used to start the fire. As he stood and dusted the dark, powdery residue from his hands onto his pants, the door of the shop swung open behind him.

A wide, blocky silhouette filled the doorway. Burden turned to find Master Josa peering into the gloom, searching for him. The man was not overly tall, and years of working metal in front of a hot fire had shaped him as surely as the thousands of weapons and tools he had shaped with his powerful hands. Sloped, rounded shoulders tapered into the impressive curve of his biceps, then trailed to the corded muscle of his wide forearms. Slabs of lean flesh wrapped his barrel chest, and the thickness of his body made him appear, from a distance, to be even shorter than his actual five feet, seven inches. The tousled black hair and wild beard put his face further into shadow, but though Master Josa struggled to see past the darkness of the shop, Burden could see him clearly.

"Boy! Are you in there? I hope you're not sleeping again when we have work that needs doing."

Master Josa was the closest thing to family Burden knew. He had been left on the blacksmith's doorstep as an infant, and the man had taken him in and raised him. Despite this relationship, Josa was not a father figure. The gruff smith had made it perfectly clear to Burden while growing up that he had no time for the niceties of family or familiarity, and while he would tolerate the youth's presence in his home, it would be only as long as he continued to earn his keep.

Even the name he had given him, Burden, was a constant reminder of his status within Master Josa's life. Not that the blacksmith bothered to call him by his name on most occasions.

"I'm here," Burden replied. He scurried to the burning lantern, grabbed up a tapir from the shelf beside it and lit it. He quickly had several more lanterns glowing and shedding light through the room. "The forge is ready, sir. The shop has been swept out and your tools are laid out as you like them."

Master Josa entered his shop, working his way around the main room and throwing open each window as he reached it. The forge emitted a sweltering heat when burning that would quickly make the shop unbearable if there was no breeze to offer occasional relief. When he finished with the windows, he next stepped over to the waist-high worktable where Burden had placed his tools in order of their most frequent use. Burden knew the order by heart and could recite it in his sleep after so many years of this daily task. Josa would find no mistakes there this morning.

Master Josa picked up a small, shaping hammer from his table and tapped it against the massive iron anvil beside the forge.

"What's this? Why do you have the number five anvil in my workspace?"

"It…it was the one you were working with last night, sir," Burden stammered.

The blacksmith turned to face Burden, placing his

left fist onto his hip. In his right, he still held the small hammer. "What was I working on last night, boy?"

"Armor, sir."

"Correct. And what did I tell you I would be doing this morning?"

"You have three customers that needed shoes for their horses."

"Again, correct. So, which anvil do I need when I make shoes?"

Burden ducked his head and stared at the dirt floor. His cheeks flushed hot, and he was grateful there was still insufficient light for Master Josa to see his embarrassment.

"You use the number two. I'm sorry, sir. I'll replace it right away."

"Where are the steel billets I asked you to bring into the shop?" rumbled the blacksmith, tossing the hammer back onto the table.

Burden winced. *The billets!* He knew had forgotten something this morning, but when he couldn't remember exactly what, he had just stuck with his usual daily routine.

"I forgot, sir. They're still out back. I can bring them in as soon as I replace the anvil."

"Leave it!" snapped Master Josa. "Gods above, boy, you are as reliable as my growling bowels. At least once each day I can depend on you to take something you touch and turn it to complete shit. No!" he admonished, when Burden took a step forward toward the worktable. "I'll change out the anvils myself. Go back to the house. I left your breakfast in the kitchen, not that I'm sure you've earned it, today, but go eat. Quickly, though, and bring the billets in when you come back to the shop."

Burden nodded but made no immediate move to leave.

"What is it, boy?" asked Josa when he noticed Burden's reluctance to go.

Burden hesitated, unsure if he should speak. He had prepared a small speech as he cleaned the shop this morning, but he had also hoped that Master Josa would be in a more receptive mood. That hope had now fled out the nearest window. He almost said nothing. Before he fled back to the house however, he gathered his courage and plunged ahead.

"Master Josa, I turn sixteen today…"

"Not today," interjected Josa. "I found you sixteen years ago today in a box with no name, no note, and not so much as a tin speck to help pay for your boarding. I have no idea how old you were at the time, so don't think I'm willing to recognise today as anything more than the day I took on more responsibility than I wanted or needed."

Burden clenched his teeth and swallowed, the familiar anger rising in him. Master Josa had never raised an overly zealous hand against him in his life, however the blacksmith's casually cruel verbal treatment was almost more than he could bear at times.

"I'm sixteen," Burden began again. "Regardless of the day I was actually born, I am sixteen now. Young men my age are typically deciding what path they will follow for their livelihood. Many are becoming apprentices and learning their fathers' trades, or they are joining the King's army and becoming soldiers…"

Master Josa barked a laugh, cutting off his memorised statement once again.

"Then you are in quite a predicament, boy. You have no father to follow, and the only fighting you've ever done is chasing the rats from out of our pantry."

"No, you aren't my father. You owe me nothing, as you have made quite clear time and again. I am not asking as your son, but rather as a person who knows the job you do and has assisted you at it for several years. Would you be willing to take me on as an apprentice? Will you teach me to be a smith?"

Master Josa ran a contemplative hand over his unruly beard, then shook his head. "No. I think not. I have just enough work to keep a roof over us and food on our table. I do not need an apprentice, and I cannot afford the lost time of watching you ruin good metal and having to fix it afterwards. I think I am better off without you."

The words stung Burden like a lash across his back. Though the refusal was not completely unexpected, he had actually let himself hope his request might find a positive response. He should have known better. Burden steeled himself, determined that he would not let Josa see his pain. His face tightened and he balled his hands briefly into fists, but he gave no other reaction.

"I'll go get those billets," he said, turning to leave.

"Go eat first, boy. I won't have you letting good food go to waste."

Burden nodded and left, heading for the two-room shack behind the blacksmith shop that he and Master Josa called home.

He ate, cleaned his dishes—as well as those Josa had left scattered about the kitchen – then returned to the shop with the iron billets fifteen minutes later. The heavy iron bars were wrapped with leather straps into two bundles of twenty and Burden hefted them easily, one in each hand. He did not have the sheer mass of muscle that Master Josa possessed, but he was no frail weakling either. Years of heavy lifting and grunt work around the shop had built up his frame to respectable proportions.

As he carried the iron through the shop's back entrance, Josa waved him over to one corner. "Just drop those over there, then join me, boy. We need to talk."

Burden did as he was bid, dropping the billets to the dirt floor and moving closer to Master Josa. Josa was standing over the discard box. Metal of any kind was too precious to ever throw away, so items that did not meet the blacksmith's standards were tossed into the box to be melted down and reused at a future time.

Josa reached into the box and removed a sword. He thrust it out toward Burden. "Take it," the stocky man ordered.

Burden accepted the blade. He turned it in his hands, examining the weapon. It was imperfectly forged; not so bad that it had cracked or become brittle, but the blade had visibly warped during the quenching phase, leaving both edges of the weapon bent significantly away from true.

"I said I would not take you as an apprentice," Master Josa said quietly, "and I will not. I don't need one and, worse, it would be a mistake for you to stay in this shop much longer. The war with Turyk is going poorly. The Landian armies are losing ground every day, and I would not be much surprised to find that by the end of the year this entire town will be learning to speak Turysh. That is if the Turysh don't simply burn everything to the ground as they pass through."

Josa sighed and sat down at the edge of the forge. He stroked his beard a few times with one thick-fingered hand. "There is no future for you here, Burden. If I kept you around, I would be condemning you to the whims of an invading army. I won't do that to you. The best chance you have is to take up a sword and join the King's army. I know you don't know how to use that thing, but they'll teach you what they can before they send you to fight. At least that way you'll have some kind of chance to protect yourself. Better that than wait to be carelessly crushed under their boots in passing."

"What about you?" asked Burden. "You could join the army with me. You could fight back, too."

Josa laughed, though the sound carried no humour in it. "I tried that once already. As a youth, I picked up a blade, and in my day, I saw more than my share of blood. I fought until I had nothing left to fight for or with. I can't stomach the thought of anymore. It's why I came here. I thought I would be able to die in peace in Landia. That was until Turyk decided they needed more room. I've grown old and perhaps become a bit of a coward. I won't raise another weapon. The Turysh can do with me as they please when they get here."

Master Josa's voice grew quiet, resigned, and his shoulders rolled forward for a moment as he spoke. Suddenly, he straightened, his back ramrod stiff, and he glared at Burden.

"But not you. No child of mine bends his neck to anyone. You are too strong for that. Gods know if I didn't break you, nobody can. You are going to leave here. Today! You will pack your belongings and join the King's army. You'll take that sword with you. It isn't pretty, but it won't shatter the first time you swing it either, not like those shiny, glass rods the army calls swords. I swear I don't know who they hire to make those things, but I'd like to wring the man's neck. He's giving all of us a bad name."

Burden lowered the sword, holding the grip and letting the point stick into the ground. Josa's words echoed in his head like a gong. "No child of mine," the old blacksmith had said. *Is he talking about me?* he wondered in numb shock. *Does he actually consider me his child? Why has he never before said anything to me?*

Instead of voicing the questions in his head, all Burden could say was, "What if I don't want to go?"

"Then you're twice the fool I thought you were," growled Josa. "Now, stop pretending you want anything to do with this place and go pack!"

Burden packed and left the blacksmith shop as Master Josa commanded, surprised at his own reluctance as he went. His entire life, he had believed Josa hated him and could not wait for the first opportunity to throw him out. Then, when it was time to actually go, Burden no longer felt so certain of the man's motives.

***

Burden travelled to Landice, the capital city, and joined the King's army. In the courtyards of the palace barracks, he received a few weeks of instruction on swordsmanship and basic military tactics before being marched to the country's southern border. Less than two months after leaving home, he found himself at the front of the battle lines with the Turysh, barely a week's march from the blacksmith shop in which he had grown up.

Master Josa had sheltered him from the reality of the war up until the day he sent him to fight in it. For over two years, the Turysh had skirmished with the king's forces practically on top of Burden's home, and he had never realised how dire the conflict had grown.

But now, his days of ignorance were over. He was

part of that conflict.

While training in the capital city, Burden had met a young man his own age, named Carno. Perhaps in another setting, he and Carno would never have become friends. They were very different from one another in backgrounds, demeanour and temperament, but both of them had arrived in Landice alone, penniless, and frightened of the future they soon would face. Their shared sense of desperation brought them together and, from their first meeting, they clung to one another's company. They claimed bunks next to one another in the barracks during training and, when it was time to leave, marched in lockstep during the long trip to the battlefront.

Burden and Carno joined the soldiers on the border along with two-hundred other new recruits sent from the capital. The lieutenant they reported to, although relieved to see reinforcements, was also clearly disappointed in the calibre of the soldiers he was receiving. Lieutenant Arlon, a gangly youth barely midway through his twenties, had been assigned to the front lines of the war eighteen months earlier as a squad leader. He rapidly ascended the ranks of the King's military, not by brilliance or distinguished performance on the battlefield, but by sheer survival. However, even he could see that Burden and his companions lacked sufficient formal training or fighting experience.

Despite his reservations, Lieutenant Arlon began breaking the recruits up into smaller groups and assigning them to fill the worst of the staffing gaps among his troops.

With great relief, Burden heard the lieutenant assign both him and Carno to the Eastern Company, protecting the left flank of the main defensive force. Burden did not know anyone here, and it was comforting to him to learn that Carno would remain close.

"How long do you think we have before we have to fight?" asked Carno, as they crossed the encampment to join their new company.

Burden shrugged. "I don't know. The war has lasted years, but I can't believe they battle every day, all day long. Somebody would have won by now if that was true. Maybe the armies sit in their camps for months at a time with no actual fighting," he suggested.

At least, I hope they do, Burden prayed, but he kept that last thought to himself.

"I can't wait to meet the enemy. You and me are going to show them what it means to battle Landia. The Turysh will never forget our names!"

"I can't wait, either," said Burden, knowing they were both lying.

When they reached the Eastern Company encampment, Burden, Carno, and seven other men from their original group reported to a battle-weary sergeant who identified himself as Brenna. Sergeant Brenna gathered them together, leading them through the campfires and bedrolls of the other soldiers into one of the large tents erected for use by the officers and sergeants.

"Everyone else in camp has already been briefed and knows what is happening," Sergeant Brenna began. "I have been assigned to make sure you men are informed of the plans for tomorrow morning. Your arrival could not have been better timed. Yes?" The sergeant pointed toward a thin, older boy in the front of their group who had timidly held up one hand. Burden remembered meeting the skinny kid during their march from Landice. He had introduced himself as Lek.

Lek cleared his throat. "Are we going to be able to eat soon? We haven't had anything since this morning before we came here."

Sergeant Brenna frowned, then decided to ignore the question.

Burden was hungry, too. It was well into the evening and the sun was low on the horizon, but he realised this was a poor time to be asking about food, even if Lek did not.

"The Turysh have been quiet on their side of the line for five days. We believe they are trying to build their numbers back up just as we are. There is no telling how much longer the break will last before they decide to come at us again. For months, we have been waging a defensive campaign, holding position as best we can until forced to retreat and re-establish a new defensive stronghold. Our current position is tenuous at best. We are too exposed and out in the open here. The next push the Turysh make is likely to drive us further back or even break our lines completely. We cannot allow that to happen.

"Tomorrow morning, at first light, we go on the offensive. We are going to lead a charge into their ranks and hopefully catch them unprepared. The goal is to drive them backwards into the foothills and to re-establish our last stronghold before we were pushed here. We held that fortification for three months before losing it, and the officers believe if we can take it back, we will again be able to offer a significant resistance to the Turysh advancement."

Sergeant Brenna paused to look at the men gathered before him, scanning through the group and meeting each pair of eyes in turn. When Brenna's stare found him, Burden was immediately frightened by what he could see in the depths of the sergeant's vacant, brown eyes. The desperation and weariness Burden found in them filled him with a sense of dread. This was a man who no longer fought for country or King, but rather because he could do nothing else. His will had broken some time ago, though perhaps he had not yet admitted it to himself, and all that remained was acceptance of his fate and hope of a swift and painless end. Burden read all of this in an instant, and his stomach began to twist inside him. To his great relief, the sergeant's gaze moved on.

"We will not be in the main charge," Sergeant Brenna continued. "We are responsible for holding the left flank of our forward forces, making sure the enemy does not circle around to catch them from behind. Our soldiers will be layered in three waves with the most experienced in the front wave. The second group will support the first, stopping any of the enemy that break through and filling any gaps that form. Everyone in this tent will be assigned to the third wave. We will pick up any stragglers that get through the first two lines. Hopefully, there will not be any. If all goes well, you may not see any combat tomorrow. I caution you, however, to not let your guard down. In war, things rarely go well."

The sergeant continued talking for a few more minutes, laying out specific assignments and explaining the basic tactics they would follow during the morning attack. When there was nothing further to discuss, and no one had any further questions, the men were dismissed.

With a pointed look toward Lek, the sergeant said, "Go back to the cook fires. The evening meal is done, but there is always something there to eat. Then get to sleep. Dawn comes early."

Burden walked out of the tent, the thoughts in his head loud enough to drown out Carno's excited chatter next to him. *We fight tomorrow morning. So soon! I just got here and in less than twelve hours I will be in the war.*

"Ten specks. What do you say?" Carno was looking at Burden with his hand held out.

"What?" Burden asked, pushing away the thoughts of battle filling his head.

"I said I'll bet you ten specks I kill more of the enemy than you do. Deal?"

Burden forced a smile and took Carno's hand. "Sure. Ten."

Ten specks was a great deal of money for Burden, but the bet was not what he most feared he might lose in the morning.

***

Burden and Carno stood together in their assigned line, waiting for the sun to break the horizon and the officers' orders to begin their first charge into the enemy's fortifications. Burden shivered, a cold sensation running through the base of his spine. Although the morning was chilly and the world around him was damp with a low-lying fog, it was not the temperature or the wet that caused the involuntary reaction.

Despite the Sergeant's assertions the night before, the planned attack did not seem to be a surprise to the Turysh soldiers. Men in the gold and blue markings of Turyk stood ready barely two-hundred yards distant in numbers equal to the Landian's own three-thousand or so warriors. The show of force by the enemy changed nothing in the minds of the Landian officers. Too much planning had been put into this endeavour to simply withdraw. Besides, regardless of who initiated the next round of hostilities, a battle was imminent and inevitable, and their current position remained untenable if they chose to hold in place and fight a defensive campaign any longer.

Turning slightly to glance at Carno, Burden saw his friend swallow nervously several times as he stared at the open ground between the Landian and Turysh troops. It made him feel slightly better to know he wasn't the only one with reservations about the coming confrontation.

No one spoke and no one moved as the first light of false dawn lightened the sky and sent the stars into hiding. The space between the armies was level and clear; some farmer's hayfield, the oat grass already cut but not yet harvested. Burden wondered idly if the cows and goats would mind the taste of blood in their winter feed. A morbid thought, and he quickly forced it away.

An eerie silence dominated the field, broken only by an occasional cough or the ring of a careless sword touching a shield. The seconds crawled by as the grey shapes and shadows of the world around them slowly resolved into colours with the arrival of morning.

Burden held his breath.

A voice cried out, a call to battle that others along the front line quickly echoed. The roar grew, spreading out from the middle of the Landian army to swallow the sides in both directions. A wave of sound crashed over Burden, sending him and the men around him running toward the enemy. The Turysh responded with a battle cry of their own and rushed forward to cover the intervening space.

As the main body of the army surged straight

forward, charging to meet the oncoming Turysh, the men in Burden's group veered left, slowing slightly to allow the central force to outpace them. They formed one wing of an extended "V," attempting to provide support and protection from any attempt by the enemy to surround them. If successful, the front of the Landian force would break through the Turysh line and divide them, forcing the enemy soldiers to flee or retreat in order to regroup. Should this happen during the disorder, Burden and the others had strict orders not to pursue, but rather to reach the foothills and set up a new defensive encampment.

Plans in a war dissolve like salt in the rain. At the first clash, it was clear Landia would not break the Turysh line. The enemy held and the Landian charge stalled, swirling and eddying in the middle of the battlefield as the two armies merged into one massive, bloody melee.

Unlike the Turysh, Landia did not have the funds to provide uniforms to its soldiers, so most of the men wore the clothing they owned before they had joined the army. In an attempt to create some uniformity, and to identify ally from foe, many of the men tied strips of red cloth to their upper arms. The red stood out plainly against the drab browns and greys of peasant clothing, but it was quickly buried in the sea of gold and blue that they faced. Burden watched the fighting unfold, disheartened by the fact that everywhere he looked, he saw only enemy colours.

Burden remained in the rear-guard of his group as directed, but he realised immediately that any hopes of remaining a nonparticipant in the fighting had already vanished. His job was to scan the lines in front of him and move to fill any gaps created by fallen soldiers, or to confront any enemy combatants that accidentally slipped past the front lines. Within seconds of the cry to arms, gaps were already appearing, and Turysh soldiers found their way behind the Landian lines.

A tall man, thin and lean, wearing a vest the colour of the morning sky, knelt and swung his sword in a low, deadly arc. The blade cut the legs out from beneath a Landian soldier Burden did not recognize. The Turyk lurched forward to drive the point of his weapon through the Landian's chest, killing his opponent. The movement left him off balance, however, and after the killing blow, the man fell to the ground.

The heart of the battle swept over and past the fallen man, who scrambled to his feet only to find himself alone in a small pocket of calm. Alone, that is, except for Burden. Dark eyes locked onto Burden, who stood with his sword in his hand but completely unprepared for what was about to happen.

The Turyk stepped forward, his own sword held out in front of him. The man smiled, showing cracked, yellow teeth through a thick patch of black beard. He could see Burden's level of inexperience; could probably even smell it on him.

Remembering what little training he had received, Burden stepped forward to meet his opponent. He gripped the handle of his blade in both hands and lunged forward. The Turyk swept his blade upward in a blurring arc, redirecting Burden's weapon, then swung his sword sideways like a man trying to fell a tree with an axe.

The sword caught Burden beneath his left arm, breaking ribs and cutting flesh. He felt it bite deep. The pain was excruciating, and he gasped in shock at the violence done to his body. Glancing down, Burden saw the sword protruding from the centre of his chest. The blade had cut halfway through him, stopping only when it had impacted against his spine.

Burden tried to draw in a breath, but his left lung had been bisected along with that entire side of his body. He could only cough, gurgling up wet gobbets of blood that poured from his mouth, ran over his chin and fell to his shirt where it joined the blood already escaping the wound in his chest.

He felt a tug, cold and agonizing. He looked up,

searching for the source of the pain, and found the Turysh soldier pulling at his sword, trying to dislodge it from Burden's ribs. It would not come free. Burden reached out with his left hand and grasped the man's sword-hand by the wrist. Pulling his murderer closer, he raised his own weapon, touched the point of the sword to the Turyk's chest and pushed it through his heart.

Stabbing a man was difficult. Meat and bone parted only with a great deal of resistance. But Burden had years of lifting and moving heavy burdens that had left his arms dense with muscle. He was up to the task.

The Turysh soldier screamed and fell to the ground; clutching at the wound in his chest for a few moments before dying. Burden pulled his sword free as the man fell. It came away much easier than it had gone in.

Burden dropped to his knees, still unable to take a full breath; still coughing out gouts of bright red blood. He fell, rolling onto his back beside the dead Turyk and panting in weak shallow breaths. Burden lay in the grass of the field, staring up at the open blue sky and wishing he had never joined the King's army. He had known it was a mistake. He was no fighter. He was nothing more than a blacksmith's assistant. And now, he was going to die in some unknown farmer's field far away from home.

He closed his eyes and wept from misery and pain.

But he did not die. Perhaps the Dark Gatherer was occupied harvesting souls in other corners of the battle and Burden had been overlooked. He could not escape notice for long, he suspected. It would only be a matter of time before the oversight was corrected.

I got one, Carno, Burden thought with grim satisfaction. *Did I win our bet?*

The battle continued for a half an hour or more, the mass of the fighting men moving back and forth over Burden's location. No one bothered him where he lay, struggling for each and every breath. Nobody had time to deal with a corpse that didn't know enough to stop moving. He listened to the cries of the injured and dying around him, the clash of metal against metal and the occasional ignored pleas for help. After a time, the sounds were almost soothing; even reassuring in their consistency.

Then it was over.

The fighting stopped. The battle was not finished, but through some unspoken agreement, the two warring sides pulled back to regroup and gauge their losses. The quiet was only a lull, rather than an ending, but the sudden silence was as startling and shocking to Burden as the initial charge had been.

"Burden! Oh, gods, Burden! What did they do to you?"

Carno was suddenly kneeling at his side. Burden smiled, touched at Carno's response to seeing him dead on the ground. Although, through some cruel miracle, Burden still had not died. The pain had eased somewhat, but was far from gone, and his breathing remained laboured.

"Carno," Burden forced himself to say. The word came out garbled, bubbling up through the blood in his throat.

"I'm sorry I didn't stay with you. Maybe I could have saved you."

"Carno," Burden said again. "The sword. Pl-please take it out."

Carno looked at the damage to Burden's chest; examined the sword sticking out of his body. "I don't know if I should," he finally admitted. "Taking it out might kill you."

"Dead…" Burden coughed. More blood erupted from his mouth. "Dead…already."

Carno nodded, understanding. Whether the sword came out or stayed in, Burden was going to die.

Carno grasped the blade with both hands and pulled. The blade did not budge. The edge of the sword had lodged in Burden's spine, and Carno was forced to rock the weapon back and forth several times to work it free. Burden opened his mouth to scream, but he did not have the breath or the strength to verbalise more than a shocked gasp.

When the blade finally came loose, the pain subsided considerably. Burden was amazed at the feeling of relief that filled him with the sword gone. Perhaps it was merely his body failing and his mind shutting down that eased the pain, but regardless of the source, he was grateful for it.

"Th-thank you," Burden told Carno.

"Is there anything else I can do for you?" his friend asked.

Burden shook his head. "Just stay until…until it's over."

Carno nodded and grasped Burden hand. Of course, he would stay, the gesture said.

Burden's breathing calmed and slowed. He spat out one last mouthful of blood, then realised his throat was clear. A human body only contained so much of the precious red fluid, and perhaps he had just run out. Another sign the end was near.

He closed his eyes once more.

Carno began to cry, laying his forehead to Burden's chest. Burden heard his friend's sobs and was grateful for the sentiment, even though he was not yet gone.

And why aren't I dead? he wondered, not for the first time. *Should it take so long?*

Burden heard voices nearby. Men shouted orders.

"I have to go," Carno whispered. The officers are calling a new line and I have to prepare for our next attack."

Without thinking, Burden sat up and wrapped Carno in his arms for a farewell hug. Carno screamed and leapt backward from his embrace.

Burden remained upright, blinking several times in surprise at being able to move. The only remaining pain he felt was a stiffness in his chest, as though he had strained a muscle lifting a much too heavy object. He glanced at Carno, who sat awkwardly braced on his palms and staring back in wonder.

"H-how…?" Carno stammered.

Burden only shrugged. He had no answer to that question. With a questing finger, Burden tugged at his torn shirt. Blood still covered his torso, but under the gore his poking and prodding found only intact flesh.

His wound had healed!

"You saw the cut, right?" Burden blurted. "I didn't imagine it?"

Carno shook his head, disbelief clear on his features. "You were dead, Burden. I pulled the sword out. Nobody could survive a wound like that."

Carno crawled to his friend and began exploring Burden's chest with his own hands.

"This makes no sense. Are you human?"

Before today, Burden would have laughed at the question. His survival after being nearly cut in two, however, made him consider his answer more carefully. "I...I think so," he said.

Angry shouts kept the two boys from any further discussion. The Landian officers were calling for all able soldiers to fall back into line. The Turysh were doing the same on their side of the field, and it was clear to all that the brief truce was soon to end.

"Can you fight?" asked Carno. "Or, do you need to find the field surgeon?"

Burden climbed to his feet. "And tell him, what? I was in two pieces an hour ago? I can fight."

Burden picked up his sword, which remained lying in the grass near where he had fallen, and swung it a few times, testing his arm. Everything seemed normal.

Which was decidedly not normal at all.

"C'mon!" shouted Carno, pulling Burden along behind him. "We need to find our company."

They found their much-depleted group forming up a new wing to the left of the main force. Perhaps five hundred men had died in the initial assault, another similar number wounded. That left two of the three-thousand men that charged the enemy that morning still able to fight. Retreat was not yet an option, as the enemy would likely follow, picking off hundreds more as they fell back trying to find a new defensible position. By necessity, there would be at least one more attempt to break through the Turysh fortifications before surrendering more ground.

Burden positioned himself in the second line of the new wing. A third line no longer existed due to casualties sustained earlier, and even shoring up the second line with all available recruits left several concerning gaps. Burden hoped the Turysh army had suffered similar losses to their own. If not, this second clash would be decidedly unbalanced against them.

Like the first, the second charge began with a cry of attack from the top officers carried along on the voices of others. Without hesitation, Burden dashed forward at the command. He felt no pain or weakness. His wounds had completely healed, but more than that, he felt alert and excited. His nerves were on fire with the thought of another chance to fight, and his body flooded with adrenaline, leaving him more than just back to normal.

He felt good.

He wanted to be back on the field, he realised. As

if a small part of him had been waiting his whole life for just this moment. All earlier doubts burned away as he ran. A cry of joy rose to his lips, and he shouted his defiance at the oncoming enemy.

The two sides slammed into each other, the blue and gold again merging and swirling into the mass of grey and brown. The armies flowed through one another as each soldier sought out a member of the opposition to face. Burden found himself facing an opponent almost immediately this time. A short, stocky boy only slightly older than himself charged directly for him.

The Turysh soldier swung his sword toward Burden's head, but he easily saw the blow coming and slapped it aside with the flat of his own blade. The boy then lowered his shoulder and rammed it into Burden's stomach, driving the air from his lungs in a hard *whoosh!* Burden staggered back a step but did not fall; his greater size allowing him to keep his feet. The Turyk followed his push with a thrust of his sword, low and straight.

Burden felt and saw the sword cut into his belly and disappear up to the hilt.

Again! he thought, disgustedly. The pain in his guts flared bright and sharp. In retaliation, he roared and swung his sword in front of him in a wild backhanded slash. The Turysh boy's head separated from his shoulders and tumbled away into the cut grass of the hayfield. The enemy soldier's body took a moment longer to fall, but it too toppled at last to lie still at Burden's feet.

Burden stared at the sword hilt protruding from his stomach. The foreign object in his body left him aching and nauseated from its presence, but Burden did not feel weak. He had no desire to fall down or quit fighting. Instead, he realised, he was angry. Angry at the soldier that had dared raise a sword against him. Angry at the army in front of him that wanted him and his friends dead. And, most of all, angry at himself that he had been clumsy enough to allow anyone to injure him.

Twice!

With the blade still buried in his torso, Burden rushed forward to find another warrior in blue and gold. The next man he faced barely had time to raise his blade before Burden cut him down. The next three fell just as quickly. He cut and slashed as he wended his way through the combatants, his weapon growing slick with the blood of his enemies. A few times, his opponents managed to strike him with their blades, but the injuries did not slow him down; they merely fuelled his rage and determination.

He turned and stabbed, dodged and thrust. Each movement faster and deadlier than the last. Men fell around him like stalks of wheat under a scythe, and still he hunted, seeking new targets even before his last victims had died. Burden's desire to kill had become unquenchable, and he felt he could never spill enough blood to satisfy his lust.

Time passed without notice as Burden mindlessly threw himself against the Turysh army. It could have been minutes, days, or weeks that passed. He could not be sure how long he fought; how many he had killed. Nor did he care. All that mattered was the feel of flesh under his blade, the taste of blood in his mouth, and the screams of dying men in his ears.

At last, the rage subsided, and Burden came back to conscious thought as he realised that there were no more soldiers willing to face him. A circle of open space widened and grew around him as both armies began to realise what was happening. Landian soldiers stepped away from him to give him room to battle and the remaining Turysh decided they wanted nothing to do with him, dropping weapons and running from the melee.

Burden lowered his sword and watched the wave of blue and gold flee from the battlefield toward their prior encampment. Bemused, he turned to face his own men and share in their victory. The looks on their faces, however, stopped any urge he might have had to celebrate. They were terrified. Afraid of the monster in their midst and, perhaps, wondering if he might turn on them next.

Pain lanced through his stomach and he looked down to find the Turysh sword still impaling him. In addition, somewhere in the fighting he had added a sword through the right hip and two daggers in the chest to his collection. No wonder they were all afraid. He was a demon; a creature that knew how to kill but that would not itself die.

Behind him, in the direction the Turysh had fled, Burden heard a voice. It was strong and clear in the aftermath of the battle.

"There you are, my son. I had feared you were lost to me, but then, like a beacon through the night, I heard you call out to me at last."

Burden spun to find a dark figure standing in the bloody, body-riddled field. The stranger was unnaturally tall, yet muscular enough to mask his height from a distance. He wore all black, with a flowing cape attached across his broad shoulders and draping to just above the ground. He wore an open-faced helmet, but inside the visor, Burden could see only shadows.

"Who are you?" asked Burden, raising his sword defensively.

The stranger moved forward, covering the distance between them quickly with his long strides.

"I am Berros. I am War. I am the god of chaos and destruction. When men of this world kill each other, they are worshipping me. And you, dear boy, you are my son."

Burden lowered his sword and stepped back as the self-described god of war towered over him. "Th-that's impossible. I'm nobody. I'm nothing to you."

The darkness in Berros' helmet remained impenetrable, but the cock of his head gave Burden the impression the god was smiling.

"You are my son. When your mother discovered she was pregnant, she ran from me. Tried to hide you. I think she hoped you could avoid your destiny. But I knew you would eventually find your way into battle. It is your nature to fight; to kill. And when you at last drew the blood you were born to take, I heard your cries. Now, I am here to reclaim what has always been mine."

Tears blurred Burden's vision and he hurriedly wiped them away. *This can't be true,* he thought. *None of this is true.*

"How am I alive?" he asked. "I should be dead."

Berros laughed, the sound high pitched and eerie. The Landian soldiers flinched and backed further away from the terrible noise.

"You cannot die in battle, my son. You are a child of War. Others die around you. That is the only outcome when you take the field. When you come to understand your abilities, nothing will ever harm you again. This…" Berros grasped the handle of the sword in Burden's guts and pulled it free. "This is just carelessness."

The god proceeded to remove the daggers from Burden's chest and the sword in his hip. The wounds closed as quickly as the weapons were tossed aside.

"I am really your son?" Burden asked.

"I would not be here otherwise," Berros said, tolerantly.

"I'm a god?"

Berros shook his head. "No. You are half god. Your mother was mortal. But it is your mortal half that makes you even more powerful than me. This means you have my strength but are not shackled by my constraints. I can only act in this world through others. I am not permitted to take a direct hand against it. You, however, being *of* this world can do as you please."

"So, what happens now?"

The god placed his hand on top of Burden's head,

ruffling his hair like he was petting a faithful dog.

"Now, you follow your destiny. You fight. You kill. You conquer!"

"Fight? The Turysh?"

"That will do to start. Defeat the Turysh. Crush their kingdom and claim it for your own. Take Landia next, if you wish. Anything you desire is yours."

"Anything?" Burden asked.

"Anything!" Berros' answer came out as an excited hiss.

Burden looked over his shoulder at the soldiers behind him. Carno stood toward the front of the assembled men; his face twisted in concern for his friend's welfare. The boy smiled tentatively when he saw Burden looking and raised a hand in a small wave.

Burden smiled back, then turned to face Berros.

"I will lead these men into Turyk, and I will break their army. The king of Turyk will swear fealty to Landia or else I will remove him and place a new king on the throne."

"A very good start," Berros agreed. "What follows Turyk?"

Burden took a deep breath. The entire world had just been handed to him. The child of War could go anywhere; do anything. Only days ago, he had feared that his only option was to die pointlessly fighting for a country that would not long outlive him. Today, everything had changed. His options were only as limited as his imagination.

If he could have his greatest wish, just reach out and take the one thing he wanted more than any other, what would that one thing be? Burden knew the answer almost before he had asked himself the question.

"When Turyk is beaten, and Landia is safe once again, I will return to my home. I wish to find Master Josa and become a blacksmith."

G. ALLEN WILBANKS is a retired police officer living in Northern California. For twenty-five years he wrote collision and crime reports during the day to pay the bills, and he wrote short fiction during his off-time to stay sane. He is a member of the Horror Writers Association (HWA) and his work has appeared in over 100 magazines and anthologies, including several publications with Black Hare Press. He is the author of two short story collections (Not for Bedtime Stories, and 13 Rooms), and the novel, When Darkness Comes. In addition to his fiction writing, he writes a weekly humor blog entitled, Deep Dark Thoughts, where he ponders life and why it apparently seems to hate him.

Bibliography

100 Word Horrors, Kjk Publishing, 2019
100 Word Zombie Bites, Reanimated Writers Press, 2019
Apocalypse, Black Hare Press, 2019
Bad Romance, Black Hare Press, 2020
Beyond, Black Hare Press, 2019
Dig Two Graves, Death's Head Press, 2019
Dragon Bone Soup, Dw Brownlaw Publication, 2019
Eerie Christmas, Black Hare Press, 2019
Gleam, Clarendon House Publications, 2019
Hawthorn & Ash, Iron Faerie Publishing, 2019
Monsters, Black Hare Press, 2019
Pride, Black Hare Press, 2020
Tall Tales & Short Stories, Escaped Ink Press, 2019
Tempest, Clarendon House Publications, 2019
The Colored Lens 2019 Anthology, The Colored Lens, 2019
Unravel, Black Hare Press, 2019

Connect

Website: www.gallenwilbanks.com
Blog: www.deepdarkthoughts.com
Facebook: www.facebook.com/gallenwilbanks/
Twitter: https://twitter.com/gallenwilbanks

BLACK HARE PRESS

DAUGHTER OF MIDNIGHT

By Erica Schaef

Cursed by ancient magic, a young sell-sword will be forced to spend eternity in a purgatorial, half-existence upon the earth, unless she can find and destroy the mysterious sorcerer whose blood ritual condemned her to such a hellish fate...

Twice the metal long-blade had punctured through her chainmail, twice it had found its mark. The soft, mangled flesh above her fractured ribcage burned and ached; two of the underlying bones had broken inward to accommodate the penetrating weapon. Her heart was torn open at the left ventricle, its dark blood spilling into her chest cavity, flooding her diaphragm and restricting the movement of her lungs.

God, it was painful, worse than having her throat slit. She teetered backward and removed her helmet, giving her opponent a raw and sickly smile.

He stared back at her, his pale eyes wide with disbelief. Blood had begun to trickle from the corners of her mouth, staining her teeth and tongue. She licked her lips malevolently, still grinning.

"What devilry is this?" the man stammered. "A…woman…a demon." He fell to his knees, his helmed face downcast in silent prayer.

She approached quietly, raising her own sword high, its hilt grasped firmly in her clenched fists.

"It is too late for salvation," she admonished, driving the experienced blade down hard into the base of his bowed neck.

She felt a pang of envy as his body collapsed lifelessly at her feet. There, at least, was peace. That expression of complete and utter relief was one that her own face would never wear.

Her troubled mind reeled with decades of pain and discontentment as she sat on the snow-frosted grass, gasping for breath.

Her young steward maintained a respectable distance, allowing her space to recuperate, as he always did after combat.

"Something to drink," she sputtered, swallowing back against the dry taste of rusted copper. "It's damned exhausting."

The curse upon her physical body began its painful and meticulous work, mending the gaping wounds, setting and repairing the fractured bones.

Her steward waited until she had recovered herself, then handed her the jug of icy spring water he'd retrieved from her cottage.

"We'll put him in the river," she instructed after a hasty gulp. "The coward doesn't deserve a proper burial."

"Very good, Milady, I will get the horses." He bowed his head at her and set off again.

It was strange, she thought, as they tied the dead man's body to drag behind her spotted gelding, *how one could get so used to killing, that it didn't excite or disturb anymore.* With every life she'd taken, her very being seemed to have numbed and callused like an overused appendage. It benefited her, in that she was now possessed of a certain moral ambiguity, one that allowed her to excel as a sell-sword.

Granted, it was not the life she would have chosen for herself, but one that had instead been thrust upon her nearly half a century ago. To think that her own father had been the one to condemn her to this eternal purgatory was almost maddening. She would find him though, one day, and have her retribution.

"This is a suitable enough spot, I think," she called back over her shoulder as they approached a wide pooling bend in the frothing river.

Her steward dismounted his ginger mare swiftly and helped her to cut the tied ropes. Together, they pulled the body down the mossy ravine, toward the sloping bank, releasing it unceremoniously into the crisp, freezing water.

Rowan Blackwood sighed, wiping miniscule beads of sweat from her brow.

"Who was it he had come to avenge, Sam? I can't recall what he told me now, when he'd called me out to fight."

"His brother, Warwick, Milady," her steward answered brightly. "The one Lord Ashford hired you to…*dispose* of."

Rowan frowned thoughtfully for a moment.

"Ah, yes" she said finally, her eyes alight with recollection. "The old brute rambled on for so long, I'd quite forgotten his reason for seeking me out. *Warwick*…that was the blackmailing fellow, wasn't it? Real scoundrel of a man."

"Yes, Milady." The steward nodded as they gained

their saddles again. "Lord Ashford paid handsomely to see him dealt with."

"It is well that he did," Rowan returned. "We ought to seek compensation from him again for the blackguard of a brother. Did you see how he charged me at the start, when my back was turned? Damned coward."

What had really vexed her, though, was that the vengeful man had been able to gravely injure her, not once but twice, in fair melee combat. She prided herself on her swordsmanship, and rarely was her curse made useful in one-to-one skilled fighting scenarios like it had been today.

"I did, Milady," Sam's voice held a distinct note of bitterness. "A despicable manoeuvre."

The pair grew quiet then, guiding their mounts expertly through the icy winter forest, back to the little cottage on its western border. Rowan had chosen the temporary residence for its proximity to a prosperous town, for though her overriding objective was to find her elusive father, she'd needed to earn living enough to support her travels. Having trained tirelessly over many decades with her heavy longsword, she found killing for hire to be both useful and an obvious choice for funding her quest.

It also allowed her to remain in the shadows, out

of the general way and mostly unnoticed. Her reputation was spread by covert whispers rather than praising shouts so that she could pass from one town or village to the next, without most of the residents having ever been aware of her transient presence.

Even when someone did have need of her services, that person dealt mostly in unsigned letters at first, then later, if necessary, with her loyal steward, Sam. Most of her *contributors* had never even seen her, and as she went simply by "Blackwood," she doubted very much if any of them thought of her as a young woman. Young being a relative term, of course.

As she was dressing for bed in the dim, fluttering light of a candle that evening, Rowan paused to run long, slender fingers over her bare chest, inspecting the now flawless, cream-coloured skin over her strongly beating heart. Tears welled behind her eyes, and she cursed her own reaction, refusing to let the treacherous drops spill outward onto her cheeks, though she was utterly alone in the room.

She put on her nightdress hurriedly, blew out the flickering candle, and got into bed. The straw mattress was lumpy and uncomfortable, but Rowan didn't even notice. She dreamt of *him* again, as she always did.

It was the night before her twenty-first birthday. Mother had stayed up to decorate a cake for her; she could smell the warm, sugary confection, even from her bedroom upstairs. Rowan was too old for such childish celebrations, she knew, a woman of her age was supposed to be married and well away from her parents' home, probably with children of her own. *They* were outcasts, though, shunned from the comfortable bosom of society since before she'd even been born. Rowan's father, a powerful Dark Sorcerer known only as Midnight, had abducted his young bride from her noble family home long ago, spiriting her away to his forbidding stronghold in the dry and nearly inhospitable Red Desert.

On that night, the eve of her birthday, Midnight had gone out abruptly, leaving his wife and daughter alone in the enormous stone structure. Rowan preferred it that way—her father was a deeply selfish and cruel man, consumed entirely by the dark magic he practiced. She and her mother lived in a small, sheltered world of their own design, bringing what beauty and warmth they could to their desolate home.

Rowan saw a green, glowing fog out of her bedroom window that night, eerie and unfamiliar, spreading out across the distant rocky plains. Something inside of her clenched and hardened, as though her body had innately perceived the strange, smoky mist as a threat. By that time in her life, she already had a crude, unrefined understanding of basic sword manoeuvres. She would be more of a deterrent than her frail mother, in any case, should there be an actual danger against them.

Slipping into her shabbily crafted armour, she crept quietly down the back staircase to avoid startling her mother. Her narrow sword was sheathed at her side, polished and ready should the occasion rise for its use.

Outside, the air was swelteringly humid; heavy and unmoving as a steel plated shield. Rowan moved stealthily in the silver moonlight, edging the blackened outline of a great rock cliff.

As she approached the rolling fog, she saw that it was issuing from a massive, dancing emerald flame. A cloaked figure stood before the fire, arms outstretched toward the purple, starry heavens. He was speaking, or rather, chanting, into the hot night air. Instantly, she knew his voice. Midnight, her father, drew a long dagger from his clothing, still standing astutely with his back toward her, as though in a trance. She watched, wide-eyed and readied to move, as he brought the dagger to his wrist and cut deeply into the stark white flesh. Blood poured from his arm, falling freely to dampen the green flames like a thick, syrupy rain.

Immediately, before Rowan had even had time to blink, the fire changed, burning a deep, mahogany red.

Her father walked *into* it, arms still cast up toward the sky. Rowan's mouth gaped open in dismay, and she waited with bated breath, expecting to see his thin, silhouetted body char and crumble to ash. To her astonishment, though, her father came out easily through the other side, his body fully intact and unburned.

The fire died down then, turning a natural yellowish- orange, and produced an unremarkable, white spiral of rising smoke. Midnight was smiling, and the sight of it turned her stomach. As she watched, he took up the dagger again—its blade having been melted slightly by the licking flames—and brought it up flush against his exposed neck. Still baring his teeth in that grotesquely pleased sort of way, he seemed to look right into his daughter's eyes as he slit his own throat.

She gasped as he fell, too stunned to move. In the next breath, before she'd had time to get her bearings, he was up again, the cut on his neck having become impossibly shallow. It disappeared altogether after another moment, and finally Rowan understood.

Her father had just performed Blood Magic, the most complicated of dark sorcery, before her very eyes. Whatever spell he had woven into those cursed flames, it, along with his own lifeblood, had apparently rendered Midnight impervious to physical harm. She sucked in a ragged mouthful of smoke-singed air, wary of the possible implications of such an act, and her heart pounded noisily against her chest wall. The black, slit-like pupils of Midnight were once again upon her, scorching into her very soul.

She woke abruptly, covered in dewy perspiration. Outside, the pale winter sun was half-heartedly casting its rays across her little bedroom, illuminating the dusty, wood plank floors of the forest cottage.

Stretching out her sore and tired muscles, she rose to dress unhurriedly, still fighting back against a sluggish sleepiness.

"Milady," Sam knocked firmly on the pinewood door to her room, "the Lord Ashford has commissioned your services again."

Rowan pulled a cloak over her thick wool nightdress, and threw open the bedroom door, unbalancing her patient steward somewhat.

"I met him in the churchyard this morning." He straightened, gaining his footing with an air of unappreciated dignity. "And told him of your trouble with Warwick's coward brother. He sent a generous reward, and asked if you wouldn't be interested in another, more challenging venture."

"Well," she considered, an index finger tapping

thoughtfully on her delicate chin, "if the pay is agreeable…"

"Most agreeable, I think," Sam went on seriously. "He plans to offer you double what he gave for Warwick."

She smiled. "I'm justly intrigued, young steward. When would he like to meet?"

Lord Ashford was one of the very few commissioners to have actually seen her in person. He liked to deal face-to-face with those he entrusted with his confidences, eliminating the possibility of miscommunication or underhanded betrayal by way of a third-party messenger.

"He said he could be here at dusk tonight, if convenient. I'm to convey your answer by letter as soon as I have it."

Rowan went to her desk, emerging from its deep cedar drawer with a long piece of parchment paper, and a drooping feathered quill. Dipping the fine point of the quill into a congealing black ink well, she scrawled a reply in the affirmative, and, leaving it unaddressed an unsigned, folded and sealed it with plain red candle wax.

"Take this to him then, if you will. Lord Ashford has proven a gracious and honest solicitor. We'll have made enough from his pocket alone to continue northward after this one is through."

Sam inclined his head at her and accepted the letter.

"Very good, Milady. You will go north and unearth the Blood Mage yet."

The look he gave her was one of such unwavering confidence, that it was difficult for her to remain untouched by the young man's pristine fealty.

"Take care, and make haste," she bade him, "I would not like to lose this opportunity."

Lord Ashford arrived at the sleepy cottage, just as evening was waning to night. A light snow had begun to fall, blanketing the darkened landscape with a fine, glistening powder.

Sam opened the front door to admit the heavily bundled man, stepping aside to assist him in the removal of his concealing wraps.

Rowan stood back, meeting Ashford's piercing grey eyes with her own easy stare.

"You made quick work of the fool Warwick." He appraised her slender form openly. "And his zealous brother."

She grinned, leaning against the narrow archway that led to her bedroom.

"I've been told that you have another proposition for me now." She motioned toward the simple wooden table at the room's centre. "Sit, please, and let me hear of this new opportunity."

He did as he was bidden, and she took the chair opposite him.

"I trust your steward has relayed information to you regarding the compensation I mean to provide you with." Lord Ashford was serious now, his charismatic nature tempered into sombreness. "This is a delicate matter of some urgency, Blackwood. It is rather…*personal* to me."

Rowan put up her hand to cut him off, "I do not require any specific details as to your reasoning, Ashford. I simply need the name, and a brief description if you have one."

"I know." The man smiled rakishly, she supposed it was his thoughtless habit when addressing members of the opposite sex. "That lack of imprudent curiosity was one of the reasons that I chose you for this request. I promise to spare you the tiring backstory, Blackwood. It was only my intention to impress upon you the importance of this particular venture to me."

"I understand." She was aware then, of the thinly veiled worry he kept back from his masculine features. It was there, just behind his storm-grey eyes, swirling like an angry sea.

"And I give you my word," she went on soberly,

"that I will hold your confidence in the utmost regard. You may rest easy on that point, Ashford. I've yet to fail."

He sat back in his chair, searching her face in the dimly lit room. "How old are you?" he asked unexpectedly. "You can hardly be more than a child, yet you seem more worldly and experienced than any young sell-sword ought to be."

She smiled. This was the very reason that she did not like to conduct her negotiations in person. Awkward questions were bound to arise.

"I've led a very interesting, very *unusual* life, Lord Ashford. To answer you simply, I am on the cusp of my twenty-first birthday."

He arched his brow at her. "A mystery, indeed," he muttered, more to himself than to her. "Regardless, Blackwood, the person I mean for you to rid me of is called Richard Fairfax. He keeps a large house in town where he stays with his wife. I would prefer the encounter to take place elsewhere, though, and during a time when I myself will be otherwise engaged. As I said, the matter is a personal one for me, and as much as I would like to handle Fairfax for myself, I must appear to be thoroughly uninvolved."

"Yes, I can see your predicament." Rowan folded her hands together on the table's rough surface. "What did you have in mind?"

"Tomorrow night," he answered bluntly. "I can arrange for Fairfax to be alone, on the wooded path just north of here, in the hemlock grove."

"I know it."

"Magnificent." He smiled again. "Shall we say, midnight?"

A chill crept down her spine at the word. She cleared her throat composedly and straightened. "Yes, that will be fine."

"Good." Ashford pulled an envelope from his jacket and handed it over to her. "Half now, half when it's done.

She accepted it with a slight incline of her head.

"And Blackwood," he said as he rose from the table, "I don't expect Fairfax to be an easy man to kill. He's damned stubborn and big as that gelding you have tied outside."

Rowan stood up too, walking around the table to lean on the door frame once more.

"No man has bested me yet, Ashford. Fairfax will be no different."

"I trust you," he said, running a hand absentmindedly through his raven coloured hair, and flashing his handsome smile again.

"I will send Sam for the rest of my due in two days'

time," she answered, her voice even and unamused.

"Very well." Lord Ashford was helped into his cloak by the waiting steward. "Bit of a pity, though. I always look forward to seeing *you*, Blackwood."

She ignored the suggestive inflection of his words. Men like Ashford flirted as easily as they breathed, but such frivolities were usually wasted upon her.

"Farewell, Ashford," she replied coolly.

"Until we meet again." He ran his eyes down the length of her once more, before departing into the cold night.

"I won't be sorry to see the last of him," Sam said with a disapproving frown when he had shut the door behind Ashford.

Rowan laughed amusedly. "As soon as we receive the next half of our compensation, we should be done with our wealthy friend for good." And on to their more pressing endeavours.

On the following night, Rowan waited in the specified grove of giant hemlocks, flanked unobtrusively by her quiet steward. The pine-scented, cool air was refreshing, even to her weary lungs. She inhaled it deeply, holding it in her chest for a measured heartbeat before exhaling it again. Overhead, the sky was clear, illuminated by a vast canopy of pure ivory stars. A crescent moon hung high and resolutely among them, shining its pale golden light onto the forest below.

Fairfax arrived just as Ashford had said he would, alone and in the middle of the night. He was very tall and imposing in size, with thick, bulging muscles, and a looming, sturdy torso.

"Richard Fairfax?" she called in a falsely gruff voice, stepping out into the clearing so that she would be visible to her unwary target.

"Aye, and who are you?" The man's speech was slurred somewhat. Maybe he was a drunkard. Rowan had come across enough of those over the years to recognise the signs with fair accuracy.

"You are challenged to combat. Draw your sword and fight," she bellowed harshly.

"Eh?" He squared his shoulders. "What is this? Who challenges me?" His hand had gone to his hilted sword's handle.

"It is I, Blackwood who calls you out tonight. Prepare yourself, Richard Fairfax. You will be defeated."

"Bloody hell!" The broad man drew his blade, its silver metal catching the twinkle of starlight to reflect it out in all directions. "It is Ashford that's put you up to this, the bumbling halfwit. I'll have his ruddy head after I've dealt with you."

His charge was steady and practiced. As he drew closer, his tightening muscles gave the impression of dormant power; their fibres having doubtlessly been formed and striated by sheer use and endurance. Her greatest advantage over him, aside from her inability to be slain, of course, was the nimble speed with which she moved. When he brought his sword down to strike her, Rowan bounced up quickly on the balls of her feet, sidestepping his attack with the graceful agility of a cat.

She danced around him evasively for a while, enjoying the morose game. Her opponent was becoming ever more agitated by her tiresome antics.

"Stand still, would you!" He cursed when she'd managed to dodge a particularly well-placed blow. "Stay where you are and fight me like a man."

Rowan held back a disparaging titter at the irony of his words.

"Here I am, Fairfax," she taunted from a narrow gap in the needled trees.

He approached her with a scowl, his barrelled chest heaving dramatically with exasperated effort.

This time, she did remain rooted to the ground, blocking his slashing great sword with her own. She was just able to withstand the brutal onslaught, her arms shaking with the effort of it. When it came down to brute strength, he had her, so she would not lend him that advantage.

Waiting for his next manoeuvre, she didn't attempt to fight back against him this time. Instead of pushing toward his massive body when she met his sword with hers, Rowan offered just a little, loose resistance, and turned with the propelling motion of his swing, spinning with its momentum so that Fairfax, losing his already unstable balance, fell forward onto the hard, frozen dirt.

He pushed himself up quickly with his big arms, but not quickly enough. Rowan knelt directly in front of him, the point of her blade sinking into the exposed skin of his neck.

"No." His eyes were saucers as she stabbed through the quivering flesh. Still, she met his astonished stare, watching the life contained like fire in their depths as it began to extinguish and dull.

Blood pumped out from the major arteries she had severed, in a pulsing, surging rhythm. It ran down to pool at her boots, staining the well-worn hide. It took no effort at all for the burly sod to die. The entire encounter had taken place in no more than a fleeting moment. He was not worth the price Ashford was paying her. She would still claim her offering, of course.

On the following morning, Sam spent longer on

his errand into town than he normally would have. Rowan had begun to grow restless in her steward's absence, wondering anxiously if he hadn't met with some trouble. When finally, she had resolved to go after the young man, donning her broken chainmail armour, he returned, red-faced but unharmed. The envelope from Lord Ashford was held securely under one of his arms, and he drew it out for her, an inquisitive expression passing over his features as he looked upon the battle-ready knight.

"Sam," she grunted, taking the payment, "you've been gone a long while."

"Yes Milady," he answered, drawing a long breath. "I made some inquiries in the town. There have been rumours of dark magic. I heard tell today of an evil sorcerer to the north, and strange smoke has been seen among the White Mountains."

Rowan clasped his shoulder. "Well done, Sam. This gives us definite direction."

The steward nodded. "Shall I purchase the usual provisions?"

"Yes, and be quick about it. I want to set off as soon as we can, before he has the chance to slip through my fingers again."

She'd been tailing her nomadic father for years without success. Every time she thought she'd gotten close to him, he had disappeared again, like a serpentine vapor.

Sam went about his work quickly and proficiently, having even commandeered the local blacksmith in the reparation of his lady's chainmail. They were sufficiently supplied and ready to leave by dawn the next day.

It was a peaceful morning, quiet and bright. The sky stretched out around them like a pink-marbled pearl, streaked with straight white clouds. They kept up an easy, steady pace, not stopping until midday, when the winter sun was at the height of its arch.

They sat together on the sturdy trunk of a fallen tree, contenting their bellies with bread and cheese.

"We will reach our destination before nightfall," she declared between bites. "I can already see the pointed mountain tops to the north."

"Yes Milady," Sam swallowed. "What will you do when you've found him?"

Rowan's eyes narrowed. Her loyal steward was the only other person who knew of her eternal plight. "I will make him suffer for what he did to me," she growled, "for what he did to my mother."

Sam nodded solemnly, his eyes fixed pointedly on the distant mountain range.

"Let us be off again," Rowan said, standing. "We

are close now; I can smell it."

As they rode on through the chilly afternoon, she allowed her mind to reflect upon the last time she'd seen her cursed father. It was on that night of the emerald flames, the one she always dreamt about. His face had been pale and bloodless, his eyes black and shining.

He'd left them for good that night, or so he'd assumed. Rowan had returned to the menacing stronghold, afraid of what to tell her sweet and ailing mother. The poor, suffering woman had lived half of her life in this hellish captivity, forgotten and abandoned by those outside who had once loved her. Her daughter had become the centre of her world, the purpose to which she devoted herself entirely.

It was with an aching heart that the young woman had watched her sickly mother waste away over the next few years, while she herself remained vibrant and strong. The prematurely aged woman would have been unable to withstand the long journey back to civilization, even if her young daughter had been sure of their course.

On the morning of her dear mother's death, Rowan, having lost her only real tie to the mortal world, had tried to end her own life, too. That was when she had learned the true extent of her father's actions on that foggy night long-ago. No matter what she tried, she could not cause enduring, fatal harm to herself. She'd hurled herself from the highest cliff, drowned herself in the small muddy lake, and stabbed through her soft torso with her own trusted sword. Nothing would kill her, because she had *his* blood. When he'd cursed himself with immortality by use of vulgar blood magic, he'd unwittingly cursed his daughter as well. In doing so, he had created his own worst enemy, one that he could not hope to defeat.

She'd set herself to combat training after that, taking her mother's surname, Blackwood, as she ventured out into wide world. Rowan, the name that her mother had given her, she kept, remembering fondly the older woman's story of a Fairy Tree, one that fiercely protected kindness and innocence.

Rowan was not so naïve as to think of herself in such a redeeming light, for she was neither particularly kind nor remotely innocent. Still the name reminded her that she carried her angelic mother's blood too, just as surely as she was burdened by that of her father.

"Up ahead," her steward's voice behind her shook her from her reverie. They had approached the snowy foothills of the white arctic mountain range, and in the distance, partially obscured by falling icy flurries, a dark human form was visible.

"Midnight," Rowan murmured under her breath, for who else would be up in this frozen tundra, alone against the uncompromising elements.

"Be cautious, Milady," Sam warned as he quickened his mount, but his words had fallen mutely upon unhearing ears.

Rowan was riding at a terse gallop, eyes set hard on the mysterious figure. As she drew near, her heart plummeted to her stomach in disappointment.

The person who stood before her in the glistening snow was not her father. It wasn't even a man.

A haggard, elderly woman regarded her with strange blue eyes. She appeared bony and ancient, with white hair that clung to her shining scalp like a wispy spider's web.

Sam, having stopped short just behind his mistress, looked down at the woman with keen interest.

"A witch, do you think, Milady?" he whispered from behind her.

"We shall determine *exactly* who she is presently," Rowan answered, unable to keep the tone of disappointment from her voice.

Dismounting from her tired gelding's saddle, she approached the stationary crone with confident purpose.

"My good lady, what has happened to condemn

you to such a cold and isolative place? Surely you will freeze to your death all the way up here, with nothing to give you shelter."

The woman's misty eyes met hers, but she didn't speak. Instead she smiled, just a small incline of the corners of her wrinkled lips, but Rowan stood back. Something about the expression rattled her to the core.

Sam had climbed down from his horse as well and approached the woman with obvious trepidation.

"You must be frozen," he said softly, extended his hand toward hers.

She moved her own bony hand, flailing out her sleeve to expose her wrist as she did so. A white, bubbling scar at its centre caught Rowan's attention. A cursed wound.

She gasped. The smile, the scar; made something inside her twist and coil like a threatened snake. They brought her back to fifty years ago, to those horrid emerald flames. Drawing her sword, she charged at the old woman, and was not even surprised to see the rounded pupils turn to narrow slits.

Midnight looked back at her now, with such infuriating smugness in his papery features that she cried out.

He put up his hands and she was knocked backward by a sweeping, invisible force.

He laughed, and she did too, though she did not permit him to hear her. As he approached, his arm made a swift, slicing motion, cutting the chapped skin of her cheek. She laughed still harder, put her hand to the wound, and whispered a string of words she had learned by heart from a spell book long ago. The crimson trickle began to emit a greenish steam. Midnight's footsteps halted. He had not expected this, she knew.

"You have spilt the blood you made immortal," she said, turning so that she could look at him.

"You have helped to reverse the unnatural magic which binds you here."

As she spoke, the blood on her face began to bubble and froth, its reaction reflected under Midnight's own pale skin. He put his hands to his face, disbelief evident on his face has the delicate capillaries began to burst, then shrivel. Rowan watched as he collapsed to the ground, then closed her own eyes, at peace for the first time in fifty years.

ERICA SCHAEF is a writer, homemaker, and Registered Nurse, living in rural Tennessee. When she is not writing, Erica enjoys spending time outdoors with her husband and two young children. Her short stories have been featured in multiple anthologies and literary journals, and she hopes to have completed her first full-length novel within the next year.

Bibliography
Colp: Solitude, Gypsum Sound Tales, 2019
Isolation, Fantasia Divinity, 2019
Issue 77, Blood Moon Rising Magazine, 2019
Issue 8, Jitter Press, 2019
Pride, Black Hare Press, 2020
Still Point Arts Quarterly: Fall 2019, Shanti Arts LLC, 2019
The Toilet Zone, HellBound Books, 2019
Volume 06, Visual Verse, 2019
What Monsters Do for Love, Soteira Press, 2020

Connect
Facebook: ericaschaef

BLACK HARE PRESS

THE SCEPTRE

By Matt Lucas

With the flames of his violent past scorched into his mind, Wilas battles through Orixe's blood-soaked arena to gain audience with the ruling Triad and fulfil an ancient prophecy by breaking their oppressive grip on the land.

Raucous cheers resonated through the arena in exhilarated anticipation of the imminent carnage. Wilas' thumping heartbeat drowned out the dissonance. His sweaty grip tightened around his war hammer's handle.

Across the sandy expanse stood a towering bronze gate. Behind that gate a myriad of sadistic terrors lurked, yearning to rip Wilas and his cohort, Klowan, to ribbons. Victory meant earning an audience with the Triad, Orixe's ruling deities, to receive their gift of magic. Defeat, on the other hand, meant death.

The sinewy, bearded Klowan twirled his battle axe and donned his iron shield. "Three hellish bouts to build a better world," he reassured himself.

Wilas placed an iron helm over his jet-black locks and adjusted his leather tunic. The flames of his tortured past blazed through his mind. Visions of charred bodies and scorched earth seared the young warrior's mind.

"Three bouts," Wilas growled through gritted teeth. He'd long envisioned the sweet vengeance at the end of this blood-soaked path.

"It's bound to be a long road," Klowan declared, "so do me a bloody favour and try to have a little fun. You're too damned grim all the time!"

Wilas smirked. "I'll do my best."

Suddenly, a booming bullhorn resounded through the arena. Chains rattled as the bronze gate crept open. Thunderous footsteps echoed from the dark corridor. The first trial began.

"What do you think our first challenge is?" Wilas pondered.

"Well, this is the dragon's trial, so something big and scary that probably wants to eat our faces," Klowan speculated.

"Esteemed spectators," the eccentric, rainbow robed arena master boomed from his raised platform, "I give you...the behemoth!"

The ground quaked. A hulking silhouette charged towards the light. A deep roar blared from the dark tunnel.

Bursting forth into the arena, the behemoth was met with cheers of awe and fear. Two, forward pointing, swirled horns jetted from the beast's brow. Deadly spikes adorned the four-legged creature's back from the nape of its neck to its clubbed tail.

The behemoth's eyes darted about in search of its adversaries. Fixating on the two combatants, the beast released a guttural growl, exposing rows of serrated teeth. The creature kicked its hind legs and snorted like a bull.

"See," Klowan observed, "big, scary, and definitely wants to eat us."

"Any other predictions?" Wilas asked, rolling his eyes.

Klowan grinned. "I'm gonna bury my axe in that damned thing's neck."

"Let's hope you're a prophet," Wilas remarked.

Tremors shook the arena as the behemoth's hefty feet galloped towards its challengers. Undaunted,

Wilas charged towards his rival with Klowan on his heels. The beast lowered its daggered horns with murderous intent.

As the deadly joust neared its inflection point, Wilas reared his war hammer back. Summoning his might, the warrior struck. A loud snap resonated through the arena followed, by an agonising screech.

The devastating collision of hammer and bone splintered the behemoth's left horn from its brow. Recoiling, the beast whirled right while simultaneously swinging its clubbed tail. Wilas ducked low to evade the assault.

Klowan wasn't so nimble. He instinctively crouched behind his shield. However, his refuge was flimsy. A deafening ring resounded through the arena when the tail's hardened flesh bashed iron and sent Klowan careening through the air.

Whirling back around, the behemoth unleashed a deadly counterstrike, snapping wildly at Wilas. Backpedalling, the warrior evaded the onslaught. Unable to restrain its bloodlust, the behemoth lurched forward with yawning jaws.

Winding his hammer back, Wilas swung upwards. Steel collided with bone as teeth fragments sprayed from the behemoth's mouth. The vicious uppercut forced the creature's head skyward.

In a flash, the behemoth exposed its fleshy neck. Wilas' hand sped to his short sword's hilt that hung from his belt. Unsheathing the weapon, the warrior took aim at his foe's neck. However, a warm splatter of black blood interrupted his plot.

The behemoth shrieked as Klowan's battle axe careened through the air and lodged itself into the creature's neck. A fountain of blood cascaded from the beast's severed jugular. Wilas turned to find Klowan triumphantly smirking.

The behemoth groaned and swayed before collapsing in a pool of its own blood. A roar of admiration erupted from the entertained spectators. The eccentric arena master bellowed in exhilaration.

"Never in the history of this prestigious arena has a behemoth been disposed of with such rapid ferocity!" The arena master lauded. "Thanks to the brave Klowan, only two more death defying trials lay between our heroes and the esteemed Triad!"

Wilas cocked his head to the side and leered at Klowan. "So I do the work and you get the glory?"

Klowan chortled, wresting his axe from the behemoth's neck. "I was only fulfilling my prophecy, old friend."

"People of Orixe, our valiant combatants felled the dragon's mighty behemoth," the arena master proclaimed. "Next, the enchantress' trial awaits!"

The sky darkened and a malevolent mist descended on the arena. A chilled wind swept through Wilas' bones. The warriors exchanged apprehensive glances. Triumphant smiles morphed into clenched jaws.

"Stay vigilant," Wilas cautioned. "The enchantress is the mistress of the mind."

Klowan's eyes narrowed with a solemn nod. As the mist descended, Wilas' companion disappeared into the fog. They were on their own now.

Wilas tread into the fog with slow, deliberate steps. He'd witnessed the devastation the enchantress wrought with her psychological warfare. She drove men mad, deceiving them to murder their kin, betray their country, or indulge their darkest desires. There was no telling what horrors might emerge from the mist.

"Wilas," a faint whisper echoed through the fog.

The warrior's eyes scanned the dense fog. Something rustled just out of view. Taking a deep breath to summon his courage, Wilas crept towards the sound.

"Come to me, Wilas," a woman's familiar voice summoned.

Suddenly a humanoid shadow formed within the

mist. It slowly floated towards the warrior. Wilas' heart pounded, his palms became drenched with sweat, and the hair rose on the back of his neck.

"Stay back!" Wilas commanded.

Undaunted, the shadow advanced.

"You wouldn't hurt me, Wilas," the shadow retorted.

"Who are you?" Wilas snarled.

A woman glided out from the murky shroud. She was beautiful, wearing a white robe that made her black hair shimmer like onyx. Her kind, green eyes brought Wilas a long forgotten sense of solace.

Wilas eyes widened with a gasp. His grip loosened on his hammer as it thudded to the sand below. "Mother?"

"Come to me, child," Elys beckoned with a stoic, unblinking gaze.

Wilas' heart leapt within his chest. His face turned flush with joy. Tears welled in his eyes as he staggered towards his mother with outstretched arms.

He wrapped his arms around Elys, though she didn't reciprocate his embrace. "What are you doing here?" She probed.

"I came to avenge you and make the Triad pay for what they've done to this land," Wilas proclaimed.

Elys' eyes narrowed menacingly. "The Triad

didn't kill me…you did."

"What?" Wilas recoiled in bewilderment.

Elys' hand sped to Wilas' throat. She effortlessly lifted him off his feet. With a scowl, her hand clamped down on Wilas' throat. The warrior wheezed, clamouring to suck down air. "Let me remind you what they did to me, what you allowed them to do," she sneered.

Blistering sores and black char slithered across Elys' skin. Her lips receded in decomposition, exposing raw sinew. Her emerald eyes morphed into bloodshot monstrosities as Elys' eyelids melted away.

"Do you remember?" the revolting husk roared. "I was mutilated while you cowered in the forest!"

Smoke singed Wilas' nostrils and tortured screams pierced his ears. In a flash, he was transported back to that fateful day. He'd gone hunting in early in the morning. However, when smoke rose above the tree line, the young boy raced home. There, he met devastation.

Flame consumed their huts. Bodies were strewn about the village. Some wailed in anguish while others were feasted upon by flesh-eating scorpteras. Vile creations of the dragon, scorpteras were vulture-sized bats with venomous scorpion tails.

Meanwhile, the mage's warlocks rounded up the

survivors for interrogation. They unremorsefully tormented with villagers with the Triad's dark magic. Spindles of lava sprouted from their black wands, constricting their victims like blazing serpents. The villagers writhed as their skin sizzled.

Hiding behind a tree, Wilas peered into the desolate ruins of his razed village. With resistance subdued, two figures emerged from the smoke. The first was an alluring woman with red hair and yellow eyes. Flames adorned her luscious figure like an extravagant gown.

Alongside the enchantress stood the mage. His pale flesh bore runes etched in flame. He wore red, flowing robes ornamented with opulent, gold embroidery. An aura of arrogance followed the bald, black-eyed mage.

"Where is the sceptre?" the mage snidely interrogated.

"We don't have it!" Arturo, the villages' husky, white bearded chieftain strained to reply.

"Come now, barbarian," the mage goaded. "Where is the sceptre Yeshu promised you?"

"It isn't here!" Arturo beseeched.

Shifting tactics, the enchantress knelt next to the chieftain. "Perhaps a kiss will jog your memory," she tantalised. Stooping low, the enchantress planted her sultry lips on Arturo's.

"Your kiss has no power here," Arturo snarled and spat in disgust.

"Enough!" the mage boomed. "I'll flay every one of these heathens until they hand over the relic!"

A sinister smile slithered across the enchantress' face. "Your magic is much too quick. Allow our brother to have some fun too."

"He'll decimate the entire village," the mage admonished. "Then the sceptre will be lost."

The enchantress scoffed. "This is the last tribe loyal to Yeshu in Orixe. When they're ashes, rumours of the sceptre will scatter like dust."

The mage ruminated on the plot before relenting with a nod.

"Come, brother," the enchantress called to the sky, "we've prepared a feast for you!"

A dark shadow blotted out the sun. The thunderous flapping of mighty wings sent potent gusts ripping through the land. With a deafening roar, the black-scaled dragon announced his arrival. He sent tremors rippling through the earth when he landed beside his kin.

"Bring forth an offering to the great dragon," the mage instructed his warlocks.

Raising his wand, one of the warlocks levitated a

body constricted by lava. Wilas immediately recognised her jet-black hair. His heart lurched in anguish when he saw the dread in those emerald eyes.

The dragon's mouth yawned wide. An orange glow emanated from its throat. A river of torturous flame erupted from the black lizard. Wilas clenched his eyes shut. He didn't watch Elys' flesh melt from her bones. However, her piercing wails would haunt him for a decade.

"Look at me!" Elys demanded back in the present. "Look at what your cowardice earned!"

Wilas couldn't tear his gaze away from the gruesome woman. Guilt, shame, and self-loathing polluted the warrior's soul. *You deserve the guilt! You deserve the shame! It would've been better if you'd burned with her that day!* A vicious voice accused.

You were just a boy, an advocating voice rose in his defence. *Let go of your pain. Give it to me, so I might fashion it into a weapon.*

A choice lay before Wilas. He could succumb to his malevolent accuser and shackle himself in the chains of guilt and shame. Or, he could cast aside his burdens and embrace redemption.

The choice was clear. Wilas drew his short sword and slashed upwards. Steel sliced through flesh and bone, severing the choking arm. Elys bellowed in agony. However, the attack only served to enflame her rage.

The wench swiped at Wilas with her left hand. The warrior ducked beneath the blow. In her overzealousness, Elys overextended herself, leaving her midsection exposed. Wilas seized the advantage. He flipped the blade to his left hand and thrust it between his foe's ribs. The ghastly wench wailed, though her aggression persisted.

Reversing direction, Elys backhandedly slashed. Wilas' right hand snatched the counterstrike. He ripped the sword from the wench's torso and severed her remaining arm.

Elys dropped to her knees. She hung her head and winced with each laboured breath. "You wouldn't kill your mother," she wept.

Wilas grabbed the wench by the scalp. He forced her tortured eyes to stare into his. His jaw tightened as he pressed the blade's point to her throat. "You're not my mother." Without remorse, he pushed the sword through her throat and out the back of her neck.

When the charred husk collapsed, its façade dissipated. Elys disappeared. In her stead lay a grotesque, emaciated creature. Wilas recognised the pale abomination.

"Banshees," a gruff voice came from behind

Wilas.

The fog began to disperse, revealing a blood-soaked Klowan. His eyes were wide, reeling from whatever horror he'd endured. He panted with physical and emotional exhaustion.

"The enchantress' masterpieces," Wilas spat.

"Bloody, psychotic bitch," Klowan snarled. "She tortures you with your greatest fear before she kills you."

"What'd you see?" Wilas probed.

Klowan's lips apprehensively pursed. "My father…mean sonofabitch. You?"

Wilas fixated on the enchantress' revolting creation. "Guilt."

Raucous cheers erupted when the mist cleared. With the bodies of two banshees and a behemoth left in their wake, only the mage's trail awaited. They were one step closer to the Triad.

A nervous shudder shot through Wilas' spine. Klowan shifted uncomfortably. Both men heard the rumours of the mage's trial. Though they didn't know what their predecessors faced, Klowan and Wilas saw the bodies of those who failed the sadistic contest.

Unsuccessful combatants returned to their families mutilated beyond recognition and drained of blood. One or two victims would always return. However, there was never a scenario where both challengers survived.

Attending arena bouts were exclusive to those who'd received the Triad's magical blessing. This gift could either be earned within the arena or bought with blood sacrifice. Since Wilas and Klowan had not yet completed the arena nor possessed the appalling fortitude to offer a human sacrifice to these twisted deities, they could only speculate what horrors loomed on their horizon.

"And now for the final trial," the arena barker adopted a solemn tone.

The two warriors exchanged stoic glances. "Whatever it takes," Klowan declared.

"Whatever it takes," Wilas affirmed.

The bronze gate squealed open. The dark silhouette of a man stood statuesque and shrouded in shadow. A tense hush fell over the crowd.

Orange symbols began glowing on the shadow's forehead and hands. The runes illuminated red robes with gold ornamentation. A reverent murmur permeated the crowd. The mage stepped forth.

Klowan crouched, readying his axe and shield for battle. Wilas quaking hand slid to a slender scabbard hanging on his belt, opposite his short sword. His fingers wrapped around the white, wooden handle, deliberating on the opportune moment to draw the weapon.

"Patience," Klowan cautioned, anticipating Wilas' plot. "Wait till we have all three."

The mage emerged to deafening veneration. The crowd of loyal followers fawned in awe of the magical deity. Raising his arms exultantly, he breathed in his subjects' adoration.

"Loyal Orixians," the mage addressed the crowd. "Two, commendable warriors stand before you! Together they bested my brother's brutal behemoth and resisted my sister's spiritual assault!"

The crowd lauded Wilas and Klowan.

However, the mage raised a finger to quell the onlookers' enthusiasm. "Still, their noble quest faces a final test! As you know, only the most ruthless are worthy to stand amongst the Triad's elect!"

Wilas gulped. Memories of his mutilated forbearers raced through his mind. He fought to control his breath as it quivered from his mouth.

"Our gift of magic comes at a price," the mage proclaimed, "and only those with the strength to pay may ascend to enlightenment!"

"I don't like the sound of this," Klowan grumbled.

"We are Orixe's *only* source of magic," the mage expounded, "and our favour must be bought with blood! Two vessels stand before you with blood pulsing through their veins!" The deity glowered at the combatants. "For one to overflow, the other must be emptied."

A stark realisation struck Wilas. The mystery of the blood-drained corpses became clear. In order to receive the Triad's magic, one had to betray and murder their partner.

Wilas turned to Klowan. He didn't see the burly, bearded man. Instead, he saw the young boy who found an abandoned child in the forest. He'd shown Wilas kindness and brought him back to his village where they were raised together. He saw a friend. He saw a brother.

"And if we refuse?" Wilas snarled.

A sinister smirk slithered across the mage's face as he unsheathed an obsidian wand from beneath his lavish robes. "We still have a show to put on. Our spectators demand entertainment. So, I will peel the flesh from your bones until their bloodlust is sated."

Dejected, Klowan sighed, embracing his fate. "It has to be me, brother. You know it's true."

"No!" Wilas obstinately refused, "I'm won't kill you!"

"We don't have a choice, you stubborn fool!" Klowan rebuked. "Whatever it takes! Remember!"

Sweat beaded on Wilas' brow. Nervous heat permeated through his chest. He could hear the drumbeat of his heart booming with fear. The hair on his neck stood on edge, like a wild animal boxed into a corner. There was only one way out…forward.

Wilas' fiery gaze met the mage's. Righteous rebellion swelled in his chest. "No. We came here to build a new world. If we're willing to succumb to depravity to seize power, we're not different…we're more of the same."

Klowan grabbed Wilas by the arm. "We get one shot at this and we need all three," he growled. "We can only get to all three if we play their sadistic game."

Epiphany struck. Wilas' grip tightened on his war hammer and his hand brushed over the white, wooden handle nestled in a scabbard. "Not if we make the dragon and the enchantress come to us."

Klowan's brow furrowed. "And how do you propose we do that?"

"They want blood, right?" Wilas pointed his hammer towards the mage. "Once we spill his…they'll come."

The mage scoffed. "So, you've chosen death? A pity. You would've made fine additions to our army."

With reckless abandonment Wilas charged the mage. The deity took aim with his wand. A beam of red energy screamed towards the warrior. When the deadly spell came within range, Wilas swung his mighty hammer.

The gleaming war hammer struck with the spell. A shockwave sent a plume of dust emanating from the collision's epicentre. The beam ricocheted off the weapon and redirected towards the arena's left wall.

Onlookers shrieked as they desperately fled the oncoming spell. A thunderous explosion rocked the landscape, tearing a hole in the arena. Smouldering debris and limbs soared through the air.

A shocked gasp pervaded the crowd. The mage stood wide-eyed and rigid, reeling from the fantastic display. Peasants from the outlying town curiously flocked to the wreckage. They were desperate to get a glimpse into the fabled arena. When they saw a mere mortal standing in defiance of a god, they were awestruck.

"Impossible!" the mage roared.

In a fit of rage the deity lashed about with his wand, unleashing a magical firestorm. The rapid onslaught sent innumerable beams of energy scorching through the air towards Wilas. Despite the assault, the warrior deftly deflected or dodged each attack.

Rebounding curses struck different areas throughout the arena. The Triad's loyal subjects stampeded from the array of explosions that rocked the landscape. Chaos reigned as the spectators trampled over each other in their frantic retreat.

"Enough child's play!" the mage bellowed.

The clouds overhead darkened and swirled as the mage lifted his obsidian wand skyward. An ominous abyss formed in the sky. Black bolts of static electricity flashed from the dark void.

The mage began chanting in a forgotten tongue. A threatening gust swept through the arena, sending Wilas and Klowan skidding backwards. Suddenly a deafening crackle rang out.

A black bolt of lightning careened towards the mage. It struck his wand. Crying out, the deity strained to control the raw power coursing through his body.

His red runes were set ablaze. The mage's body trembled, teeming with dark magic. With a roar, he thrust his wand towards Wilas.

The bolt of black lightning screeched from the wand. A jagged stream of energy sped towards Wilas. The time had come to show Orixe that magic didn't belong to the Triad alone.

Wilas drew a white wand from its scabbard. A gilded river of energy burst forth from the wand. Darkness and light collided.

The ground quaked beneath their feet. A plume of

sparks erupted from the duelling energies epicentre. Light pushed back the darkness until it struck the mage. The Triad's magical deity launched through the air before landing with a thud onto his back.

Sitting up, the mage gawked at his adversary. "How?"

Wilas glowered at his foe. "I'm the flame you couldn't stamp out, the ember that will grow into a wildfire!" The warrior raised his wand once more. His hand trembled as he readied the spell he'd dreamt of casting since the day his village was razed.

An earthquake rocked the arena, interrupting Wilas' killing spell. The dragon burst skyward from behind the bronze gate, leaving heaps of rubble in his wake. He swirled above the arena before landing between Wilas and the mage. The scaled beast released a menacing roar as his sister climbed off his back.

"Looks like your plan worked," Klowan pointed out. "Let's just hope it doesn't get us killed."

"I see we haven't quite eradicated Yeshu's stain from Orixe." The enchantress leered at her rebellious adversaries.

"We must burn away this infection before it festers," the dragon snarled.

"That is your area of expertise, brother," the enchantress goaded.

"It would be my pleasure," the dragon avowed.

He reared his serpentine neck back. An orange glow blossomed within his throat. Smoke billowed from his nostrils and out the sides of his mouth.

"Get behind me!" Wilas shouted to Klowan.

With a roar, the dragon hurled a stream of dragonfire towards them. Klowan dived behind Wilas. The wand wielding warrior looped his wand to his side before whipping it upwards. A shield of water manifested before the warriors.

Steam sizzled, but the watery safeguard refused to yield. Wilas resiliently dug in his heels. The dragon advanced in a futile effort to push back his foes.

With the dragon fire held at bay, Wilas countered. He launched his hammer towards the dragon from behind their defence. The steel sung as it sped through the air. A loud clang erupted when the hammer bashed into the dragon's jaw.

In a flash, the fiery blast ceased. The hammer blow forced the dragon's head skyward. As the black scaled creature recuperated, Wilas thrust his wand forward. An invisible grip latched onto the hammer, halting its momentum. Pulling his wand back towards himself, Wilas summoned the hammer back.

When Wilas' weapon sped back to his hand, the dragon lashed out in anger. Rows of serrated tear barrelled towards the warrior. Thrusting his wand towards the lunging beast, an unseen force restrained the onslaught. With the dragon suspended before him, Wilas struck.

His hammer crashed into the side of the dragon's face. Bone crunched as the beast's orbital bone caved. Releasing a shrill groan, the dragon tumbled onto his side and writhed in agony.

"An impressive display." The enchantress feigned applause.

"I'm not here to impress you," Wilas growled.

"No, you came to destroy us." The smirking enchantress arrogantly wagged her finger at Wilas, "but, you won't."

"Doesn't look that way to me," Klowan retorted. "Your brothers might disagree."

"Two trinkets don't make you a god-killer!" the enchantress snapped. "You know the prophecy. 'With shimmering rock and the sun-washed branch Yeshu shall forge his sceptre, severing the Triad's grip on Orixe and calling his people back to him.' I see no sceptre, just two fools."

The dragon stammered to his feet. The mage rose to re-join his siblings. Though bruised and battered, the Triad remained far from defeat.

Klowan glared incredulously at his cohort. "You

told me Yeshu appeared to you! You said he promised victory!"

Wilas' guilt ridden heart sunk as the colour drained from his face. His faith waned. Noxious doubt infected his soul.

"I-I was certain," Wilas stammered while staring at his weapons. "He told me I'd understand at the appointed time."

"Why would he send us here without the sceptre?" Klowan held out his arms in outrage.

"Yeshu has forsaken you!" the mage taunted. "He sent you here to die! Soon your mutilated bodies will stand as a reminder of what happens to those who rebel against the Triad!"

The enchantress' gaze shifted to the commoners peering through the hole in the arena's wall. She saw how these rebels' resistance caused hope to swell in the downtrodden. "Hope is a dangerous thing," she observed. "Come, brothers, it's time we quench this ember."

Without warning, the dragon's tail whipped towards Wilas. The warrior instinctively held up his hammer to block. However, the beast's powerful tail knocked the weapon from Wilas' grasp.

Wilas thrust his wand out to call back his hammer. Suddenly, a searing pain scorched his wrists, and the stench of singed flesh infested his nostrils. Two fiery whips lashed from the mage's wand to restrain the warrior. Bellowing, Wilas' hand jerked open and his wand fell to the sand below.

Holding her hand out, the enchantress summoned the hammer. It flew into her clutches and she tossed it to the ground before the dragon. "Destroy it."

Wilas fought to wrest himself free from the mage's bonds, to no avail. That's when a stream of dragon fire sped from the dragon's mouth. The glimmering metal glowed red, then orange, before it melted into a shapeless mass.

Cackling triumphantly, the enchantress stooped down and picked up Wilas' wand. She glared at her foe. "Magic belongs to the Triad *alone*."

The white wood bowed. Splinters snapped from their source. Wilas lurched forward against his restraints, but the magmatic shackles only dug deeper into his wrists.

A defiant battle cry resounded from Wilas' left. With his axe high, Klowan charged the enchantress. She sent a cockeyed glance towards her assailant, though she made to move to evade.

Before Klowan could reach his target, the dragon's powerful jaws launched forward. A grisly symphony of teeth screeching against metal and crunching bone tortured Wilas' ears. The dragon lifted Klowan and violently shook his head like a dog snatching a rat. Wilas watched in horror as Klowan's limbs limply flailed before being thrown at the enchantress' feet.

Klowan's breastplate had caved against the dragon's mighty jaws. His lifeless eyes stared hopelessly skyward. Blood pooled beneath his corpse.

A mournful cry blared from Wilas. His closest friend, the man he loved as a brother, was gone. The war hammer he'd held since the day his village burned was reduced to a smouldering pile of melted rock.

The enchantress delivered the final blow. She snapped the white wood and tossed it before the dragon. The beast's fire scorched the wood until it dissolved to ash. Wilas was undone. He'd failed, and it cost him everything.

The shackles left Wilas' wrists. He dropped to his knees and hung his head in defeat. Tears fell to the ground, intermingling with sand and Klowan's blood. He heard the mage shouting a curse, though the noise was muffled by the warrior's grief. A red light flashed. Everything went black.

Sunlight trickled through the towering treetops. The light stung Wilas' heavy eyes as they peered open. He sat up and surveyed his surroundings in bewilderment.

Somehow the warrior had been transported to a small meadow surrounded by a lush forest. At the clearing's centre stood a humble, white tree with a shimmering, silver boulder at its trunk. Wilas recognised this place.

A man with a wavy head of dark brown hair and a beard stood atop the stone. He was pruning away the tree's withering branches so its budding fruit could grow unimpeded. The gardener wore a simple tan tunic bound by a leather belt. Wilas recognised the man as well.

"Why are you here?" the gardener inquired without breaking concentration on the task at hand.

The question drew Wilas' ire. "I should be asking you that question," he growled. "You're the one that sent me into a battle I was destined to lose!"

"Have you lost?" Yeshu replied with scepticism as he hopped down from the rock.

Wilas leapt to his feet. Teeming with anger, he pointed an accusing finger at Yeshu. "They took everything! My hammer! My wand!" A lump developed in Wilas' throat and his fist clenched in a futile effort to quell his swelling emotion. "They murdered Klowan right in front of me…"

Yeshu hung his head and began to weep. Tears trickled from his kind eyes. When droplets struck the ground below, a colourful array of flowers bloomed. "Klowan will rise again," Yeshu proclaimed with certainty.

Despite Yeshu's genuine grief, Wilas remained indignant. "Why should I believe that? Tell me why I should believe any of your promises! You promised victory over the Triad and then sent me into battle without the one weapon that could defeat them! How dare you mourn Klowan! If it weren't for you, he'd still be alive!"

Yeshu absorbed Wilas' rage in silence.

"You were supposed to protect us! Look at the world you built! You let the Triad in and left us with no way to protect ourselves…just like you sent me into that arena without your precious sceptre!" Wilas spat in anger.

"Everything I've done, I've done to break the bonds of evil on my people," Yeshu justified. "I will redeem all things, even the worst things. I promise you, soon, you'll understand."

"Enough of your promises! I was loyal! I did everything you asked, and you still sent me to my death!" Wilas snapped.

Yeshu shook his head. "I gave you exactly what you needed."

"Except for the sceptre!" Wilas snarled, "You

neglected to give me the key to accomplish the task you entrusted to me!"

"Do you remember what happened the day I brought you here?" Yeshu asked rhetorically. "I found you standing in the ashes of your village amongst the dead. I wiped the tears from your eyes, took you by the hand, and led you to this very meadow."

"I remember," Wilas replied through gritted teeth.

"From the boulder I carved your war hammer and from the white tree's branch I cut your wand," Yeshu expounded.

"And now they're gone," Wilas rebutted.

"Because you misused them!" Yeshu countered. "You idolised them as if they were divine! You replaced me with the very gifts I gave you! They were tools so you could harness the power I gave you, not the source of that power!"

"It doesn't matter now," Wilas lamented. "The wand is gone. The hammer is gone. The sceptre is gone, if it even existed at all."

"Are you still so blind?" Yeshu reprimanded. "With shimmering rock and the sun-washed branch *I* shall forge *my* sceptre, severing the Triad's grip on Orixe and calling *my* people back to *me*."

"I know the prophecy," Wilas begrudgingly confirmed.

"You don't," Yeshu corrected. "I cut your hammer from that shimmering boulder to forge your strength. I fashioned your wand from the sun-washed branch so you might harness the magical power I entrusted to you."

Wilas' eyes widened as epiphany struck. His heart skipped a beat. "The Triad thought they were looking for a weapon that day…"

"You are the sceptre," Yeshu revealed. "You are the one I will wield to severe the Triad's grip on Orixe and call my people back to me."

"But, I'm dead," Wilas reminded Yeshu.

Yeshu smiled and stooped down. He plucked one of the colourful flowers that grew out of his tears. "The Triad's magic can only destroy, but my power gives life. Today, you will show Orixe a new path."

A renewed faith bubbled within Wilas. "What happens now?"

"My spirit runs courses through your veins," Yeshu explained. "I will fight through you. You need only to let me."

A gasp of air filled Wilas' lungs. His eyes jerked open to meet an empty, grey sky. Raucous cheers resounded in the warrior's ears, and his hands stroked the arena's coarse sand.

Peering towards his feet, Wilas observed the Triad

drinking in their followers' admiration. The mage and enchantress waved to their fawning followers. The dragon took flight for a victory lap high above the arena.

Wilas sat up with a groan and gingerly worked his way to his feet. Like smoke being swept away by wind, the applause gave way to a shocked hush. Sensing the shifting tone, the mage and enchantress surveyed the scene for the source of their followers' astonishment.

The enchantress' smile fell into a frown. Her yellow eyes narrowed, and her jaw clenched. "Are you so stubborn that you won't even do us the courtesy of dying?" she sneered.

The mage shoved his sister aside. He angrily paced towards Wilas with his wand raised. "You mock me with every breath you draw!"

The enchantress snatched her brother's arm before he could cast his spell. Her teeth gritted as she shoved him backwards. "Clearly you're unfit for this battle," she growled.

Above their heads, the dragon roared. The beast looped behind his siblings and set course for Wilas. With two mighty flaps, the dragon sped towards his prey with smoke billowing from his nostrils.

Taking a deep breath, Wilas closed his eyes. *I will fight through you. You need only let me,* Yeshu's voice echoed through the warrior's mind.

Wilas obediently turned his palms up. A gentle breeze comforted him. The hair on the back of his neck stood on edge as Yeshu's familiar presence entered his midst. A euphoric wildfire blazed within his soul.

Smoke singed the warrior's nostrils. A heated gust blew against his face. The temperature grew hotter and the dragon's beating wings grew louder.

Now, Yeshu whispered to his sceptre.

Wilas' eyes shot open. They glowed gold as Yeshu's power teemed from his spirit. Light cloaked the warrior like armour. A triumphant shout bellowed from the deepest reaches of Wilas' being.

Dragon fire scorched the sand as it sped towards Wilas. Nothing stood between the beast and his prey. Suddenly a crackling boomed from the sky above.

A gilded pillar of light ripped through the grey sky. The beam sped earthbound with a thunderous hum. Onlookers screamed in terror.

A high-pitched squeal emanated from the dragon. A fountain of black blood saturated the sands below. The beast's body fell limply behind the pillar with flame spouting from its neck while his head continued soaring forward.

Blood spurted from the severed head as it bounced across the arena before skidding to a halt at Wilas' feet.

The warrior lifted his gaze to the mage and enchantress. The deities were wide-eyed and rigid.

"You murdered countless innocents to find Yeshu's sceptre," Wilas taunted. "Now you've found me!" The sceptre's fists clenched. Golden sparks of jagged electricity flashed from his palms.

The mage stepped forward. He raised his trembling wand. Sweat beaded on his forehead, causing steam to rise from his head where the moisture contacted his fiery runes.

The enchantress put her hand on her brother's arm. She slowly lowered his wand. "This war has only just begun."

A black portal, much like the one from which the mage called the black lightning, formed behind the deities. The remnants of the Triad slowly backed into the abyss. Once they entered, the portal rapidly shrunk and disappeared into thin air.

Throughout the arena, Triad's loyalists followed suit. An array of black portals popped in and out of view as onlookers fled. Soon the stands were empty. However, the arena was not.

Droves of peasants from the surrounding villages tentatively crept towards Wilas. He exhaled and relaxed his hands. The sparking lightning ceased, and the luminous armour dissipated.

"Don't be afraid," Wilas beckoned them to come closer.

One of the children stepped forward. Her face was smeared with dirt, and her clothes were ragged. "How did you do that?"

Wilas' lips pursed as he considered how to respond. "I let someone stronger fight through me."

"What kind of warlock are you?" An elderly man with a crooked back wagged his cane at Wilas. "The Triad's magic didn't do nothing but destroy! We don't need another tyrant!"

Wilas cocked his head towards Klowan's lifeless body. Without answering, he strode towards his oldest friend and knelt next to him. The sceptre placed his hand on Klowan's bloody and broken chest. "The Triad only brought death, but Yeshu sent me to show you life."

A light spread from Wilas' palm. Klowan gasped and lurched forward. His bewildered eyes darted about. "What'd I miss?"

"One or two things," Wilas affirmed, glancing over towards the dragon's head.

"How did—? I remember— How did you—" Klowan stammered feeling around his torso for broken bones.

"All you need to know is that we won," Wilas

answered, patting Klowan on the back.

Klowan's eyes narrowed. "What about the enchantress and the mage?"

"Fled," Wilas answered.

Leaving Klowan's side, Wilas picked up his melted war hammer and the remnants of his wand. Light emanated from his palms. The hammer's shimmering metal regained its original form. The wand mended to perfect condition.

"What do we do now?" Klowan probed.

Wilas looked out towards the crowd of peasants. "We do what we came here to do…we build a better world."

MATT LUCAS writes varying forms of speculative fiction, including urban fantasy, paranormal, sci-fi, and horror. He is represented by Labyrinth Literary Agency and his debut novel, The Shadow Gospels, is in process for publication.

He's had several short stories published with Black Hare Press, Blood Song Books, Eerie River Publishing, and Fantasia Divinity Magazine. As his career progresses, he's always seeking opportunities to expand his resume. Writing is his passion and he hopes to spend his days cultivating captivating stories with impactful messages.

Bibliography
Angels, Black Hare Press, 2019
Apocalypse, Black Hare Press, 2019
Beyond, Black Hare Press, 2019
Flashes of Fantasy, Fantasia Divinity Magazine, 2020
Forest of Fear, Blood Song Books, 2019
Forgotten Ones, Eerie River Publishing, 2020
What If? , Black Hare Press, 2019
Worlds, Black Hare Press, 2019

Connect
Amazon: www.amazon.com/-/e/B07TKDMZWL
Twitter: @MattDLuke

MOUTHPIECE

By Annie Percik

Lissandra has grown up far from the capital in a convent, with only her maid for company. But, when the king dies, she is called to claim her birthright and discover the origins of the voice in her head.

I speak to her at night, whispering strange words deep into her mind, where they mingle and breed as she sleeps. Tendrils of thought and idea combine to form solid strands, twisting themselves into a stream of words. All of this is at my command, her slumbering self my conduit. She will be my voice, my means of communication to the masses, the tool through which my message will be heard. My plan has been long in the making, and I am impatient for it to come to fruition. For now, though, I will plant the first kernels in her mind and wait.

***

The morning bell woke Cerrise from a sleep troubled by formless shadows lurking in the corners of her mind. But the sense of dread rapidly retreated with the early sunlight as the events of the day ahead pushed themselves forward for attention. Clambering out of bed, she winced her way across the chilly, stone floor to where a basin of water sat on a table, upon which a film of ice had formed overnight. She washed briskly, then pulled her indigo robes over her head. The rough wool scratched at her skin as the fabric settled into place, and she thought back to a time when she habitually wore silk and had a lot more than one outfit in her wardrobe.

Sighing, she twisted her greying hair into a simple braid and tied off the end as she moved to where her sandals waited by the door. She fastened the straps around her ankles with practised fingers, even as her back protested the stooped posture the action required. Resigned to face the day, Cerrise pulled open the heavy wooden door of her room and walked down the hallway to knock on the next door along. Unsurprisingly, there was no response, so she pushed the door open and stepped inside. An unmoving lump in the narrow bed told her she had her work cut out for her. She moved to the window and pulled open the drapes to let the early morning sunshine into the room.

There was a protesting moan from the direction of the bed.

"They won't hold up morning prayers for you, Lissa," Cerrise scolded. "And you don't want the mother superior to reprimand you again."

There was another moan and Cerrise wondered, not for the first time, if the duty she had been performing for the last fifteen years was a terrible punishment meted out for some unknown transgression in a past life.

Before she had to resort to stripping the blankets from the bed, though, her charge emerged, long sable hair in disarray, expression resentful. Lissa pouted, then reluctantly pushed herself upright and dragged herself out of bed. Cerrise considered that her job description from their life before hadn't changed much since their arrival at the convent. Their accommodations, clothing, and lifestyle might have altered beyond all recognition, but she was still basically waiting on Lissa hand and foot, even to the extent of helping her dress and brushing her hair. It was possible that this continued service had contributed to the girl's almost total lack of humility. Perhaps if she had forced Lissa to fend for herself in their new surroundings, the girl might have developed some new attitudes. But old habits were difficult to break and Cerrise had never learned to be anything other than a servant. Still, it was important to remember that their fortunes would one day change again, and Lissa would need to be prepared for that far more than she needed to fit into life at the convent.

***

Years before, and miles away, the palace was in a state of fevered anticipation as news spread that the queen had gone into labour. Phylos, the King's Chancellor, waited anxiously for an update from the birthing chamber. The king had been reassuring the council for years that the succession would not fail, even as his hair turned to grey and the lines on his face multiplied and grew deeper.

Faith in the king's connection to the god, Athras, was strong, so the council was willing to accept that the king's protestations were backed by divine assurance. But Phylos had begun to worry that even this faith might begin to crumble in the face of the king's continued childlessness. When the queen finally fell pregnant, there had been celebrations throughout the land, and the people had followed the development of the child obsessively. There had been a resurgence in the worship of the silent goddess, Arla, as the people prayed for the health of both queen and baby. But the strain of the nation's expectations on the queen had been considerable, during a pregnancy that had also proved physically debilitating.

Now, the day of the birth had at last arrived, and the entire nation was holding its breath for good news. Royal criers were stationed at the palace gates, ready to ring any announcement around the city, and mounted couriers were gathered in the palace courtyard, preparing to transport proclamations to the surrounding countryside. So, when Cerrise, the queen's young handmaiden, emerged from the birthing chamber, Phylos rushed up to her eagerly.

He noted with apprehension the weariness in her posture and the way her hair was escaping from its usually neat bun, but then she smiled.

"Twins," she said. "A boy and a girl." The sound of infants crying reached them from beyond the door behind her and she smiled more widely. "Both healthy."

Overtaken by the moment, Phylos grabbed both

her hands and squeezed them tightly.

"That's marvellous!" he exclaimed. After such a long wait, the god had provided a son to take the throne and a daughter to capture the hearts of the people. The outcome couldn't have been better. "And the queen?"

Cerrise's expression sobered. "She's exhausted and I can tell the midwife is worried. You know she was already weak, and the labour was a difficult one. But, hopefully, with rest and good care, she will recover."

"I must tell the king," Phylos said. "The nation will rejoice with him. Praise Athras!"

"Praise Athras," Cerrise echoed, though without the same level of fervour.

Phylos assumed that was simply due to her fatigue, and he was already planning the wording of the proclamations that would need to be written. He released Cerrise's hands and hurried off to attend to his joyful duties.

***

Once Lissa was finally ready, Cerrise led her towards the prayer hall. It was quiet in the hallway; there were not many members of the convent, and they would all be gathered for the morning service already.

The convent's corridors were chilly in the wan morning sunlight, their breath collecting in clouds before them as they walked. Cerrise did her best to hurry Lissa along, only to find their entrance to the prayer hall blocked by an imposing figure. As they approached, Cerrise recognised the mother superior. They came to a halt in front of her and both woman and girl bowed their heads in respectful greeting.

"Blessed be thou at the break of day," Cerrise intoned and heard Lissa barely whispering the words along with her, just a beat behind.

The mother superior's face was stern. She was a hard woman, and Cerrise was certain she disapproved of their presence there, even though she had never said as much. Cerrise couldn't blame her, since neither of them were exactly model devotees. She often wondered what the mother superior had been told about them, to persuade her to accept them into this isolated community. Even out here, so far from the capital, there must have been rumours.

"There is a visitor for you, waiting in the cloister," the mother superior said stiffly. "This is highly irregular, but I will allow you both to miss morning prayers. Go now, so you do not disrupt the entire convent."

Lissa looked at Cerrise with wide, questioning

eyes, but Cerrise had no answers for her. They had been secluded here for so long, and she had not yet begun to prepare for any change to their now ingrained routine. They made their way to the covered cloister, eventually emerging into thin sunlight and a sharp breeze.

The visitor, robed and hooded in the familiar purple hue of the convent, was sitting on a wooden bench close to the wall, but rose swiftly as the two women came into view. Large, strong hands reached up to push back the hood and Cerrise felt a stab of painful recognition. Lissa gasped in astonishment beside her, at the unexpected sight of a man. She had been so young when they first arrived here, and her interactions had only been with women since that time.

Phylos stepped towards them and Lissa shied away from him. Cerrise put an arm around her in reassurance, though she was shaken by her own feelings at seeing him. He represented everything she had been forced to leave behind, and everything that was waiting for her in the nebulous, long-imagined future she had constructed in her mind during the long winter evenings at the convent. She yearned for that life, but also feared it, and she knew she and Lissa were not ready to step back into it yet.

Complex emotions played across Phylos' features, as well, as he held out a hand in greeting.

"It's time," he said.

***

The little prince and princess grew quickly, cosseted and spoiled by everyone in the palace and allowed to get away with almost anything. Phylos knew Cerrise tried to instil some sense of decorum in them, but she was fighting a losing battle as the only disciplinarian in their young lives. The queen's health had deteriorated rapidly in the days after the birth, and she had eventually slipped away in her sleep one night. With the loss of his wife, the king might have shunned his children as too painful a reminder of her death, but instead he clung to them and indulged them in everything.

The palace servants pitied their motherless status and plied them with sweets, while the guardsmen developed elaborate games to keep them entertained. They had the run of the palace and made good use of it, tearing through the hallways and getting into every tower and cellar. They were inseparable, almost to the extent that Phylos couldn't remember ever seeing them apart. So alike in form and feature, it was only the difference in the style of their dress that allowed him to tell them apart in their early years.

It was when the twins were about four years old that Cerrise came to him. He was surprised to see her in his office and could tell from her expression that she was worried about something. She hovered in the doorway until he invited her in, and then she looked very uncomfortable in the chair on the other side of his desk. She fiddled with the hem of her bodice in silence until he spoke.

"What is it?" he asked, smiling in an attempt to put her at ease.

She looked up at him, uncertainty clear in her eyes.

"The princess told me something, and I don't know what it means."

Phylos didn't know what to make of this. What could a four-year-old girl possibly tell her nursemaid that would result in a visit to his office in such consternation?

"Oh?" he prompted.

"She's been having strange dreams for a few weeks but hasn't really been able to tell me what they're about before now. But, this morning, she said she heard a voice talking to her in her head."

Phylos felt apprehension building in his chest. He had been waiting for just this kind of news from Cerrise, or someone else close to the children, but it should have been the prince imparting such information, not the princess. He tried to laugh it off.

"She must be picking ideas up from her brother," he said. "It's not unusual for her to want to copy him."

"But the prince has never mentioned anything of the sort," Cerrise said. "I've asked him about it, as I know you've been expecting it to start happening any time now, but he's never shown any sign that he understands what I'm talking about. And now this—what does it mean?"

"I don't know," he replied, his brows lowering in consternation, "but nothing good."

***

In the convent cloister, Phylos gave a heavy sigh.

"The king is dead," he said.

Cerrise stared at him, unable to process what she had just heard.

"But how?" she asked. "When? Why hasn't there been news of this?"

Phylos sighed again, and Cerrise noticed for the first time how much older he looked. She knew he must be thinking the same thing of her, but it was more than the passage of time that had marked his once strong features with such weariness and worry. For the first time, she wondered if her quiet existence at the convent might have been a blessing compared to what he had been dealing with back at the palace.

"The council decided to keep it a secret for the time being until we could decide what to do. They knew all was not well with the prince—"

"The prince?" Cerrise interrupted. "What's wrong with the prince?"

"He's spent all the years you've been away, knowing he is supposed to hear the god, waiting for the voice to come to him, and never experiencing it. It's an impossible burden for a young man to carry, and he hasn't dealt with it well. He is reckless and selfish. He drinks too much, and he does not care for the wellbeing of the kingdom."

Cerrise thought back to the happy, boisterous little boy she had cared for in his infancy and felt a pang of sorrow for all the years of his life she had missed. Perhaps if she had been there, she could have helped him, guided him through his struggles. The goddess knew she hadn't been much help to Lissa during that time.

Phylos continued. "When the king died, I knew something would have to be done. So, I revealed to the council what the princess told you all those years ago, and what we did. Some said the tradition of male succession was sacrosanct and should be maintained no matter what. Others said the princess hearing voices was a sign from the god that there must be change. The first group argued that the word of a four-year-old girl could not be relied upon to make such a momentous decision. And so it went on, until I volunteered to come here and bring you both back with me to the palace."

Lissa had been silent up till now, presumably entirely bewildered by the conversation. But this last part piqued her interest and she spoke up.

"The palace?" she echoed. "We're going to the palace?"

Phylos ignored her, keeping his focus on Cerrise. "What have you told her?" he asked.

"Nothing," Cerrise replied. "As we agreed. She thinks she is an orphan, raised by the convent because her village was too poor to support her."

"And am I not?" Lissa's tone was gaining in intensity, and she pulled on Cerrise's arm to turn her around.

Cerrise looked into the young woman's face, seeing all the years of tantrums and disobedience, but also the potential for great strength and purpose. She wanted to protect Lissa from the world, keep her safe here at the convent, in peace and isolation. She didn't want Lissa to be cast against the rocks of the outside world and forced to fight for her place in society. But

Cerrise knew there was no way to resist the pull of the past. She had known all along this day would come, and she also knew the part she had to play in it.

"No, Lissa," she said. "You are not."

***

"What does it mean?" the king asked, his expression guarded.

"We don't know," Phylos admitted. "I've tried to speak to both children about the matter, but I haven't been able to get much information from them. It seems clear the prince has had no contact from the god thus far, and I really don't know what to think about what Cerrise reported about the princess." He paused, trying to dredge up the courage for what needed to be asked next. "Hasn't Athras told you anything about what's going on?"

The king slumped in his chair, eyes downcast, demeanour utterly defeated. Phylos was disturbed; the king had always been a strong and commanding figure, even in their private conversations, and it frightened him to see his monarch so vulnerable.

"I've been trying to hide it," the king said, "but I suppose now I must tell you." He looked up and met Phylos' gaze, his own expression one of mingled fear and despair. "I haven't heard the voice of the god since the children were born."

Phylos stared at him. The entire foundation of the kingdom was built on the people's faith that the god Athras spoke through the monarch and thus guided and watched over them. If the news got out that the king's connection to the god had been severed, it would be impossible to predict the consequences. This was potentially far more catastrophic than the idea that the god was now speaking to the princess, rather than the prince. Phylos tried to think of something positive to say.

"At least, if what the princess says is true, it means Athras hasn't abandoned us altogether," he managed.

The king nodded. "I hope so," he said. "But she's only four years old. She can't rule now, even if the council and the people were to accept her as heir. What are we going to do in the meantime?"

Phylos was thinking hard. "We need time to decide on a long-term plan," he said. "Athras has put this challenge before us and we must rise to it. But if the princess starts telling stories about voices in her head, we won't be able to control the situation. We need to send her away, somewhere safe, where she'll be protected but won't be able to cause any trouble."

The king stared at Phylos in open despair for a long

moment. He doted on both his children, and the thought of having to send the princess away was clearly painful to him. Then he let out a heavy breath.

"All right," he said, his voice weighed down with resignation. "But what about my son?"

Phylos was thinking fast, the plan developing in his mind as he spoke it aloud. "He will stay in place as heir for the time being. We'll have to pretend all is well and that the god is still in communication with both of you." Phylos fixed the king with a hard stare. "I know it won't be easy, and I know we won't be able to keep up the pretence forever, but we have to think of what's best for the people. Perhaps the god's plan will become clearer in time."

"Yes, we must trust in Athras to show us the way," the king said, though Phylos thought he sounded less than confident.

***

"So, the god has been silent all this time?" Cerrise's body trembled at the rough passage of the carriage, even as her mind trembled at what Phylos was telling her.

There had been neither tears nor heartbreak at their departure from the convent. Lissa was eager to see the world she had no memory of, and the mother superior was clearly delighted to see them go. Cerrise's own emotions were more difficult to define. She had never felt at home at the convent, but at least it was safe and predictable. Now, she was being thrust back out into the world of political intrigue and societal uncertainty with no preparation, and she was frightened of what might happen.

"Yes, the god has been silent," Phylos confirmed, "and things have been slowly unravelling for some time. Crops have failed in various parts of the kingdom, and people in the more rural areas are struggling to survive. The poor in the cities have increased in number as those who could no longer make a living farming have headed there to find new lives. But, as supplies from outside have dwindled, life in the cities has just kept getting harder, too. At first, the people looked to the king to help them and to tell them what to do, but his mind started to crumble under the pressure of keeping up the lie, and after a while, he was no longer able to make public appearances. The council and I tried to keep it quiet, but it was difficult to hide. We turned to the prince for help, but he was suffering a similar mental burden, with the added sense of failure that the god had never chosen to speak to him. When the king eventually died, it forced my hand. It was almost a relief to have to take action at last."

Cerrise knew how hard it must be for Phylos to admit those feelings. He had always been a faithful servant to the king, and it must have torn him apart to see the monarchy falling to pieces like that. She glanced over to where Lissa was asleep on the opposite bench of the carriage.

"But what do you expect her to do?" she asked.

"I don't know," Phylos admitted. "But Athras must have a plan. He spoke to her as a child, so he must intend great things for her. Does she mention hearing him speak often?"

Cerrise was troubled. "I believe the voice is still with her," she said, "but she doesn't confide in me. She has always been secretive about what it says, so I have no better idea than you what the god may have in store for her—and for us."

"Let us hope things will become clear when we reach the palace and reveal Lissa's connection to Athras," Phylos said. "We need a sign of how to proceed; otherwise, the kingdom may quickly fail outright."

It is a tremendous amount of pressure to heap on a young, untried girl, Cerrise thought. But surely the god would guide and protect her on the journey. This must have been his intention all along, though why he was forcing the people to endure this trial, only Athras knew.

***

Cerrise bundled the little princess into a warm coat, struggling to get her arms in the sleeves, while the child wriggled and tried to get away.

"But I don't want to go outside!" the girl wailed. "I want to play in here!"

Cerrise didn't blame her. There was snow on the ground outside and the sky threatened more at any moment. The little girl had never liked the cold, and the room they stood in had both a roaring fire and many beautiful toys scattered about. Cerrise herself would much rather stay, too. But she also agreed with Phylos' analysis. They couldn't remain in the palace and pretend nothing was wrong, nor could they conceal the problem of the god speaking to the wrong child for much longer. One word from Lissa to the wrong person and the whole secret would come tumbling out.

"We're going on an adventure," Cerrise said, attempting to make the words sound enticing. "Don't you want to travel further than you've ever travelled before and see parts of the kingdom you never knew existed?"

Their 'adventure' would actually be a very uncomfortable carriage ride to a small convent of Arla up in the north, far away from the palace and all the comforts they had previously known. Nobody there would know their true identities, and they would be forced to live in seclusion and simplicity for an unknown number of years. But Cerrise wasn't going to tell the princess that, not when she was already struggling with the idea herself.

"No!" the princess said firmly, sitting down on the rich carpet and folding her arms in defiance.

Cerrise felt sorry for her. She would be leaving everything she had ever known and would not see her brother again for who knew how long. She wouldn't understand what was happening, and Cerrise wouldn't be able to explain it to her. But, at the same time, she was acting like the spoiled brat she was, and Cerrise was growing impatient. She reached down and lifted the princess into her arms, holding Lissa close to stop her from breaking free. She ignored the child's cries as she carried her through the palace and into the cold afternoon and the waiting carriage.

The following day, to explain their disappearance, the royal criers would announce a terrible accident that had claimed the lives of the young princess and her faithful nursemaid. Cerrise and Lissa would be far away by then, beginning their new lives at the convent.

***

As the carriage drew closer to the palace, it became clear that something strange was going on in the city. It didn't appear to have changed much in the fifteen years Cerrise had been away, though there was more litter and the people she saw were dressed more poorly. It was the people that drew her attention. There were many more of them out in the streets than she would expect to see this late in the day, and the crowds got denser as their journey progressed.

"What's going on?" she asked Phylos, who was looking out of the carriage window in consternation.

"I have no idea," he said, "but I can't imagine it's a good sign."

Lissa, too, had her face pressed against the window, on the other side, taking in the unfamiliar sights.

"This is my city," she murmured, and Cerrise and Phylos exchanged an uneasy glance.

By the time they drew up outside the palace gates, the carriage had slowed to a crawl, and the driver was having difficulty avoiding the mass of pedestrians that practically blocked the road. The guards opened the gates at the sight of the liveried driver, but had their work cut out for them to stop any of the other people from swarming inside the palace grounds along with them.

Phylos, Cerrise, and Lissa climbed out of the carriage and were immediately approached by a harried looking young man in expensive robes.

"My lord Phylos, thank Athras you're back," he said breathlessly. "The whole city has gone mad. The people are on the verge of storming the palace."

"What's going on?" Phylos asked.

"They're demanding to see the king!" the young man replied. "They want to know why he hasn't been seen in so long, and they want to know why the god has abandoned them."

"Summon the council," Phylos ordered. "I have important news that may lead to a solution. We'll meet them in the conference chamber as soon as they can convene."

Cerrise picked up her skirts in preparation for climbing the steps to the palace doors.

"No."

Cerrise looked round in surprise at the single, forceful syllable from Lissa. The girl stood strong and straight in the purple robes of the goddess and something like authority shone from her eyes. She fixed the young man with an arrogant stare.

"You will bring the prince immediately, and this council as well, if you think it wise. I will address them and my subjects together."

The young man glanced fearfully at Phylos, who didn't look much more certain about what was happening. He nodded, though, and the young man went scurrying off. They didn't have to wait long. After only a few minutes, a group of men wearing chains of office emerged from the palace and joined them in the courtyard. Among them was a tall youth with dark hair and a regal bearing. Behind the sullen expression and uncaring attitude, Cerrise could see the shadow of the little boy she had once loved.

Lissa took up a position on the palace steps, facing the gates where the populace still gathered. She beckoned to the prince with an imperious gesture, and Cerrise was surprised when he simply stepped forwards to stand just below her. Then, Lissa spread her hands wide and spoke in a voice that was amplified beyond normal human volume.

"Citizens, hear me! I know life has been difficult for you these past years while I have been away, and for that I am sorry. The road to the death of the patriarchy has been hard on all of us, but today marks the beginning of a new age. The king is dead and the false prince, Lithandathras, has no claim to the throne, as the god, Athras, has never spoken to him."

There were gasps and shouts from the crowd, both outside and inside the gates, but Lissa wasn't finished.

"I am the princess, Lissandarla, returned from exile to become your queen and lead you back to glory and prosperity. For his crimes against the nation, the pretender prince will die."

A purple light flashed in her eyes, and Lissa brought one of her arms around to point directly at her brother. She flicked her fingers and a bolt of lightning shot from them to strike him square in the chest. Screams erupted from several directions, as the prince collapsed to the ground, his body smoking.

Cerrise and Phylos looked on in horror, unable to comprehend what had just happened. They had brought Lissa back to be the people's salvation, to heal the breach between the monarchy and the gods. But she had begun her rule with an act of fratricide. How could this be what the god wanted?

***

I speak to her in the day now, shouting familiar words out of her mind, where they combine to direct the way she thinks and feels. Thoughts and plans come together to create solid intentions, weaving themselves into a series of actions. All of this is at my command, her waking self my conduit into the world. She is now my body, my means of revelation to the masses, the tool through which my plan will come to fruition. After so long, plotting and scheming, preparing the way for my rise to power, my time has finally come. I am the silent goddess no longer, and she is my puppet and partner, destroying her brother as I have destroyed mine, so that the age of the goddess can truly begin.

ANNIE PERCIK lives in London with her husband, Dave, where she writes novels and short stories, whilst working as a University Complaints Officer. She writes a blog about writing, makes a media review podcast with her husband, and publishes a photo-story blog, recording the adventures of her teddy bear. He is much more popular online than she is. She likes to run away from zombies in her spare time.

Bibliography

Alternative Truths III: Endgame, B Cubed Press, 2019
Apocalypse, Black Hare Press, 2019
Beyond, Black Hare Press, 2019
GEEK OUT!: QUEER POP LIT, ART & IDEAS, Qommunicate Press, 2019
Hate, Black Hare Press, 2020
Life Plus 2M Volume 2, Life Plus 2M Project, 2018
Life Plus 2M, Life Plus 2M Project, 2016
Love, Black Hare Press, 2020
One Hundred Voices Volume 2, Centum Press, 2016
Pride, Black Hare Press, 2020
Slave to the Axe Song, Shreyer Ink Publishing, 2018
The Wishing Star, NAWG, 2017
Unravel, Black Hare Press, 2019

Connect
Website: www.alobear.co.uk
Bear Blog: www.aloysius-bear.dreamwidth.org
Twitter: @apercik
Twitter (Podcast): @loveittomorrow

CORVALO AND THE OUTSIDE WORLD

By S. Gepp

Corvalo does not want the cloistered life of his tree-top village. Not knowing what lies beyond the forest, he ventures forth only to find a world that he does not—and cannot—understand.

Corvalo didn't want to go in, but it was his duty. Until he reached his twenty-first summer, he was not considered an adult and so, with all the other youngsters, this was where he had to go each full moon. Next summer it would be all over, but for now he was forced to be here.

He paused and looked out over their village, high

in the canopy of the trees. Two days before, he had joined the men in a hunt, bringing down eight birds on his own; now he was entering the temple with the other children. No longer a child, not yet a man. He did not like this half-life.

"Are you awaiting something?"

Corvalo looked at the young woman beside him and smiled happily. Carinna. Her hand took his briefly and squeezed. Like himself, come the next summer, she would also be an adult. They had promised themselves to one another, and their families had approved; if any of their parents or family members knew just how physically they had promised themselves, they may not have been so pleased with their decision. But Corvalo and Carinna already considered themselves adults, and their love was merely a part of that.

"I do not want to go in there," Corvalo muttered. "Sukhio treats us all like we are still amongst the youngest."

Carinna grimaced; this was a conversation they'd had before. Corvalo and Carinna were the eldest amongst the children by two summers, yet it felt like ten or more. The rest all seemed so young and childish. But Carinna knew this was important. This was their knowledge of Zilozium, their town in the trees, knowledge passed on from the shaman to the youngsters. They had to know about their lives and their city. It was all that existed in their world.

Corvalo, she knew, did not feel that way. He wanted to know about the world beyond, if there was such a thing, about other towns, about other peoples. She just hoped that once they were considered adults, his love for her and their desire to be together would overcome all his doubts.

Corvalo finally sighed heavily and indicated that Carinna should lead the way into the wooden temple set into the fork of an ancient tree, spanning three other trees in size. The building was large enough for every member of their town to fit into for the rituals that occurred periodically throughout the year, the canopy of their forest home dropping away far below to a view of green and brown. For the two dozen youngsters, it hardly felt warranted that they be in such a large hall. But Sukhio lived here, in quarters set above the rear of the structure, and it was down the wooden ladder the old man now came, dressed in the garments all knew as his—all made of leaves and bird feathers, the skull of a mighty eagle on his head. He shuffled across to the centre of an empty area and stared at those gathered, sitting on mats made of woven bark.

"There are two of you who will very soon take the final steps into adulthood," he intoned in his deep, slow voice. All turned to look at Corvalo and Carinna who smiled awkwardly back at them. "As such, I feel now would be a good time to reiterate all I have told you. Our world is the world of the high trees where, by the grace of the goddess Artema, our town of Zilozium has lived in peace and thrived for many generations. The trees provide us with fruits and edible leaves and give a home to the birds and beasts we eat. We get water from the rains, from the leaves, from the very branches. We have all we need in the trees. Here, our lives are complete.

"But there is a world beneath. There is a bottom to the trees, where they sprout from the body of the giant Jimir, whom Artema slew countless aeons ago. The men who live upon the body of Jimir are degenerate and care not for their world. They only care for themselves. These people are to be pitied, but also feared. They know not peace and kindness, but kill one another for sport and fun. They spoil their world and they destroy the worlds of others.

"That world is not for us. While we stay here, we are protected and hidden, and their lives do not matter to us. Our forest is vast, and they do not come near to us. When we look across the expanse of our green world, we can see the mountains of Jimir's bones thrusting into Artema's breath that is all about us, but what we cannot see are the signs of their smoke and what they call civilisation rising up into the air, polluting Artema's breath. We are alone above the ground of other men, and that is for the best for all of us."

The sage nodding of the youngsters greeted his speech, Carinna's eyes particularly wide. But Corvalo's gaze drifted to one of the large, octagonal windows. All he could see were trees, leaves, branches and more trees. That was all he could ever see. His world felt too small.

No, he did not care what Sukhio said, there had to be more to life and the world than just Zilozium.

***

It was always colder at the top of the trees, especially at night. But it was also quieter, and away from everything else in his world.

And the older he got, the more Corvalo wanted to get away from this place.

He had to see the world, had to see what was beyond the trees. He could tell that the shaman wasn't telling the whole story. There was something else there. For all his words to the youngsters in the temple, what he described could not have been all that was out there.

Sukhio was hiding something, and Corvalo wanted to know what it was.

His eyes drifted from the stars down to the tops of the trees, to the thickness of green and brown beneath his feet. Somewhere down there was the body of Jimir, the ground. That was something very few of his people had ever seen but that none had ever stepped upon. That was where he knew his destiny laid.

He heard the rustling of leaves behind him and didn't have to look to know who had scaled the high branches to be with him. "What troubles you?" Carinna asked as she slid in beside him, wrapping her arm around his waist.

He smiled at her. "Nothing," he muttered before kissing the top of her head.

"I know that's not true," Carinna murmured. "You were distracted at the temple tonight, and when I tried to kiss you afterwards, you were not with me. What is wrong?"

"You would not understand," he replied. "And, really, it matters not."

"I have left my home tonight to find you," she stated. "If my father finds me missing, we will both be in trouble. It matters to me."

He sighed. "I feel I must leave Zilozium," he said quietly.

"What?" her voice was no more than a sharp exhalation of air.

"Tomorrow after evenmeal, I think. Then I shall go. I need to see this world that Sukhio is so afraid of." He stroked her hair. "I was going to come to you tonight, to tell you, then we would leave on the morrow when the moon is at its zenith. We have been avoiding the sentries for years, so it would be simple for us to climb down and disappear. Then we could—"

"We cannot," Carinna whispered. "You have heard what Sukhio has taught us for years, about the evil that exists in the world beyond."

"But they are just stories," Corvalo said passionately. "I need to know."

Carinna stared at him and he saw her eyes welling with tears. "You cannot leave me," she sobbed. "We know the stories of those who have gone in the past, who have not returned. Not one has returned. If you go, I will never see you again."

"That is why I want you to come with me." He smiled hopefully at her.

"I cannot."

"Please." He took her by the hands. "This is very important to me."

"I will keep your secret, but I cannot go with you," she said quietly. "But I will always wait for you. I will never give up hope."

"Then come. We can face that world out there together."

"I cannot." She didn't even look at him as she descended, leaving him all alone at the top of their world.

***

Corvalo could not get Carinna out of his head as he climbed slowly down. The trunk of the tree grew wider and wider, the branches he leapt on thicker, sparser, but just thinking about Carinna made the descent seem secondary.

She did not want to join him. Was it her fear or was it him? He had not really pressed her, to give her a chance to explain; he had waited only a short while after she had left him before returning to his parents' dwelling and placing his few articles of clothing into a pack.

Now he was here.

He gazed up, half-hoping to see Carinna pursuing him, but knowing she wouldn't be there. Zilozium was her entire world; she—like so many others in their treetop town—did not want to discover how much truth was in Sukhio's words. Of course, there were the tales of those who had fled to Jimir's body; none had ever returned, as far as anyone knew. Whether they had perished, or they had joined with and become a part of the degenerate world, none could ever know.

He stopped, and for the first time, looked down. He could see the green tops of what he assumed were smaller trees. But around that was a darker substance. He looked around and saw that a nearby tree was growing out of that dark material. He understood—the body of Jimir, the ground. He could see the ground.

He paused and stared at it for a long time. It was dark with only a little of the light from the full moon filtering through, but he could still make out the surface. A childhood myth entered his mind and would not leave him. It was a story told to stop inquisitive youngsters from venturing downwards: that the body of Jimir, the ground, was too soft to support weight, and that a person would become stuck, ready food for the raptor birds and large lizards and snakes that populated their world. It was only the children who were born imperfect or those who died who were allowed by Sukhio to drop down to become as one with Jimir—their bodies would feed the animals they themselves fed upon, and so they helped keep the population of Zilozium strong. It was the way of their world, something Corvalo just accepted as a part of life.

Only the strong could survive high in the trees.

A sound reached him, coming from somewhere down below. He froze and waited. The animal that appeared was tall and graceful, walking on four legs, covered in fur like the many fruit, nut and insect-eating animals of the high trees. It moved slowly along the ground, pausing only to nibble at leaves from a small tree. Then it stopped and seemed to sniff the very air. Its head jerked up to gaze in his direction, then it bolted into the darkness, disappearing amongst the trunks and shadows of the nearby trees.

Corvalo nodded to himself and scurried the rest of the way down, leaping the last two body lengths to the ground beneath before he could think about what he was doing.

It was certainly soft, but it could hold his weight, and that was all that mattered.

He was standing on the body of Jimir. He had taken that final step away from Zilozium. He had left his home, his life... Carinna.

And he knew there was no going back.

**

Corvalo stared at his fire, watching the small lizard he had caught as it slowly cooked. For six nights he had journeyed, heading northwards. He had climbed trees to sleep during the day and had scaled the highest plants to survey the scene, but still he could not see the edge of the forest. The greenery was not thinning and there were no signs of anything to indicate the presence of other people.

He was wondering if the tales were really all just myths and legends, designed solely to scare children. Were the people of Zilozium the only people in the world? But Sukhio had insisted there were others, degenerate peoples living on the ground. Where were they?

He took the stick from the fire, snapped the head off the dead reptile and bit into its charred corpse.

How could the world be this empty?

He extinguished the fire and resumed his travel. The sounds were just as he had grown used to in his life—the wind and the animals and nothing else. He climbed up the nearest tree and journeyed forth, leaping from branch to branch, tree to tree.

He stopped suddenly.

There was something out of place. He made his way a little to his left and peered down at a small clearing. A group of three men were packing up a camp. He smiled to himself and started to climb down towards them when one of the men dragged a net out of the underbrush. Tangled up inside of it was a young woman. One of the men kicked her in the side before they forced her to her feet. The four of them then started to walk along the ground. Corvalo just stared. Why would they have a person wrapped like a trapped animal, and why would they kick someone who could not fight back? It made no sense to him, but it did make him very wary of approaching these people.

Corvalo stayed hidden in the branches, making sure he was not seen as he tracked them. It was slower and they covered very little distance compared to his travel through the trees, but these were the first other people he had seen and so he continued to follow them. He tried to listen, but what they said made very little sense. They spoke in a tongue as foreign to him as the screeching of the lizard-raptors that flew overhead at the height of the hottest days of the year. He took that as another reason to be wary of them.

It took five more days of this slow journeying before he noticed that the trees were thinning, making it more difficult for him to remain hidden as they moved. They hunted their food with more luck than skill and abused the woman in the net often. Corvalo was not sure what these people were doing, but nothing about them seemed to be calm or at peace.

The trees thinned considerably over a short period

of time, giving way to a large, green area. Corvalo had never seen such an expanse of empty land. It did not seem possible, and yet here it was. The men accepted it as part of their world and set up a camp on the edge of it, securing the woman's net to a tree, and then one of them ran off across the emptiness.

Corvalo merely stayed in the trees, too afraid to move.

***

It was another day before the man returned, leading some large animals Corvalo had never seen before, riding one and with another man seated upon the back of a second. Corvalo dropped down out of his tree and watched them carefully. He could sense a tension in the air immediately.

The one who had been constantly kicking the woman started to yell something at the two men on the beasts. The newer one, the one who hadn't been in the forest, seemed to get very angry and dismounted his beast. They were large men, but their bodies did not seem to have the agility or muscle of one who had lived his whole life in the trees.

The new arrival suddenly pulled out a long, shiny object, made of a hard material Corvalo had never seen before. The other instantly did likewise and the two hand-held things were struck against one another with a loud, ringing sound. Again and again these objects met before the one who had been in the forest ducked a stroke and thrust forward, skewering the other through the chest. All movement ceased for just a moment. Then he twisted his weapon—for it could be nothing else—and jerked it out, releasing a brief fountain of blood as the man toppled backwards, lifeless.

Corvalo's mouth fell open. That man had killed the other as though he was no more than an animal! How could a man do that to another?

Then this clearly-sharp tool was held to the throat of the netted woman. Words were exchanged and foot connected with her face hard enough to spray blood from her nose.

Corvalo leapt forward without thinking. These were not men, they were little more than talking animals, and so had to be treated as such. With his short wooden hunting spike, he dived into their midst.

The man nearest him stood in his way and grabbed his wrist. But Corvalo was stronger and used the man's momentum to lift him up and slam him down on the ground as hard as he could. Corvalo then spun quickly.

The wooden club sailing towards his head filled

his vision moments before it struck him, bringing pain and blackness.

***

Corvalo blinked against the bright light and instantly recoiled against the putrid, unfamiliar odours in the air. It took him a short while to get some sense of his bearings, and when he did, he realised that this was not a good situation. He was hanging across the back of one of the animals, hands and feet tied by thick bindings. He lifted his head and saw a building made of a material he had not encountered before. It looked like someone had taken the distant mountains and somehow constructed a building of that material, of Jimir's bones.

One of the men dismounted from the animal he was riding and entered the structure. He heard voices coming loudly from inside, and then the sounds of ringing clangs as Corvalo had heard before the man had been killed, only faster and louder. A cry suddenly emerged, and a young woman walked out of the doorway, holding two of those shining things, one long and one short, both tipped with fresh blood.

She pointed one of them at something Corvalo couldn't see and said some words calmly. The other two men did not hesitate; they leapt to the ground and rushed her. She was much smaller than both of them, but she quickly disarmed one and used her foot to knock the other into unconsciousness. She held the longer of her shining objects at the throat of the one she had disarmed and growled at him.

He nodded before replying quickly and fearfully. The woman slid one of the things in her hand into a long, stiff container at her hip and said something else. He laughed and spat at her feet. She shifted the other object quickly, opening up a long gash across his cheek. He climbed to his feet, staring at her with wide eyes, and stumbled away, clutching his face.

The woman watched him go, then moved out of Corvalo's sight. He heard more voices—calmer this time—and then he was shifted. The sharp, shining object slid downwards, slashing through the bonds that held him. The woman smiled at him and said something, her tone of voice almost pleasant. Beside her was the woman from the net, her face purple from bruising and caked in dried blood.

Corvalo simply stared at the two of them before he gathered the courage to ask, "What is happening?"

The two women exchanged an uneasy glance before the one who had saved them looked back at him. She said something, but it still did not make any sense.

He shook his head helplessly. She said something else, then something else, but he could understand none of it. Then she pointed at her chest. "Natalie," she said, before pointing at him and gazing at him quizzically.

He understood this time. "Corvalo," he replied slowly.

"Corvalo," she repeated. He nodded. She pointed at the battered woman next and said, "Kulpra."

The one called Kulpra smiled at him and said something quickly that made him just shake his head again.

Natalie gazed at him for a few moments longer and then tried speaking again, this time with a much more guttural tone to her voice. He still did not understand.

"What is happening?" he asked again. They just shook their heads. Why didn't they understand him? "What is this place?' he tried, but still they clearly had as much trouble understanding him as he did them.

Natalie sighed heavily and shrugged helplessly. She turned and gave Kulpra some assistance onto one of the large beasts, then swung herself up onto another with practised ease. She indicated one of the other animals, but all Corvalo could do was shake his head. She sighed and slid down, then stood behind him and lifted him up. He stared at the animal. She growled something and pushed him against its flank. He draped a leg over it like Kulpra, and Natalie hefted him the rest of the way, then handed him the ropes attached to its snout.

He took them, but just held them as though they were covered in slime.

Natalie sighed and muttered what could have been a curse under her breath, then took one of the ropes from his hand and tied it to a rope attached to her own animal before she remounted.

She said something else, louder and sharper, and the three animals started onward. Corvalo held on in a panic as he was bounced up and down uncomfortably, but he said nothing as he let this woman called Natalie lead him further away from the only home he had ever known.

***

More and more structures came into view as they travelled, becoming denser the further they moved on, but the main things Corvalo noticed were the smells and the sheer number of people everywhere. He felt like he was being smothered and had trouble gasping for air. His eyes watered with the smoke all about, and the noises that filled his head were like clouds in the sky.

He hardly noticed when the animals stopped and Natalie almost dragged him down from his beast. His legs buckled beneath him, but Natalie held him up. She might have been smaller than him, but she was strong, like a woman from Zilozium. She led him in through a door into a building that was dark and dank and smelt terrible. He balked a little, but the woman's firm hand guided him ever onwards. He looked for Kulpra and saw that she had covered herself with a hood and a cloak that concealed her identity completely. But Corvalo had little time to contemplate her as his surrounds got the better of him.

The place was even more crowded than the outside world. Corvalo moved right in close to Natalie and noticed her laugh as she took him and Kulpra to a table in a corner. They sat down, but he refused to leave Natalie's side. He wasn't sure why, but so far, she seemed to be the only person who was even interested in helping him.

A large man came across to them after only a short time and Corvalo shrank down. Natalie nodded at the new arrival and he disappeared. A few moments later, two other men came across. On seeing them, Kulpra moved her hood back just enough to reveal her face.

One of the men stared at her and touched her bruised cheek, then he started to weep. Kulpra did the same thing before they fell into one another's arms. Then the man looked up at Natalie and smiled warmly. Words filled with joy were exchanged. He reached down and grabbed a pouch which he dropped onto the table. It made a strange, heavy, jingling sound which caused Corvalo to jump. Natalie and this man exchanged some more words through kind smiles, and then the man offered his hand to Corvalo.

Corvalo looked at it. He recognised this gesture and only hoped it meant the same thing in this world. He grabbed it and the handshake was firm. He did not understand, and understood even less when Kulpra reached across to kiss his cheek. She embraced Natalie for a long time and the man did the same before they made their way through the crowd to the rear of the room where they disappeared from view.

Natalie said something that sounded to Corvalo like a question, laughed at herself, and then held her hand up as she gazed into the throng. The same man who had come to them when they had first entered reappeared, and the two spoke briefly. Natalie took a round, shining object out of the pouch and gave it to the man, who then walked briskly away. As soon as he was gone, she tied the pouch to her belt, below the table's edge. Corvalo could not help but wonder just what it was he had witnessed, but Natalie was once more staring at him. She tried to speak again, and again, but still to Corvalo it sounded like little more than the chatter of animals.

The man soon reappeared with a small plate of cooked meats and other foodstuffs, as well as two mugs of liquid.

Corvalo looked at Natalie who smiled at him and nodded, taking one of the mugs and sipping it. Corvalo took a deep swallow of the fluid but spat it across the table. It tasted bitter and burnt his throat. He stared at Natalie forlornly. She grimaced and shook her head, then downed all her drink. She took a tall container from the other end of the table and poured it into her cup, which she offered to him. He just stared at it. She said something soothingly and offered it again. He took it reluctantly and sipped it. There was still a hint of that awful taste, but to his relief he found that it was primarily water. He drank it greedily.

He turned to thank Natalie and found her eating from the plate. She offered him a piece of meat. He took it and bit into it. It tasted of charcoal, was chewy and the flavour was quite strong, and he found he could not bear the feel of it in his mouth. He spat it out. "What is this?" he demanded.

Natalie sighed and grabbed another piece, which she ate slowly. Corvalo just stared at her in confusion.

What was this place? He suddenly stood and vaulted over the table, flying through the air to land right beside two men dressed in identical clothing, their torsos and heads covered by the same shiny, hard substance as the weapons he had seen.

One glared at him and suddenly a burly fist was swung at Corvalo's face.

Corvalo dodged sideways and grabbed the forearm of the man, flipping him over onto his back. The second started to slide his weapon out of the long holder at his hip, but Corvalo's foot connected with his jaw before he could move it more than a hand-span.

The taller man stumbled backwards, crashing into a table, then the first of the men grabbed Corvalo from behind. He tried to struggle out of the strong grasp, but the second bounded forward and buried his fist into Corvalo's stomach. He wanted to double over as all the air was forced out of his body, white dots appearing in front of his face, a sour taste rising in his throat. He looked up and saw the man getting ready to strike again.

And then Natalie was there. She spoke quickly to the two men, standing in front of Corvalo as she did so. The two of them glared at her, and the second suddenly punched forward again. Natalie caught his fist in her hand and growled something, her voice low and even.

The two men exchanged a quick glance, then one of them barked something gruffly. Natalie nodded once and let go of the hand as Corvalo was also released. Before Corvalo could do anything else, however, Natalie had hold of his hand and dragged him to the front door of this establishment.

Once outside he coughed and tried to catch his breath, but she grabbed him by the upper arms and pinned him to the wall. She drew her face in close to his, and spoke to him again, slowly and firmly. He tried to get out of her grip, but she held him tight. He suddenly shifted sideways, but she flipped him over, slamming him against the ground.

Corvalo struck out, his foot aimed at her face, but she blocked it with her forearm and hooked his heel in the crook of her elbow. He cried out as she twisted it sharply.

"Please!" he cried. "Just let me go back to Zilozium! I need to leave this place. I need to get out of this world. This is not my place! I don't belong here. I want to go home. Please help me get back home!" And he started to cry.

"It will be all right, young one."

Corvalo turned with a start. The man staring at him was dressed in rags, his arms and legs hidden from view, his long hair unkempt, his beard a woolly mass.

"Who…?" Corvalo tried to ask, but the man was already talking to Natalie. Corvalo watched as their communication became a back and forth affair, Natalie's face softening with every word spoken.

Then the man with the wild hair held out a hand. "Come with us. We will talk." Corvalo took the man by the arm and allowed himself to be led even further into this strange town by a man he didn't know and a woman he couldn't understand.

***

The building they entered was large and nondescript and, to Corvalo's relief, almost completely empty. "What is this place?" Corvalo whispered.

"This is a temple, one dedicated to the great god, Secludos," the man said. "Here we can talk and be safe."

"Who are you?" Corvalo asked nervously.

"Deror." The man tried to smile. "I left Zilozium many summers ago." The grin finally touched his mouth. "Like me, did you listen to Sukhio and wonder what the world was like out here?" Corvalo nodded slowly. "It is a dream many have, but only few dare to follow. A very few. Most do not survive." He paused. "I know of no others. Most who survive the trek through the forest and across the great plain come to this very city. They understand nothing, cannot survive, and are unfortunately killed. I have seen two come since I was here. One was killed by a soldier"—the word meant nothing to Corvalo—"the other by a thief in a side street. Or maybe there are lucky ones who go on to survive. But I have not heard of any."

"So why do you not return to Zilozium?" Corvalo asked. "They will take you back."

Deror's faint smile disappeared. He lifted an arm and shifted his tattered cloak over one shoulder. His other arm ended in a stump, the leg of that side of his body a withered stick only able to help support his weight by the pieces of wood attached to either side of it. "I cannot live in the trees like this. I would be cast out like the weak at birth, and as the elderly are when they can no longer live in the trees, to fend for myself only if I survived the fall. Begging on these streets, at least I have some chance of living."

"What do you mean?" Corvalo whimpered. He felt so much like a child at that moment, he might as well have been going to Sukhio's lessons for the very first time.

Deror's smile returned, a slight one, filled with sadness. "There is so much you do not know, that very few in Zilozium know. The weak children, you know that they are given to Jimir. But the same happens when the elderly can no longer swing or climb or hunt."

"Sukhio says they are taken to Artema," Corvalo muttered. "She sends the lizard-raptors to take them to her side."

Deror sighed. "Sukhio says many things, young man." He smiled a little wider. "The things he says—the tales of the outside world, the offerings to our goddess—all of it is designed to make you fear, but also to protect you."

Natalie spoke then and Deror responded, but Corvalo was not concerned with them. Deror had told him one simple truth, and yet that and what he had encountered away from Zilozium told him so much more about Sukhio and his people's life in the trees than he had ever wanted to know.

"She wants to know if you wish to remain here, in this city," Deror said suddenly.

"What does she know of Zilozium?" Corvalo asked.

"Only what I have told her briefly. She knows not where it is located." He looked around at the empty room they were in. "I feel it is best for all in Zilozium to remain hidden for as long as possible."

Corvalo looked at Natalie who returned his gaze without emotion.

"Will you come also?" Corvalo asked.

Deror sighed and bowed his head. "Just to the edge of the forest," he replied. "Zilozium is not my world any longer. For all its strange ways and the terror of this small part of the outside world, this is my home now."

Corvalo looked upwards, a single tear creeping down his cheek. "But how can I return?" he muttered.

"Oh, you can. This world, these people…" Deror shook his head. "This is not our world. We do not really belong here. This world does not understand us. I can live here. This is certainly not your world." He placed his good hand on Corvalo's shoulder. "You have seen this small, tiny part of the outside world. You would have been killed many times over were it not for Natalie. But she cannot be your Artema. So go home, to those you love and to those who love you. Let this place become just the stuff of your dreams and your nightmares and nothing more."

Corvalo stared at him. He had been in this world of other men for less than a day and already it felt like an entire summer had passed. Deror was speaking the truth.

"I shall return home," he finally muttered.

***

Corvalo climbed off the animal with Natalie's help and looked at the trees that stretched as far back as the eyes could see. The mountains of Jimir's bones thrust up out of the sea of green to break the view, and no sign of other people could be seen anywhere.

He was making the right choice.

"Have a good life in Zilozium," Deror said, clasping Corvalo by the shoulder.

"And good luck to you as well," the young man responded. He looked at Natalie. "Can you tell her thank you?" he asked nervously.

Deror nodded and the two spoke briefly. Then Natalie kissed Corvalo's cheek. "Take care," she said in his tongue.

He smiled, turned, and clambered up the nearest tree. He cast one last glance back at the pair and then jumped back into the safety of Artema's world.

***

Zilozium was shrouded in the darkness of the night. The few sentries on duty—more interested in keeping warm than watching for any danger, which, truth be told, had not come to the town in living memory—did not notice the black shadow slowly climb down through the highest branches of the trees before dropping silently onto the roof of the living quarters attached to the top of the temple.

Corvalo peered through a window. Sukhio was sitting at a table, holding a mug of water, staring at nothing. His partner was not visible; Corvalo guessed she was sleeping. That made this a little easier.

He slipped inside and stood in front of the town's shaman, scowling. Sukhio opened his mouth to speak, but Corvalo instead stepped backwards into a small antechamber and dropped down the ladder into the temple beneath before any words could come out.

Corvalo stood in the middle of the vast, empty hall that seemed so much smaller now, looking at the undecorated walls and leaf mats upon which they all sat during the town worship times. It all felt wrong. It was like a childish version of reality. It now seemed so pathetic and useless.

"You have returned."

He turned slowly and faced Sukhio but did not reply.

"Not many do," Sukhio muttered sadly.

"Do any at all?" Corvalo asked.

"Oh yes," the shaman smiled. "Yes indeed." He sat on the floor and stared at the young man. "What did you see on your journeys?"

Corvalo opened his mouth, but nothing came out.

He did not have the words to describe the small portion of the world he had seen outside the confines of Zilozium. He could not begin to explain the people, the smells, the feel of even that tiny part of the outside world. Instead he just covered his eyes and shook his head.

"I do understand," Sukhio said soothingly.

"How could you?" Corvalo muttered.

"I do, and that is all that matters."

"I met a man named Deror," Corvalo said suddenly. "He told me things about this place, our home, that I did not want to hear."

"Deror. He lives?" Sukhio was genuinely curious.

"He is damaged, but he does indeed live. He begs amongst the others to survive."

"He would have been your age when he left here, maybe sixteen summers ago," Sukhio mused. "I thought him dead. He must have a truly strong will."

"He said most who leave die out there," Corvalo muttered. "Do many leave?"

"Every three or four summers one will travel out. It is nearly always a youngster, a male, about your age. And it is only very rare ones that ever return."

"Why do we not hear of them?"

Sukhio indicated the floor in front of him. Corvalo sat with some reluctance on one of the mats. "Because those who return are very rare indeed. And if they have not had their minds damaged by the experience, then…" He grinned a little. "How did you survive? Did Deror come to your aid?"

"I was helped by a woman named Natalie."

Sukhio nodded sagely. "Thirty-two summers ago, I was helped by a man named Voldon, an old and powerful priest of Secludos."

"Secludos? That was the god whose temple Natalie took me to."

"Maybe Secludos watches over Artema who watches over us," Sukhio said quietly.

"Maybe…" Corvalo's brow furrowed. "You were helped?" he asked with a gasp.

"Yes, young man, and I returned. Like you."

"Oh." They both fell into silence.

"You now know so much more than most of those in Zilozium do," Sukhio went on suddenly, "and I shan't be here forever."

"What are you…" Corvalo's voice trailed off. He didn't have to ask—he understood completely what the older man was saying.

"Next summer you reach adulthood. If you wish, you can start to train with me, to become the shaman when my body fails and I am taken by Artema." He reached across and touched Corvalo on the knee; both knew the truth of his words. "Only one who has seen the real world can do this and understand what they are saying in here and why they are saying it."

"But so much of it is untrue."

Sukhio sighed. "Would you like any of your family or friends to experience what you experienced?" he asked carefully.

Without hesitation, Corvalo shook his head.

"Right," Sukhio nodded. "And would you like your friends to even know the truth, to question this world and all we have here? What if they told someone, who told another, and then more tried what you and I have tried? How many would have a Natalie or a Voldon to save them? How many would end up like Deror? How many would actually die?"

Corvalo bowed his head. "I understand," he muttered.

"I shall tell your family you took a pilgrimage, to be as one with Artema, that you have chosen, and have been chosen, to follow me in this calling." He smiled. "And I shall tell Carinna that you could not tell her because that is the way of Artema. She knows, I am sure, that you were talking of leaving; now she will understand why."

"Carinna?" Corvalo whispered.

"I know of your feelings for her," Sukhio said,

"and I know how far those feelings have progressed." Corvalo's face flushed red. "It matters not. In time you will also learn how to know these things." He stood and offered Corvalo a hand. The young man took it and was helped to his feet. "Our life here is cloistered and hidden for a reason. Even though we cannot live like this forever, we can try to preserve it for as long as possible."

"I understand," Corvalo repeated.

"Does this mean you accept my offer?" Sukhio asked with an apparently casual air.

Corvalo looked all around at the empty temple. Yes, it was a hollow place, as hollow as the stories he had grown up hearing, but it was filled with something he could not have imagined a moon before—safety, security, peace.

Sukhio's tales might have been borne of fantasy and superstition, but for Zilozium they were all the hope the town needed to survive. They needed to believe.

He now knew that better than most.

"It would be an honour to follow you," Corvalo said firmly.

He held his hand out. Sukhio took it and shook it. And both closed their eyes to pray—not to Artema, who neither was really sure even existed, but to

Secludos, thanking him for saving them and, through them, Zilozium and all its inhabitants for some time yet.

S.GEPP is an Australian who has been writing for a number of years in the horror, fantasy, sci-fi and humour genres, as well as poetry. Tertiary educated, former acrobat and professional wrestler, a father of two, well past 40 years old, and with more than 100 publication credits to his name, he hopes to be a real writer when he grows up.

Bibliography

Broadswords and Blasters, Issue 12,2020
Crypt Gnats, Jersey Pink Ink, 2019
Curses and Cauldrons, Blood Song Books, 2019
Eerie Christmas, Black Hare Press, 2019
Fated, Stormy Island Press, 2019
Fire and Brimstone, Specul8 Publishing, 2019
Flash Fiction Addiction, Zombie Pirates Publishing, 2019
Lovecraftiana Magazine, Candlemas, 2019
Monsters, Black Hare Press, 2019
Non-Binary Review Issue #22: The Odyssey, Zoetic Press, 2019
Rex the Rotten, Alban Lake Publishing, 2019
Sins of the Fathers, Grinning Skull Press, 2019
The Ginger Collection Issue 9, 2019
The Haunted Life, Alban Lake Publishing, 2019
The Rabbit Hole Volume 2, Writer's Co-op, 2019
Thema Vol. 31 No. 3, 2019
Through Death's Door, Monnath Books, 2019
Trembling with Fear Valentine's, Horror Tree, 2019
Under Ground, Black Hare Press, 2020
Worlds, Black Hare Press, 2019

THE COLLECTOR OF SOULS

By Lynne Phillips

When an evil wizard seeks to destroy the kingdom, can an albino sorcerer defeat him and lock his malefic soul away forever?

Weary from fighting, Karma's foot soldiers trudged on resolutely through the long grass of the Great Shifting Plains. Ominous black clouds filled the sky, and the stench of some unknown, but slightly familiar, source filled their nostrils. Karma and his knights held the reins tightly; something had frightened the horses. Ears back, they rolled their eyes and fought to get away.

"What do you think has spooked them?" asked Stefan of Eragon as he struggled to control his mount.

"Could be wolves, they'll set the horses off. The stench could be the rotting carcasses from their kill," Rupert the red-headed archer suggested.

Karma sniffed the air. "I think it's more than that. Have the troops take up a defensive position. I suspect some of Malevolence's Vilemen monstrosities are somewhere around."

Thomas of Argonfort and the other knights deployed their troops.

"Cuthbert, have your archers cover the left flank. Arthur, the right is yours. Pikemen, back them up. Swordsmen, get ready. Axemen, fall back!" Thomas shouted as he rode towards the back of the line.

The Vilemen attacked the rear ranks before he got there.

They stood only five feet tall with short stumpy legs. Their hairless bodies shone like burnished ebony. Muscular arms bulged as they ripped men apart with their bare hands.

Cuthbert's archers swung around in a line and rained arrows down on the seething mass of black bodies. The arrows failed to penetrate the tough, smooth skin, and the enemy advanced implacably.

The archers fell back, regrouped, and allowed the

pikemen to replace them in the front line. Lances were more effective and the Vilemen squealed like stuck pigs as the pikemen ran them through and tossed them aside. Their sticky black blood smelled like tar and stuck to the lances of the pikemen.

"Get off, you filthy beast!" Gilbert of Cornwell Castle yelled as he tried to shake off one which got stuck and prevented him from spearing the next wave as it rushed in.

Thomas rode back to Karma. "You were right; it's the Vilemen!" he shouted. "The pikemen are holding, but we'll need your magic to defeat them. There's twice as many as before, and they've grown stronger."

The Vilemen, created by Malevolence's warped mind, were something only a madman could conjure. Their faces appeared to be featureless until they opened their yellow cat eyes and blinked.

The last time the Vilemen attacked on the Eastern Plains, they ran amok amongst the villages, slaughtering hundreds. Only his sorcerer's power held and sustained those whose resolve wavered at the horror of being eaten alive.

Karma rode to the rear as the battle hung in the balance. The Vilemen's muscles bulged as they continued to dismember Karma's men with their bare hands. The troops fought valiantly but were seriously outnumbered.

Karma's eyes glowed red with anger as he removed the Ark from the folds of his coat. He held it high and spoke a command to the magical artefact.

"Give me a weapon to end this battle."

Instantly, a giant ball on a long chain appeared in his hand.

He swung it around his head with tremendous strength. The two nearest Vilemen collapsed, crushed to a bloody pulp, brain matter mixed with black gore splattering Karma's face. He reeled back as the stench of tar hit his nostrils. Karma steadied, reached into his cloak, and took out his enchanted pocket watch.

"I want the souls of those two!" Karma said as he pointed to the two Vilemen he had killed. The watch began to gather their spirits. As it sucked in air, wisps of the Vilemen's souls drifted towards it.

The souls screamed in protest and struggled against the pull of the watch, but its power was too strong, and they were sucked in, unable to escape. Karma held the watch to his ear and smiled with satisfaction.

The remaining Vilemen watched the scenario unfold, their yellow eyes blinking rapidly. They bayed and howled in anger, stamped their legs and beat their chests, before they surged forward again.

Karma yelled, "Ark, arm all my men!"

His army cheered as ball and chains appeared in their hands and they attacked in frenzy. The Vilemen had no defence against the Ark's weapons, as the ball and chains smashed into them. Shattered bones, brain matter, and black oozing blood littered the ground.

When it was over, the reek from the black gore of the Vilemen, the stench from the decimated corpses, and the emptied bowels of his dead troops remained in the air until Karma's men buried their dead and he charred the remains of the Vilemen. Only the smell of burned tar remained when the army moved on.

***

Karma stood on the crest of the hill and viewed the carnage below. The screams of those dying in the castle echoed in his head, but he had become immune to the sounds of death. There had been so many in the last three years, he was numb, almost beyond feeling anything but anger and revenge. A sweet, sickly smell of burned flesh permeated the air.

In a past life, only a few years ago, he would have mourned the loss of his friends and relatives, but there was nothing he could do to save them now. The inferno was of such intensity, even his most powerful magic could not quell it.

Karma's army had finally crossed the Great Shifting Plains, the gore from the Vilemen dry on their tunics when the call for help came by messenger from Lord Henry's castle.

Karma conjectured Malevolence, the megalomaniacal wizard, would have already attacked the castle, but he never denied a call for help. When his army was several leagues short, even before they crested the last hill, they saw the ball of black smoke and bright orange glow.

"We're too late," Karma fumed.

The fires lit by Malevolence's henchmen and fuelled by the wizard's potent magic, had engulfed the castle.

When dawn crept over the horizon, only the four corner stone turrets and the grand granite entrance would remain to indicate that there was once a castle. There would be no evidence it had once been Lord Henry's happy and vibrant community.

It was a scene repeated across the kingdom many times. Karma's army had encountered burnt out castles all across the land during their quest. They had fought swarms of Malevolence's repulsive creations, and defeated each of his armies, but had not been able to defeat Malevolence himself. Finally, they knew he was near. Tomorrow, Karma hoped to end The Quest and save the Wizard Kingdom.

***

"My Lord, come have something to eat and warm yourself."

Karma turned. His most loyal knight, Stefan of Eragon, held out a cloak.

"The knights are waiting for you," he said.

"Thank you, Stefan," Karma murmured as the knight disappeared into the gloom.

He wrapped the cloak tightly against the bitter cold. The black and green images of smoke, depicted along its hem, swirled in a mesmerising pattern as he strode back to camp to discuss strategies with his knights.

Cold rain fell intermittently, but the skies predicted sleet or possibly snow before sunrise. A bitter penetrating wind whipped across the land and leached into his bones. He chanted softly and created some warmth as he waved his wooden stave to ward off the iciness which threatened to freeze his balls.

The pallid, silvery full moon, which washed over the landscape with an eerie hue, emphasised the paleness of his skin and highlighted his long white hair.

It reflected off the wolf skull mask, which his men eventually found familiar but his enemies still cowered from in fright. He had worn it for many years, and the memory of how he obtained it was still vivid in his mind's eye.

It was a moonless night soon after his army was first formed. Karma and a small band of his men traversed through Devastation Forest to acquire supplies from Lord George's realm. He always preferred to move under the cover of darkness whenever possible because of his sensitivity to sunlight. They had left the main army to recover from battle, sharpen and clean weapons, and prepare for the next challenge.

"I smell the musky scat of wolves," the lead scout whispered and held up his hand to indicate for them to stop. "I think they're close."

The archers moved forward to defend the group, although without the moon, they would have to fire blindly.

A wolf howled close by and another answered with a mournful cry. It raised the hairs on the nape of the men's neck. They looked around, trying to judge the direction of an attack. The sound of snarling and snapping jaws could be heard as the wolves jostled for dominance.

"Prepare to fire," Stefan of Eragon whispered to the archers.

"We can't see."

"Tarkin Turin Glow!" Karma uttered and an eerie green light filled the area. The bowmen, able to see clearly, released their arrows and killed all six wolves as they leapt.

The men skinned the demon wolves. Twice the size of normal wolves, their long shaggy coats would provide warmth against the chill of winter.

Stefan cut off the head of the largest wolf as a trophy. Later he boiled it clean, and when they were back at camp, he presented it to Karma.

"My Lord, this might protect you from the sun," he suggested.

Karma placed it on his face. His men recoiled in fear as he grinned at them.

Once he only wore it into battle, but he had fought for so long and hard now, it had almost fused onto his face and become part of his persona. He appreciated its dual purpose; it provided protection for his sensitive pink irises and pale albino face from the harsh sunlight, but more importantly, it terrified the enemy

***

Korben walked into the room where Katherine lay bleeding after a long and difficult childbirth. The midwife had been unable to stem the flow and had called for a physician, but he was a long way off.

Korben cradled his wife in his arms.

"Katherine, my love, please don't leave me," he pleaded.

She smiled at him and touched his face. "I'm sorry," she said with a sigh, closed her eyes and stopped breathing.

Tears ran down Korben's face as he glared at the newborn; a puny, albino child that looked at him with unblinking pink eyes.

"That's no child of mine. Put it out in the snow. It will be dead before dawn," he ordered the midwife and strode out of the room expecting his order to be obeyed.

The midwife wrapped the small boy up tightly. The pink eyes looked at her solemnly.

"I don't have the heart to obey Lord Korben's orders," she said to him. "You might not last the night, but your mother would want you to have the best chance to survive."

She took him to his grandfather, Flame-fire, a master sorcerer, who lived in the realm of the Endless Forest. He found a wet nurse and a nanny for the child, named him Karma and raised him.

His grandfather was the only one who understood the anger which simmered beneath the surface from the time Karma was old enough to understand his father's rejection and the malicious remarks of others.

When Karma turned fifteen, Flame-fire said, "It's time you fulfilled your destiny. I've arranged for you to be apprenticed to Wolfgang Firebrand, your uncle, an omnipotent sorcerer, who lives fifty leagues past the furthermost edge of the Endless Forest."

"Grandfather, you have taught me so much. I feel safe here. Can't you teach me more?" Karma begged.

"I've taught you all I know. He will teach you the advanced skills of a multiple master sorcerer. Be brave, Karma. Wolfgang won't be concerned with your demeanour, only what's in your heart and your mastery of skills," he answered as he hugged his grandson.

***

Karma watched silently as his knights entered the tent hastily erected against the rain and bitter cold wind which blew from the south. The wind howled and shook the tent, and a single lantern cast a shadowy light in the semi-darkness.

The knights, normally a handsome group—tall, dark complexioned, broad shouldered and hair neatly plaited—stood before him exhausted; long hair untidily held back with a single leather thong and clothes splattered with mud and the black gore from the Vilemen.

They were fatigued from fighting and living rough, but despite all their hardships, they remained fiercely loyal to Karma; something they had proved to him many times during the last three years.

They could have been clones except for the distinctive crest embroidered on each man's chest, unique and special, each representing their realm of origin. Individually, each had volunteered to represent his lord's castle to support Karma in The Quest to defeat Malevolence and save the Wizard Kingdom.

Every knight had arrived with a fully equipped army of support over the last three years. Many more men had joined them as they became dispossessed by Malevolence's forced take-overs or news of his atrocities spread across the land.

The meeting was brief. Each knight recounted loses and gains and the major points of the battles they had fought during the last thirty-six hours. Karma looked at their tired drawn faces, etched with pain and loss. Some of their most valiant fighters had been slaughtered and eaten by Malevolence's Vilemen monsters. Karma knew his knights carried the burden of responsibility for their deaths and defilement. He decided strategies could wait until dawn.

As he spoke, the lilt of his voice raised their spirits.

"Thank you, my loyal friends. You fought well today, but we need to be ready at first light. Try to get some sleep. Tomorrow we face our biggest challenge. We will meet at dawn to discuss strategies."

He waved his hand. "Tarkin Turin Release," he chanted. A blue light washed over them. It eased their exhaustion and guilt. Their faces relaxed, shoulders firmed, and their faith in success for The Quest was restored.

"My Lord." Each knight acknowledged Karma's authority with a hand clasped to his heart as he left with quiet stealth and disappeared into the darkness to check on the troops.

Karma stood perfectly still, as if in a trance, closed his eyes and sighed. The stench from the black gore of Malevolence's monsters, which splattered the knight's tunics, lingered in the tent.

His mind turned to the task before them. At last the end was in sight. Malevolence and his army were holed up against the base of Mount Cracken. They had no escape, and he would have to face Karma's army and fight the next day.

Unexpectedly, Karma felt exhaustion wash over

him. He turned the lantern down low and dropped into a meditative state where he remained for several hours while he centred his core using the skills Wolfgang Firebrand had taught him.

Later, when he was unable to sleep, he thought about his time spent with Wolfgang and the special powers he had mastered. Karma knew his followers and enemies alike were fearful of his powers. He was known by several names: Runner of the Night, The Watcher, and The Collector of Souls. But the name he preferred, and was probably the most apt, was given to him by his grandfather when he turned twenty.

The Volatile.

***

Three years previously.

Wolfgang Firebrand stood facing Karma, hands lightly resting on his shoulders. His penetrating sapphire-blue eyes stared into Karma's, not seeing the pink hue of the albino, only the steely determination that was hidden behind them. He knew Karma was ready.

"You've trained long and hard. I'm proud of what you have achieved. You are now a skilful sorcerer. There is nothing left for me to teach you. The skills you have will evolve more. You will develop and discover skills of your own as the need arises," Wolfgang stated as he reached into the folds of his crimson robe and produced a small spherical object, half the size of a man's fist. He handed it to Karma. The energy it emitted pulsed silently but vibrantly as it glowed in his palm.

"What is it?" Karma asked, enthralled by its uniqueness.

"It's the Ark. It belonged to your great-grandfather, an incredibly fearless and potent sorcerer, who bequeathed it to me on the understanding I would pass it on to someone who needed it more. That person is you. It will help you in your quest to defeat Malevolence."

Karma turned the small orb slowly in his hand. The energy and warmth it emitted felt familiar, like a message from his great-grandfather.

"It can transform into any weapon you conjure and is activated by your command," Wolfgang explained. "Try it."

"Ark, I need a strong, sharp dagger," Karma said.

Instantly a double-sided dagger, sharp and lethal, appeared in his right hand. He smiled with satisfaction. With a wave of his left hand, it morphed back into the Ark.

***

The memory of that day was strong. Karma was grateful to Wolfgang for such a precious bequest. He slipped the Ark out of the folds of his cloak and held it gently in his hand. It shimmered with a soft green glow and emitted tiny sparks of energy. Its usefulness had been proved over and over again during the quest.

He replaced the Ark and took out the pocket watch, his most valued treasure, which was given to him by his grandfather when he turned twenty-one. That memory was even stronger.

"Grandfather, it's magnificent," he exclaimed as he looked at the intrinsically carved silver case and dial adorned with mystic symbols. He turned it in his hand and held it to his ear. The sound of moans and screams could be faintly heard. He looked puzzled.

"It's a special pocket watch called a Soul Collector. Use it to capture the wicked souls you destroy during The Quest so they don't return to do evil again," his grandfather had explained.

Now Karma turned it over in his hand. Its present count was one thousand two hundred and fifty-six. Sometimes, when he held it close to his ear and everything was quiet, he could hear their death screams; it reminded him of how much evil he had taken out of the world and why he was still fighting. He hoped one day Malevolence's soul would be the prize in his collection.

Karma closed his eyes and slept until dawn.

***

Malevolence, named Malevich at birth, ruled the Realm of Glome, far away from the Endless Forest. His father was a strong yet fair ruler, loved by his people.

When his father died Malevich became Lord of Glome. He ruled by might and cruelty and was detested by his people. He delved into dark magic. As his spells became blacker, so did his heart, and his avarice grew until he wasn't satisfied to only control Glome; he wanted to rule the whole Wizard Kingdom.

He mustered armies of evil with promises of power and wealth to achieve his goal.

***

Lord Morton glared at the intruders.

"Get off my land," he demanded. Malevich's ogres glared back. Arms crossed, they stood defiantly in Lord Morton's Great Room.

"Our master, Malevich the Great, rules this land

now," the head ogre stated. "He demands taxes in the form of gold, jewels, livestock or farm produce, or you will be beheaded and your wife and daughter raped."

The ogre grabbed Lord Morton's daughter around the neck and pulled her close.

"Let her go, take what you want," Lord Morton conceded. He valued his family's lives more than any possessions.

The ogres ransacked the castle. They hauled away caskets of gold and jewels and filled carts with livestock before they set the barn on fire and left.

Other lords weren't so fortunate. They resisted and retribution was swift. Estates were burned to the ground and people executed, sometimes in horrific ways, just to satisfy Malevich's thirst for cruelty. He amassed enormous wealth and power.

He created armies of evil monstrosities, of increasing depravity, and became known throughout the Wizard Kingdom as Malevolence.

***

Malevolence sat in his study beside the fire. As he twirled the wine around in his glass, he contemplated his next move. Across from him sat his mother, a witch, who supported her son's endeavour to control the

Wizard Kingdom.

"What monstrosities have you created today in the dungeon, Malevich? They smelt putrid when I walked past," she cackled.

"I haven't given them a name yet, but I guess Putrid Ones is as good a name as any," he said as he threw the empty glass into the fire and laughed.

***

Karma's army advanced through the thick undergrowth. They had waded through The Great Mire and approached Malevolence's new army from the north. They could smell the putrid flesh of the foe long before they reached the enemy camp.

"The messenger was certainly accurate about the stench. No wonder he called them the Putrid Ones," Maxim, the leading knight, said as he held up his hand to signal the troops to halt. "It was easy to find them."

A villager had arrived at their last camp only hours previously. He had ridden long and hard to find Karma's army and was breathless on his arrival.

"A horde of putrid beings have arrived on Lord Alfred's land," he gasped. "They slaughtered a score of my lord's sheep, lit gigantic bonfires and roasted them. They still feasted when I left, but my lord fears what they will do when their hunger is sated. He begs your help."

It would have taken Karma's army a day to march to Alfred's castle, but by approaching through The Great Mire they had arrived in under two hours. It was difficult to transverse the mire. The mud sucked at their legs; each step took enormous effort.

"Tarkin, Turin Release," was repeated over and over again as Karma used his magic to get them all through the most impenetrable places.

When they finally breached the mire, the thick undergrowth hid them as they watched the Putrid Ones, but it didn't protect them from the nauseating smell which turned their stomachs and caused many to retch.

Tarkin, Turin, Aroma," he whispered as he washed a soft blue light over them which abated the stench in their nostrils and settled their stomachs.

The Putrid Ones were slow to realise they were under attack as Karma's men crept up behind them. They lolled around the fire, their enormous bellies bulging. They looked surprised to see the intruders.

"Ark, I need a broad axe," Karma commanded.

When it appeared in his hand, he hefted it above his head and swung. It sliced through the air, decapitating the first Putrid One. As its body released an acrid smell, Karma reeled back. The sickening stench hit his nostrils and bile rushed into his mouth as the Putrid One's body disintegrated and scorched everything it touched.

"Stand back," Karma shouted. "Don't let it get on your skin. It's acid and will burn you."

"Tarkin, Turin, Abate," he yelled as he cast a spell to neutralise the acid which allowed the troops to withstand the putrefying mess as they moved in to kill the other Putrid Ones.

Karma gathered the soul of the Putrid One he had slain, locked it away in his pocket watch. He held the watch to his ear. It sounded like the new soul had to fight for survival.

He turned his attention to the fight and admired the skill and tenacity of his men as they slaughtered all the Putrid Ones and left them to rot on the edge of The Great Mire.

***

A lad on a black steed with a white blaze on its forehead rode into Karma's camp. The horse quivered and trembled with exhaustion; it was near collapse. White foam lathered its coat, mucous and blood dripped from its nose. The rider fell from the horse and lay there, unable to stand. Stefan stepped up to the lad, pulled him to his feet and supported him as he drank in great gulps from the flask the knight offered him.

He managed to hoarsely croak, "Where is Karma? My master begs his help."

"State your case," Stefan replied. "Karma is not to be disturbed."

Hearing the commotion, Karma emerged from his tent.

"Let the lad speak," he commanded.

The boy looked at Karma's wolf skull and cringed in fright, but his master's need was greater than his fear.

"My master, Lord William, says to tell you Malevolence's army of malignant goblins are only ten leagues from the Keep. He begs your help to defend his realm," the boy managed to blurt out before he collapsed on the ground exhausted.

"Have cook bring this lad some food, and prepare our troops to march within the hour," Karma ordered his knights before he turned to the boy.

"Come lad, tell me where your lord abides."

Karma and his troops crested the hill above Lord William's castle. The sight daunted them, but they held. They had faith in Karma's magical powers to keep them strong.

Thousands of goblins, clad in multi-coloured

leather tunics and wielding long staves, stood shoulder to shoulder, three rows deep, facing Lord William's castle.

Karma turned to the bugler. "Lord William needs to know help has arrived."

A strident blast echoed across the valley and the goblins turned as one towards Karma's army. Their wizen faces, covered in warts, beamed in delight as they advanced.

Stefan quickly took control. "Herbert, cover the left flank with your swordsmen. Hector, cover the right, take the axemen," he ordered. The other knights deployed their troops.

The largest goblin, which stood proudly in the centre of the horde, emitted a raucous, maniacal laugh, and the mass of goblins rushed forward in a vee formation. The goblin leader led the attack, swinging his stave and baying like a demented madman.

Karma drew his long sword from its scabbard and held it lightly in his hand. When the goblin was nearly upon him, he swung it wide and deftly severed its head. It flew through the air and landed in the middle of the following throng, which howled and roared in anger as they surged forward.

"Arkin, Turin, Thrive," he yelled. His pink eyes turned red with anger and he grew in stature until he stood head and shoulders above his tallest knight.

"Your evil will not be allowed to fester," he roared. The wolf mask glared at the remaining goblins as they approached. They faltered, cowered in fear for several seconds before they overcame their trepidation and rushed forward again.

Karma released his pent-up power. The fireball hit the front line of goblins. Their bodies flew into the air from the force. They cried in pain as their bodies disintegrated, blown apart by his chaotic magic.

His knights murmured amongst themselves. "The Volatile has spoken."

The remaining pack of goblins hesitated, stunned by Karma's furious outburst. Their indecision allowed Karma's troops to move in for the kill. They released their own bloodlust and anger as they attacked with swords, maces and axes.

Karma's energy continued to blast goblins close to him for several minutes before he managed to control his anger. He stepped back and watched his troops decimate the goblins while he collected the souls of those killed by his blast. The stunned spirits whooshed into the pocket watch with little protest.

Lord William's troops emerged from the castle, clad in full armour. Some wielded long lances, others swords and longbows. His bugler announced their arrival with a long blast on his horn as they joined the fray. William's archers released a volley of arrows and his foot soldiers used their swords and axes to hack at the goblins.

Even though the goblins still outnumbered both attacking armies, they fled in all directions from the onslaught.

Karma's troops, who strategically protected the flanks, butchered them as they fled.

Karma raised his hands and shouted, "Tarkin Turin Poison!" A wave of poisonous smog formed and raced after the central fleeing horde.

The knights held their men back and watched impassively as the goblins succumbed to the deadly gas. As a final insult, Karma charred the goblins with an intense flame, which burned until only a pile of blackened bones littered the landscape.

"Karma, you and your men are welcome to be my guests," Lord William declared as the triumphant army were escorted to the castle where they feasted, drank, and were entertained before they rested their weary bodies in comfort for the first time in several months.

***

It was during the penultimate battle the foot

soldiers saw their leader without the mask for the first time. Haunted by adverse reactions to his appearance, Karma loathed to expose his albino guise to scrutiny. Only his trusted knights were privy to his vulnerability.

Karma stepped up to face the Undead as they lurched towards his men. Pieces of skin and flesh hung off their faces, arms, and naked chests. Eyes sunken into their hollow sockets, they stared at him without blinking. Even the sight of his wolf mask received no reaction from them as they slowly advanced with arms outs stretched.

"Take aim, fire!" Rupert the Red ordered his archers. They released a stream of arrows from their longbows, but the arrows disintegrated on impact.

Karma stepped forward and created a powerful wave of energy which hurtled towards the leading Undead, but they continued to advance relentlessly.

He took the Ark out and angrily growled, "I've had enough of this, Ark, produce the appropriate weapon."

A wooden cross appeared in his left hand and a sharp, pointed wooden stave in his right. He looked perplexed until he remembered his uncle's words from his training: "If you meet the Undead, only a wooden stave through the heart will kill them, and a cross will protect you from becoming Undead too."

He held the wooden cross before him and moved

in to kill the leading Undead monstrosity, which wielded its long stave and knocked his wolf mask off his face. It fell to the ground and shattered into a multitude of small pieces.

"No!" his knights gasped as one and surrounded him to protect his masquerade, but Karma pushed them aside, determined to kill the Undead.

Avoiding the shards of bone, he stepped up to the Undead and thrust the sharp stave through its heart. The Undead collapsed at his feet, truly dead.

Karma hesitated for a few seconds before he collected the soul of the Undead in his pocket watch. The soul moaned in agony as it was sucked into the abyss to be locked away forever.

His army momentarily focussed, not on the Undead, but on the exposed face of their leader. Whereas before they were fearful of the wolf mask visage Karma portrayed to the world, they were surprisingly tolerant of the sight of his albino features. All they saw was a strong, passionate leader whom they trusted multiple times in battle, and who inspired them to maintain a belief in the final goal of The Quest; to restore the keys to the Wizard Kingdom.

"Ark, arm everyone," he shouted.

The Ark produced crosses and sharp stakes for everyone. His men held the crosses in front as they thrust the staves into the hearts of the foe. Karma fought on bare-faced, side by side with his men. They fought until every Undead was destroyed.

Before the bright sun came over the horizon the following day, Stefan had searched the nearby forest and found a more gruesome demon wolf skull to protect Karma's vulnerable skin and eyes from the sun.

***

As the faint light of dawn washed away the last vestiges of darkness, the knights filed into Karma's tent to discuss strategies for the final battle. They argued between themselves about the best way to attack. Karma was impressed with the acumen they had acquired during The Quest and the intelligent way they argued each proposition. He stood back and allowed them to formulate the final plan of attack. Based on knowledge of Malevolence and his armies, Karma thought their plan had merit, and his sorcery should be able to fill any unforeseen circumstances Malevolence created.

Tactics finalised, the knights left the tent to inform and prepare their troops.

A blood red corona ringed the sun, giving everything a crimson hue as they advanced up the hill to meet the enemy—hopefully for the last time.

Karma and his men arrived at the crest and looked down into the valley at the base of Mount Cracken. The sight below daunted even the bravest of them. A horde of one-eyed dwarfs, short and squat, clad only in green leather tunics, and armed with double-sided axes and shields, stood shoulder to shoulder, five rows deep, like a dense forest. The line extended for a quarter of a league across, almost filling the whole valley.

Amidst the mass of green, only their singular amber eyes shone with an intense glow. There was no sign of Malevolence's presence. The knights turned towards Karma for his reaction.

"How do you want this lot annihilated? Do we follow the plan?" asked Robert, the knight from King's Close.

The wolf mask grinned back at him. "Show no mercy. If we fail, the Wizard Kingdom will be lost forever.

Robert beamed. "My lord, it will be our pleasure," he declared as he turned his horse and rode off to convey Karma's orders.

The first line of the dwarfs raced forward. They yelled and hollered as they advanced, only to be met by a torrent of poison arrows. Many fell, moaning in agony, others staggered back. The pikemen followed, using their long lances to spear the dwarfs who shrieked in pain.

As each wave of dwarfs fell, Karma used his powers to blast their bodies aside. More filled the void but, following their plan, the knights waded in with their double-sided swords and wiped out more of the vile green enemy.

Pandemonium ensued. Some dwarfs realised that, without Malevolence magic to support them, they were doomed. They turned and fled.

"Cowards," Stefan yelled, carried away with the frenzy of battle. "Stand and fight," he demanded as the knights pursued them with vengeance. They reeled their horses and raced after the fleeing dwarfs slashing at them with both sides of their long swords.

They showed no mercy and slayed dwarfs in their thousands. More one-eyed monsters waded into the battle, screeching and swinging their double-sided axes with abandonment, but Karma's men defended well.

Dwarfs on the flank swarmed in, wielding their double-edged axes in frenzy, swinging left and right rhythmically. Some men fell, mortally wounded. Others received deep cuts and lacerations and fell back.

Karma could see his men were still severely outnumbered and their energy was flagging.

"Tarkin, Turin, Freeze," he yelled as he evoked a

spell which froze the brains of the dwarfs. They hesitated just long enough for Karma's army to regroup.

"Tarkin, Turin, Strength!" Karma reenergised his men and gave them the incentive they needed to sustain the upper hand. The battle continued for several hours until Karma's army was victorious.

The air was filled with the sound of the dying dwarfs. The stench of emptying bowels and spilled guts permeated the area for hours as the knights moved through the carnage to ensure no dwarf remained alive.

The men gathered their dead and dying, although the death rate was not substantial. Many were badly injured. Karma moved among them. Some had deep cuts from the dwarf's axes, others superficially lacerated but bleeding. He used his powers to stem the flow of blood and start the healing process, but even his strong magic was not always enough and a few score of men could not be saved.

Karma walked through the mass of dying and dead dwarfs. He felt no remorse for so much slaughter. He considered burning the bodies but decided, as a final insult, to leave a feast for scavengers.

Before the troops had moved a hundred yards away, vultures had landed on the bodies of the dwarfs, eager to get the tastier pieces. Eyes were their preferred delicacy. They squabbled and jostled each other, large wings extended as they fought to gorge their fill.

Long, lean shaggy-coated demon wolves entered the arena. They forced the vultures to abandon their prize. The wolves favoured the intestines, liver and heart, which they ripped out and devoured before they slunk away leaving the vultures to move back in and pick the bones clean.

Karma's men moved well back, away from the mass of dead dwarfs and feasting scavengers. Exhausted, they fell to the ground. No one had the energy to talk, but in the back of each mind was the thought, *The fight isn't over yet. Where is Malevolence, and when would he strike?*

They cleaned their weapons, chewed on dried meat, and drank deeply from their water flasks. Some walked to a nearby stream and filled water skins. Karma walked among them. He spoke softly to each man, commending their efforts. He placed his hands on shoulders as he spoke, and his magic rejuvenated them.

Some of the foot soldiers set about the grim task of burying their dead, understanding that no man was to be left for the scavengers.

Each one was buried deeply, and their grave covered with stones. The task was onerous. It was hard to find enough stones to make the graves safe from marauders, but they did it willingly, knowing someone would do the same for them if needed. Karma washed a blue light over them as they worked. It strengthened their resolve and lightened the load.

***

Malevolence stood camouflaged half way up Mount Cracken. He looked down at the disaster below. He fumed with rage and paced as he planned his revenge. The dwarfs had been his finest and largest army. He had been certain they would obliterate that albino freak's supporters.

The blood sun disappeared. The sky turned inky black with a tinge of green as ragged clouds raced across the sky and massed above his head. Karma looked up and saw the unusual phenomenon and knew Malevolence was nearby.

A jagged lightning bolt shot into the ground ten yards from Karma's feet. A bombardment of lightning strikes ensued, each closer and more forceful. Malevolence's outline appeared in the glare of the lightning flash but disappeared immediately. More lightning with brighter flashes burst around Karma.

"Ah!" he screamed and clutched at his eyes as the lightning burned into his retinas, making him momentarily blind.

"Circle," Thomas yelled, and the knights reined their horses in tight, surrounding Karma to protect him while he was vulnerable.

"Defend and protect!" Stefan ordered the troops.

They quickly formed an extra barrier around Karma while he regained his equilibrium.

The troops rested nervously in position, aware that the next attack could come from any direction and in any form. No one underestimated the ability of Malevolence to appear in an unknown guise.

A pack of enormous hyenas with long shaggy grey coats, fiery red eyes, and sharp teeth loped in from the left flank.

"Repel the monsters," ordered Rupert of Lord Hector's Realm. His swift thinking troops swung their lances into position and thrust at the hyenas. They dissolved into a cloud of grey haze and floated away.

"It's Malevolence!" Rupert shouted. "Be alert!"

An accumulation of black, sooty dust appeared a hundred yards ahead. It swirled and formed into the shape of a giant eagle and swooped down on the army. Its shadow loomed above them.

"Watch out!" Rupert exclaimed as its talons extended towards Karma. The archers fired at it, but the arrows passed right through it.

"It's Malevolence again!" he yelled.

The eagle flew back and reformed into a swirl of dust. Malevolence appeared in its midst.

The men knew the next battle would only be fought between their leader and Malevolence.

Karma forced his way through the protective ring and faced Malevolence. The evil wizard pointed and called his challenge.

"Wolf mask man, Night Watcher or whatever your rag tag band of followers call you, the ultimate moment in time has come. We will battle at last, and when I win, the Wizard Kingdom will be mine, forever. Prepare to meet your doom!"

He swept his hand across in front of him and giant, jagged hail stones rushed at Karma, who sent them hurtling back with a word of power. Malevolence countered with a succession of lightning bolts that singed Karma's hair and clothes.

Karma created a tornado, which raced towards Malevolence, hit him full blast and swept him off his feet. The evil wizard quickly recovered and evoked a plague of vicious wasps. They flew at Karma, their giant stingers protruding.

"Tarkin, Turin, Return," Karma roared as he swiped them away with his hand. They raced back towards Malevolence who howled in pain as they stung him.

Malevolence disappeared in a puff of smoke, only to reappear close to Karma. He raised his hands and began to invoke a powerful spell.

Karma took a step back. "Enough," he stated as he withdrew the Ark from deep inside the folds of his cloak. It vibrated with a fierce intensity, eager to assist.

He held it firmly and yelled, "Malevolence's magic is evil and potent. I need a sword like no other before, one with the power to defeat him forever."

The Ark shook and emitted a high pitch sound before it morphed it into a potent sword. The sword was twice as long as Karma's arm, double-bladed and smouldered with an intense scarlet radiance. He held the sword in both hands. It felt heavy yet comfortable.

With one final effort, Malevolence raised his staff and threw an intense bombardment of lightning bolts, which forced Karma to stumble. He followed it with a black cloud of poison, but Karma waved it aside with the sword.

Karma stood still and evoked the words Wolfgang Firebrand had taught him.

"Power and might, I call on all my ancestors to give me strength to defeat this megalomaniac, Malevolence."

Wolfgang's words washed over him and increased

his strength enough to lift the sword high. He swung it at Malevolence who hesitated for a second as he sought to conjure more magic to strengthen his own power.

Karma's sword sliced through the air, straight towards Malevolence's head. Karma's troops cheered as Malevolence head flew into the air and landed in the mire. His body remained erect, quivering, for several seconds before it, too, joined the head on the ground.

Karma took his pocket watch out and held it high above his head. "Give me the soul of Malevolence," he ordered.

A loud screeching and wailing filled the air as Malevolence's soul resisted. It moaned and screamed as it fought against the power of the watch, but the soul collector's might was stronger.

A cloud of black mist formed in the air, and Malevolence's soul was sucked in, yelling, screaming and cursing, to be contained forever with the other evil souls Karma had gathered.

Karma held the watch to his ear and listened to the collection of souls as they fought for superiority within. He grinned in satisfaction before he turned to his men.

He took off his wolf mask and addressed them.

"The Quest is over. The Wizard Kingdom is safe. You have fought hard and long. Your Lords should be as proud of you as I am. You can all go home," he declared. His knights lifted him high and cheered.

The army began packing for the return to their homes, cheerfully talking about the anticipation of seeing their families again, or just a good romp with a pretty lass, fresh food, and warm beds.

Karma distanced himself from the group as he preferred to be alone. The things his men craved were foreign to him.

Stefan appeared at his side. "My lord, I've packed your gear. We are ready to depart," he stated, holding up the wolf mask.

Karma waved the mask aside. He placed his hands on Stefan's shoulders. "You have been a loyal companion, Stefan, I just need to be alone for a while."

"Yes, my lord." Stefan returned to the main body of troops.

Karma walked away, deep in thought. He recalled all the evil he had encountered during The Quest. He was not comfortable with what he had become and how much he had enjoyed the killing towards the end.

He looked at the pocket watch. It buzzed and vibrated in his hand. He could hear the evil souls he had collected, aggressively struggling for control. The watch slipped from his hand and landed on the ground near his feet.

There was a loud whooshing sound and a strong

force gripped Karma's heart. He could feel his heart disintegrating as the watch continued to exert pressure and pulled at his core being.

"No!" he wailed as he fought to resist.

Unable to withstand the force, Karma's heart imploded, and his soul was released. It formed into a fine white mist before it rushed into the watch to be collected too.

His desiccated body fell to the ground and dissolved as Stefan approached and picked up the pocket watch.

"A fine addition to my collection," he said, his face flickering for a second before the magic reasserted itself.

Behind the disguise Malevolence grinned.

LYNNE PHILLIPS, a retired teacher, lives in the beautiful Northern Rivers Region of New South Wales Australia. Her stories, across all genres, have been published in anthologies and various online magazines. Her priority is spending time with her family. Her passions are reading, writing and keeping fit.

Bibliography

Beyond, Black Hare Press, 2019
Clockwork Dragons, Zombie Pirate Publishing, 2020
December Issue, World of Myth Magazine, 2020
Dragon Bone Soup, Our Wonderful Anthology, 2019
FLASH FICTION ADDICTION, Zombie Pirate Publishing, 2019
FULL METAL HORROR 2, Zombie Pirate Publishing, 2019
Grievous Bodily Harm, Zombie Pirate Publishing, 2019
Hate, Black Hare Press, 2020
Jibbernocky, Black Hare Press, 2020
Key to the Kingdom, Black Hare Press, 2020
Love, Black Hare Press, 2020
Oceans, Black Hare Press, 2020
Relationship Add Vice, Zombie Pirate Publishing, 2017
The Collapsar Directive, Zombie Pirate Publishing, 2017
Treasure Chest, Zombie Pirate Publishing, 2020
Twenty Twenty, Black Hare Press, 2020
Unravel, Black Hare Press, 2019
Winds of Despair, Fantasia Divinity, 2020
Worlds, Black Hare Press, 2019

Connect
Facebook: lynne.phillips.505

AZKOMAR

By Sam M. Phillips

A shape-shifting vampire seeks the energy he requires to take on his true form, but to do so he must hunt a terrifying prey: the full-blooded dragons.

Sky like pitch, with no moon, no clouds, just an infinite void of blackness, stretching into forever. A bleak forest where no birds stir, long overcome by fear. The trees—pine, birch, teak—cover most of the valley and up to an omnipotent mountain, wreathed in smoke. Smaller mountain ranges stretch down either side like the wings of a dragon. The mountain, with its sharp crag bent over like a hook, points down at a placid lake, cold and uninviting, where the fish are skittish and avoid the surface.

In the middle of this timeless scene is a village, with burning fires and glowing lamps, set like a shining jewel in a dark crown. Even now, late at night, the village is bustling with noise, the people drinking in the taverns, and the sound, or rather the energy, of these boisterous, celebrating people, wakes me from the slumber of my long hibernation. Even if it rouses me, it does not disturb me, for I must stir and go forth to hunt, driven by my thirst for magic.

Overlooking the village, a shadow in the black night, is a castle. A squat block of iron and stone, black and rusting, uninviting, perched menacingly on the valley's single hill, with its river snaking past like some demon made of liquid energy, ready to pull you in to drown.

This is my home, where the crest of my family—a sleeping maiden with a winged demon rising from her chest, framed by bats and featherless birds—hangs either side of a sombre gate, through which very few visitors pass. Inside, the halls are lavishly decorated with tapestries and glittering jewel chandeliers, precious artefacts and finely crafted furniture. These objects still bring me pleasure, but mostly they are just memories now, their usefulness long sucked dry, and I look to the future for my next find.

Beyond all the splendour of my halls, there is a labyrinth of tunnels which burrow down into the rock and dirt of the hill on which my home stands. Deep in this maze, beyond the reach of prying eyes and inquisitive fingers, lies my chamber, simple and unadorned, its wall lined with slabs of black onyx.

In the centre of this room is my coffin made of soft green jade, opaque walls to let the energy of the Forever Moon subconsciously filter in, the onyx walls trapping and focusing this power upon my sleeping form. It is here that I go to rest and recharge, to harbour what energies I have and to feel the echo of eternity in my bones, my immortality often a curse, but part of me I must acknowledge and to which I pay homage.

In my dreams I do not feel the thirst, the Forever Moon comforting me in her womb of pale white light. If it weren't for her, I'd surely go mad in my desire to feed, and I am thankful my ancestors perfected this energy bath to at least make eternal life bearable. The hunt is always on, but here, in my chamber, in my jade coffin, I can find real respite.

I suppose this is why my little village celebrates so often. There was a time, and not so long ago that they cannot remember and appreciate it, when they were the focus of my deprivations. I soon learned why my forebears left them alone; they are weak morsels, unfit for consumption. Flesh and blood is nothing, a single soul unsatisfying, and while humans contain magic, it is not enough for me, and I would soon glut myself on every man, woman, and child, and this would not do. For a lord without a village is no lord at all, and they provide cover, justify my existence, and keep others out of my valley.

They do keep me up at night though, but this is the prodding I need, so safe and warm in the Forever Moon's glow. I must rouse myself or I would eventually starve, the subtle subconscious energies not enough to sustain immortality, only to slow down the creep of inevitable death.

There is no lid on my coffin, and I open my eyes, the purple irises spread wide in the dark. There is nothing to see in this black chamber, just the soft green glow of my coffin, absorbing the Forever Moon's energy, and the slight sheen of the black onyx as it traps and focuses that energy on my sleeping form.

I lie there for a long time, traversing the infinite void between the dead and the living, from sleep to full wakefulness. I am sad to be leaving the Forever Moon, to leave *her* behind, and it takes time to mourn the loss. It is a process which I go through every night, but one which never becomes any easier.

Eventually, with my waking conscious coming to

the fore, and my moon mind, my subconscious depths, receding, I am no longer satisfied by the weak, yet constant flow of soft white light. The hunger grows in my belly like a stoked fire, bursting up into my brain and setting off fireworks of need and want.

My craving for magic becomes everything and, fearing the slow decline of my immortality, sinking into an abyss of death, I am propelled from my jade coffin, suddenly repulsed by its promise of a mere morsel to sustain but never satisfy.

I seek expansion. I want *more* life, and so I must feed. The hunt begins.

***

Creeping through the dark passages, my eyes dull with thirst, I feel weak and desperate. The search of my vast home turns up nothing and I'm angry with myself, knowing my greed has left me vulnerable. There should be *something* left over from my previous feeding frenzy, but there isn't. Not a single kobold to tide me over, give me back my strength.

"Master, you're up," says a voice like a creaking door. I turn, my skin like flaking parchment, my breath a hiss of steam, and look at the silhouette made of light in confusion. I lift my decaying hand to shield my eyes.

It is my assistant, the pathetic mortal Holstein.

"Where are the spare kobolds?" I ask, reaching out with claws on trembling fingers.

"You used them all up, Master."

"And it's your job to get more!" I take an ominous step towards the man, but he retreats, holds the lantern up protectively.

"There's none to be had. There was blight in the wild mushrooms and they never migrated from the mountains this year."

"No mushrooms either?" I gather up my strength and march menacingly towards Holstein. He drops his lantern; sharp, bright smashing tinkle of glass and a tiny fireball as the dragon scale oil catches. There is the barest whiff of magic in that essence of the great reptile, and as I catch it in my nostrils, it sends me half mad with thirst.

"You fool! What have you been doing all the time I have been slumbering? Using up the precious dragon scale oil to get your own fix, I'm sure. I should gut you and use up your magic, pathetic morsel as it would be."

"Master, have mercy upon my soul. I only lit the lantern now, suspecting you were up. I have lived in darkness these past months."

"You'll live in darkness forever if you don't help me get some magic."

He sees the ominous flare of my eyes in the darkness and rushes from the room. I want to give chase but I am too weak, desperate to conserve my energy. Simply rising from my coffin has sapped the base reserves which maintained me. Every moment now my immortality is slipping away. True blackness, the darkness of the abyss, sweeps over me as the light in my eyes dims. I go into a trance and dream of kobolds, fresh and juicy. Draining the magic from just one would allow me to transform, to *hunt*. A part of me knows this is my fault, but still, as I enter second sleep, the sleep of the dead, I whisper over and over, "Holstein."

It is an accusation, dissembling my situation, reinventing the past. It is transference of guilt, as if Holstein placed this curse upon me, not *her*. But I cannot blame her either, nor can I blame myself, for this would be to admit that I am weak, that I gave up my will so easily.

She said she loved me… I needed her strength. I am weak…

Weak…

A deep abyss gathers around me, and I see her face for a second. It tugs at my heart. She created this creature I see in the deep pools of memory, my own self, now being absorbed by the Forever Moon, snatched away, never to live again, never to taste magic once more.

Where is she now? I struggle to see her face, to remember the manifestation of her energy given form. Is this the fate which awaits us all?

Sinking…

One more taste.

***

Sharp tang of acid blood, the hint of metal and the warm goblet; there is something entering my system, something long forgotten. It is flavoursome but flat, not much magic in it, but it is the start of a cascade, a catalyst towards being reborn.

A soft moan of pleasure with a groggy dose of pain mixed in. I open my eyes to reveal the beauty of a woman. She stands, or is held, over me. Her eyes meet mine, but they are glazed over. My eyes drop to the cascade of blood flowing from her neck. A single fine cut across the throat, the warm liquid pouring into my open mouth. I almost gag; the foul liquid tastes earthy like shit. I hate myself, but through the disgust I recognise the glimmer of magic and I gulp greedily, pushing through my repulsion of humanity and finding the acquired taste I had forgotten. There is base joy in feeding like this, I realise. I have too long become accustomed to turning kobolds to crystal and smashing them into a magical powder to snort.

The woman runs dry and she disappears from my view. I feel my limbs starts to revive, my heart to beat in my chest. My brain clears and I sit up. There is a small stack of bodies nearby, used up. Holstein in dragging up a fresh one and I feel a touch of feeling for the man.

It is quickly replaced by anger.

"What is this, Holstein?" I whisper, my voice venomous. I haven't fed on the villagers for many years; I didn't want to start now.

"Just the scraps from the heap, Master, best I could do."

"Are these...?" I look at the bodies. They are all beautiful women, scantily dressed.

"Yes, Master, walkers of the night."

"How did you get so many so quickly?" I ask, and Holstein looks abashed.

"They are used to coming here, Master, to sample the potions."

I laugh, but it is a dark laugh, full of menace.

"You've been tempting wenches up here in exchange for the drugs in my collection?"

"Yes, Master." His head sags, resigned to his fate.

"You could have just left me," I say. "Or lied…"

He looks up, shocked. "I could never leave you, Master, nor could I lie to you. You see into my soul. You know my weakness. I fight it, I swear I do. I just get…bored…over the winter months. I'm sorry I took liberties."

"Pass me a fresh one," I say, reaching out with a hand, slowly regaining its strength.

Holstein smiles sadly and drags the woman over.

"You did this… gave up your whores, for me?" I ask, genuinely touched.

"I'd do anything for you, Master."

"Good," I say, cutting the lass open and beginning to drain her magical essence, "then get my carriage ready, I'm still not strong enough to transform."

***

Whips crack against the hides of my trolls as they lumber through the forest, Holstein pushing them hard as they tow my carriage sled. I lie in the back, trying to conserve my energy but finally coming back to life once more. The blood of those women might have been tainted with drugs and enflamed by the hormones of passion, but it still contains magic, the fuel of my power, and it warms my dark soul and brings relief from the thirst.

Now I just have to find a richer source, expand my cape of energy, live in the true splendour magic could bring.

Holstein is taking me towards the mountains. If I hadn't been so greedy in the previous thawing season, smashed up all my kobolds, I would have had the magic reserves to make me whole again, to allow me to transform, spread my wings and fly across the mountains to the magic rich plains beyond. As it is I'm going there like a peasant, dragged by lowing beasts, just my manservant to aide me.

"Damn, Holstein, can't you go easier on the bumps?"

He mutters something I don't catch; the words snatched away by the rushing wind.

"What was that?" I ask, sitting up.

"You asked to make great haste, Master."

"Yes, make great haste, but avoid the ruts in the track."

Holstein's shoulder's slump wearily and he goes back to lashing the trolls.

We pass by a village, and I see the bright lights and hear the carousing. It is like a beacon, guiding me, tempting me. It is everything I can do not order Holstein to take us towards it. I would throw the wooden door of the tavern open and it would be a feeding frenzy.

But then they'd all at the gates of my castle next slumber with the pitchforks and flames like the old days.

And besides, I bet a drunk's blood tastes even worse than that of a whore. I need kobolds to feast upon or, even better, dragons.

I huff on the fumes of a snifter of dragon's scale oil held under my nose and remember the pleasure of the taste of pure magic. A shiver runs through me, another memory crowding in, but I ignore it, blinded by my thirst, my greed for power.

***

Holstein and I are laughing, and the kobolds are screaming.

We had to leave the carriage in the foothills of the mountains, steep and perilous trails blocking the passage of the bulky vehicle. Now we ride on the shoulders of the trolls, long spears in our hands, hunting the kobolds as they cower and caper amongst the rocks.

"Well done, Holstein!" I cry happily as my servant spits a crying reptile with his weapon. "Only a baby, but still a catch."

I squeeze my knees around the neck of my troll as it lashed out, tossing boulders aside, revealing a dense huddle of cowering kobolds. They scatter and I lash out, skewering three in quick succession, my troll lumbering after the rest, gathering them up in massive hands. We fall back, happy with our catch, but Holstein is still hunting, plucking the baby kobold from his spear and dropping it into the bag on his back.

"Let me down," I say to the troll in a magical language of a mind pulses. Dismounted, I pull the dead kobolds free of the shaft of my spear, nod up at the troll. The beast reluctantly lays its catch down on a flat bounder, pens them in with its long, thick arms. They panic but they aren't going anywhere. I toss the dead ones in with them just to let the fear peak. The magic is tastier when mixed with terror.

"Grind them up," I say to the troll telepathically, and there is an awful crunching noise as it goes to work, his giant fists like the pestle, the boulder his mortar. I almost weep with joy to see the pile of magically infused powder their bodies create. It is golden and shining, and rainbow oil slick patinas leap across its surface as I circle the heap in awe.

Then I consume, pulling the powder powerfully up my nose, the magic going straight to my brain. It is a vast rush, pulling me into a limitless heaven. My jaw clenches and I go numb all over. I can feel it going into the cells of my body, infusing me with ancient magics.

I nod, satisfied. I look up at the expectant troll.

"Feed," I think, and take a large handful, give it to the troll. The simple beast smiles and licks it from my hand like a grateful pet. I smile as the small pile is quickly gone. Then I'm feeding again myself and I'm so lost in the pleasure of my thirst being obliterated that I nearly don't hear Holstein's panicked cry.

"Master!"

Heavy thumps; Holstein's troll is running towards me, my manservant clinging to his back in fear. I quickly see why.

Behind them is a pack of fully grown male kobolds, armed and armoured, ready for battle.

Holstein pulls up his troll behind me, cowering protectively. He looks down and sees the godlike glow in my eyes, and he smiles, sighs with relief. He sees the pile of crushed kobold and knows what it means.

I have fed and I am charged with magic.

The kobolds advance in a phalanx, dull breastplates strapped onto their powerful torsos, wickedly curved blades in hands, reptile heads snapping a challenge, bolstering their courage with oaths of vengeance for the women and children I have harvested.

I laugh and close my eyes, go into the deepest recesses of my body, and will the change, fuelled by magic.

The ranks of kobold warriors pause, milling in confusion, uncertain of their foe as I begin to transform. I stretch out above them, my silhouette blocking out the sun, my shadow draped upon them like a death shroud. Fear dawns on their collective faces, reptile eyes narrowing as they look up at my awful majesty.

They break and run in panic. I sweep after them, smash them to dust, my body thrilled by the magic coursing through my veins.

***

We are descending the far side of the mountains on the back of the trolls. Each giant fist of the massive creatures holds a sack of magically infused powder, the remains of the feeding frenzy. There were so many kobolds to consume, but I can only take so much and now I'm dizzy with magic, my mind fuzzy and overwhelmed with pleasure and power.

I could have remained transformed, carried us down the mountain swiftly, but I need time to recuperate from the overwhelming rush of battle and the quenching of my thirst. I have enough magic to carry me for a time. Not enough to go home, satiated, and feast for the rest of the waking season, but enough to carry out my quest, enough to carry me into the realm of the dragons to hunt the real prey.

I smile, very content, and rock with the motion of the troll, tapping a tattoo upon its head happily. It hums an earthy tune, rumbling deep in its throat, and this soothes me. Even Holstein looks happy, but he's just a human, and the slightest taste of pure magic is enough to keep him high for days. His eyes are wide as he looks at the landscape in awe and wonder. I wish I could match his simple mind, be as easily impressed as he is, but I need more. Already, the thirst is calling, never truly satisfied, and I have to resist calling a stop, reaching into the sacks to feed again. I need to wait. I will need that power when the times come. If I cannot transform, I will be squashed as a kobold is before my terrible might.

We are in the land of the dragons and I need to be very wary.

***

The night comes, and as the moon rises my dreams are prised from my head like the moving images of a magic lantern. I see the past, with all the hunts gone before, my ancestors and their timeless battle against the full-blooded dragons. It is a tapestry of tragedy and triumph, a test of will not all of them were equal to. I also see the future, the generations marching out before me, all bearing my face, and more importantly, my mask, the visage of the demon, bursting from the body, stretching its wings, born on the power of magic.

Holstein sleeps a drugged sleep, and I can see his dreams, too, but they are simple and animalistic, full of lust for flesh and power. Seen from far away, they give me pause. I wonder if I'm really so far above such a creature. I have long life, immortal as long as I have magic to fuel me, but I hunger, I thirst, and I can be killed by the strike of a dragon's tail just as surely as any, and my desire to dominate others is no different than a man.

For once I was a man, until *she* found me.

Crowned Empress of my soul; I feel the mourning loss of love snatched away too soon. I gave myself in thraldom to her so easily. Now she is gone, taken on the wings of an angel to a nightmare, and knowing this is my fate, the fate of all those whose abuse magic, I shudder, wanting my love back, but also fearing the curse she has placed upon my soul.

I'm so lonely now.

The trolls grunt as they shuffle and crash through the woods. I want to kill something, and for a moment I consider joining them in their hunt, crushing wild dogs, or digging up porcupines, or whatever it is they are doing, but it won't help me. Nor can I kill one of the trolls. I look at the sacks of magic, and they are everything to me, but really, they are just a down payment on the real treasure. There are dragons here, and I will need every ounce of kobold magic to defeat them. Then the magic will pour over me for a hundred years and I can truly rest. Not this seasonal hibernation I have known, hunting the kobolds as they migrate and then sleeping through the summer. No, with dragon's blood and dragon's flesh I will be sustained for so long the Forever Moon will forget me and I will no longer need it its weak light as my surrogate lover.

In my dreams I shall be a prince. In the inverted reality of the abstract astral plane, I will join the other demons and, finally, I will be with *her* once more.

The trolls flatten a tree as they return, and Holstein sits bolt upright. His knife is out, eyes wide with fear, sharp pinprick skin, hackles rising as he jumps to defend me.

I laugh and he looks around groggily, lowers the dagger as the trolls dump lumps of broken flesh and bone on the fire, chargrill their disgusting meal.

"We'll be off soon, then, Master?" asks Holstein, munching his meagre rations of nuts and berries, eyeing the burning carcasses with a mixture of fascination and revulsion.

"Yes, Holstein, as soon as the trolls have replenished themselves," I say as I lean back, smoking a few choice rocks of magic in my pipe.

***

Endless desert of dust, only broken by outcrops of rock soaring into the sky, scoured by the biting wind; this is the landscape of my heart, mirrored so perfectly in the land of the dragons. We ride on the backs of the trolls as they trudge on into this inhospitable environment.

"How are we ever meant to track them, Master?" Holstein asks, a rag tied around his face uselessly, the dust filling his ears, nostrils, mouth, and eyes. I am slowly burning magic to keep the elements at bay, a shimmering field of energy around me like a soap bubble. There's none to spare for the likes of Holstein.

"They leave their magical spore. I can smell them."

"In this wind?" Holstein says through a mouthful of dust.

"The ether realm of magic is beyond the mortal elements, Holstein. In the astral plane, I can see their taste clearly. They are large creatures, rich in magic. They leave a very obvious wake."

"But you said they're smart, Master, wise as wizards."

"What?" I turn on him, reach for him, wanting to bite him, but he just beyond reach. The trolls bellow and start to slap at each other sympathetically.

"Surely, they know they leave such a wake, that they can be tracked. You said your ancestors have been here before?"

Holstein is only mortal, this is his first hunt, but his father, his grandfather—a long line of pathetic creatures—served my kind as well.

"I have been here before, myself," I snap, reaching for him. He pulls his troll away.

"Yes, when you were in thrall to the Empress," says Holstein.

"You dare speak of her?" I almost lose myself to a bitter rage, but I try to contain myself, wondering if it is the comedown from the magic. The sacks are growing light once more, and I have been trying to go without. I know I am…unhinged…and perhaps Holstein has lost it, too.

"Master, the dragons are cunning. Could they…

could they be hunting *us*?" he asks. His eyes are wide, and I can see his frazzled, magic addled brain through the cracked lenses.

"No," I say, the lie true even to my own ears. "The Empress taught me everything she knew of dragons."

"The Empress suckled you like a babe at the teat."

A red curtain cuts my vision. Holstein is dead before I come to my senses. Standing over his corpse, the wind sucks the blood away, a twisting whirlwind like cloth caught on a breeze. It wraps around me and then dissipates. I feel sadness and summon a troll.

"Open the sack," I say, and reach inside to quell my guilt.

***

I'm going mad. The trolls are dead. I don't know if I ate them, or if they ran away as I slept, but I am alone. My clothing, once so rich and fine, has been torn to shreds by the cutting wind. I no longer have magic to spare to waste on my own protection. A small pouch of it hangs inside my meagre rags, tied to a thong around my neck. I clutch at it protectively and enter a cave in a rocky edifice, following the scent of magic, but also just wanting to be out of the elements.

Echo chamber, pulsing rhythm, the mechanism

deep in the soul counting down to my death; I know it is my heartbeat, but I feel hollow and corrupt, like an evil spirit has wormed its way into my being, and is now possessing me totally. I exist as an embryo in the egg of the world, inside this stone structure, formed naturally by the magics of those who live here. I realise now it *is* a trap. I am not strong enough. My mind flashes back to the death of the Empress, and I realise it was not her choice; she was prey to her hubris. She carried me only so far, like an infant, but then she went away and I felt abandoned. I told myself it was the natural order of things. One cannot hunt dragons without eventually being consumed, without eventually *becoming* one.

"Azkomar…" a voice whispers, shuddering around the chamber like a snake. I feel it wrap around me, and it is sensual and horrific, suffocating and comforting.

"Empress?" I ask the darkness, my eyes filtering the merest slither of light so I can see a play of shapes and shadows, dancing against the back of my retinas. I do not know if they are real or illusion, the scaffold of reality or the reality itself. I question my very existence.

"I made you," says the voice. It sounds so much like her I want to believe. I fall into its coils, so warm and inviting. I'm numbed by her soporific scent and don't feel the life being squeezed out of me.

"I didn't come here to kill *you*," I say, my eyes hanging heavy, my head lolling.

"It's okay, we shall be one again."

A tongue licks at my neck, and I feel it searching, eager and hungry. It flicks its forked, black flesh into the bag around my neck. The scent of magic fills my nostrils and I start. Bolt upright, I am awake.

The snake has me grasped tight and I bite viciously at its tongue as it tries to steal my last reserves of magic. Heavy flesh and bitter blood fill my mouth. The snake shrieks in pain as my teeth tear.

The coils slacken just enough for me to get my arms free. I greedily grasp the bag of magic around my neck and thrust it into my face, snuffling and swallowing the contents like a hog feeding on slops.

My body courses with angry energy. The bag is only small, but taken quickly, all at once, it gives me a vast burst of power. I scream as the beast in my mind takes over and the cells of my body transform.

Scales replace skin, bulging tendons of muscles beneath. Wings burst from my back as my face elongates. I'm already slashing with my new claws, biting with my dagger sized teeth, as I take on my true, magical form, a terrible monster from the abyss of my imagination.

I am the were-dragon Azkomar, demon spawn of the Empress, created by her half dragon blood.

The giant snake hisses in terror and pain, slashing at me with its fanged jaws, spitting venom at my red eyes. The rocky chamber echoes with my roar as I grasp the writhing, slithering body. It tries to wiggle free of my grasp, but I am too fast, too strong. I snap the snake like a twig. Rainbow blood gushes from the cleaved halves and I open my gullet, let the magic pour into me. It pulses in my soul and sustains my form. No longer a burst of energy from a tiny, wretched bag, I am now able to hold this form and hunt.

I drop the body of the snake to the ground and it withers, becomes the body of a woman. I see *her* face there, for a moment, and I realise I knew all along, and didn't care. She left me to fend for myself, and now the Empress is dead.

Did she give her life for me or was this a trap gone terribly wrong?

The face of the body flashes like light on a mirror and then dissolves, and I stare at the puddle of liquid, rainbow patina like an oil slick, and wonder if it was all an illusion, or if this really was the one who made me, cursed me with the thirst for magic.

Either way, I feel freedom flood the base of my brain. I am an animal, unleashed, and now I must *hunt*,

I must *feed*. I look deeper into the darkness of the cave, down into the black abyss which the snake was guarding. I know that down there I shall find myself, my match, my *mirror image*, and it will be glorious, even if it destroys me.

Into the heart of the world I descend to hunt the full-blooded dragons, to exorcise my past or be consumed in the fire of my own desires.

SAM M. PHILLIPS is the co-founder of Zombie Pirate Publishing, producing short story anthologies and helping emerging writers. His own work has appeared in dozens of anthologies and magazines such as Full Metal Horror and World War Four. He recently published his debut novella, *SCIENCE FICTION DOUBLE FEATURE: Phosphorus & Into The Eye*.

He lives in northern New South Wales, Australia, and enjoys reading, walking, and playing drums in the death metal band Decryptus. He is also a prolific poet and his poetry can be read on his blog.

Bibliography
SCIENCE FICTION DOUBLE FEATURE: Phosphorus & Into The Eye, Zombie Pirate Publishing, 2019
FULL METAL HORROR 2: A Bloodstained Anthology, Zombie Pirate Publishing, 2019
WORLD WAR FOUR: A Science Fiction Anthology, Zombie Pirate Publishing, 2019
WITCHES VS WIZARDS: A Fantasy Anthology, Zombie Pirate Publishing, 2018
PHUKET TATTOO: Crazy Tales of Far Away Places, Zombie Pirate Publishing, 2018
FULL METAL HORROR: A Monstrous Anthology, Zombie Pirate Publishing, 2018
Relationship Add Vice: A Thrilling Mashup of Romance and Crime, Zombie Pirate Publishing, 2017
The Collapsar Directive: A Science Fiction Anthology, Zombie Pirate Publishing, 2017
FLASH FICTION ADDICTION: 101 Short Short Stories, Zombie Pirate Publishing, 2019

Connect
Blog: www.bigconfusingwords.wordpress.com

THE PRINCESS OF THE TREES

By Cecelia Hopkins-Drewer

A faerie princess naturally expects her life to be one of endless parties and parades. Instead, Elorah finds herself thrust into intrigue as she attempts to bring a villain to justice and foil pernicious power plays.

The bark cut into Elorah's arms as she wrapped them around the birch tree. She had not intended to get caught. Trespassing onto the enemy lands was a little bit of fun, but being caught was another matter entirely. The tough rope bound her body tighter, squeezing it to the trunk.

"What do we have here?" a voice spoke from

behind Elorah. The voice was melodious and fluid, pleasant to the ear, but hated despite that. "Princess?"

"Don't bother yourself, Florian," Elorah muttered. "I'm just a trespasser, like any other."

She had met Florian before. When the territories had been at peace, the faerie prince had been a contender for her elder sister's hand in marriage. He had been impossibly arrogant, and solely focused on Meanderer, whose hand came with the throne, should their father ever pass. He had barely even noticed the tomboy sister who had developed a huge crush upon him. After the feud broke out, the marriage plans had been abandoned, and Meanderer had been married off to a much richer and more suitable prince.

"Just a trespasser, eh?" Florian's voice sounded amused. "You could be a spy. I think I ought to check."

Spying was a far greater offense than trespassing. Firm but gentle hands patted her down, searching for weapons. Elorah shuddered.

"Knock it off Florian," she ordered.

Florian found Elorah's personal dagger and confiscated it. Elorah clung closer to the tree trunk. It must have been a friendly tree, because it softened, taking her into its trunk. Inside the tree, Elorah shook herself off and thanked the plant profusely. Then she rematerialised into a tree much closer to home. Florian was left clutching her dagger and looking confused.

"To think I almost married the older sister," he murmured. "The younger one is far more interesting!"

***

Elorah was shocked when she entered the palace of the trooping faeries to find that her father was laid on a stretcher in the middle of the hall. At first, she thought he was dead, and then she noticed that the doctors still buzzed around him.

"Father," she cried, dropping to her knees beside the pallet.

"He has been attacked." Meanderer's eyes were fierce.

"Who by?" Elorah asked desperately.

"Prince Florian," Meanderer replied.

"Impossible," Elorah said. She had been with Florian herself a few minutes prior, but she did not want to explain the nature of her activities. "It must have been someone wearing Florian's armour."

"Either way, he is responsible," Meanderer was convinced.

"Will father die?" Elorah stammered.

"It takes more than a stab wound to kill a faerie king," Meanderer replied. "Unfortunately, the dagger was also poisoned. A slow acting poison that is hazardous to us faerie."

"I know that Florian did not do it," Elorah persisted. "I have a report upon him." She neglected to say that the informant was herself. "Florian may be a womaniser, but he is not a murderer."

"He is no longer my concern," Meanderer said firmly. Her engagement to Florian of Angor had been negated long ago, and she was now happily married to Trystane of Gelane. Normally she lived in Gelane with her husband, but they were in Releaf on a state visit.

Elorah hurried to the barracks and demanded that the captain show her the weapon with which her father had been stabbed. It was of Releafian manufacture. The plot thickened.

"We have traced the poison back to an apothecary in the south," the Captain said.

"Good work, Captain," Elorah said.

Duke Mikolo of the South believed he ought to have been king, instead of duke of a providence. Although Mikolo had been married to a trooping faerie, his solitary nature made him unsuited to leadership, and he was not a popular governor. The Duke was also the instigator of the feud between Angor and Releaf, although few faeries knew the origins of his malice. There was the culprit if Elorah could make Meanderer believe her reasoning. She sighed in frustration.

*****

Elorah retreated to the privacy of her room, closed the door and checked that she was alone, before translocating into a tree close to Florian's palace. She was taking a risk in coming to warn him. To his people, she would be an enemy intruder. To her own people, she would be a traitor for warning the accused prince. Yet, she had to do it, her heart demanded justice.

Luckily, Florian was strolling in his palace grounds. He grinned at the sight of Elorah. "Come back for more?" he asked teasingly.

Elorah shook her head, and at the sight of her tear-dimmed eyes, Florian became serious.

"What's wrong?" the Prince demanded. "Was I too rough before?"

"Rough, never you!" Elorah refuted. Now was not the time to admit she liked his hands on her body, or was it? She longed for a comforting hug. "My father has been stabbed."

Florain looked shocked. "I'm flattered that you have come to me for comfort." His arms closed around her.

"It's not that easy," Elorah sobbed. "You have

been accused of the attack."

Florian tensed. His voice was angry. "I know the marriage to Meanderer was called off – but why would I harm your father?"

"The assassin was wearing your armour," Elorah sobbed.

Florian led Elorah through the back corridors of the castle into the armoury. "My armour is right here!"

"Perhaps a replica?" Elorah ventured.

"Serious indeed." Florian was thoughtful. "And what are we going to do about you? You cannot go home, your life might be in danger too."

"I will be alright," Elorah said. "Meanderer will be regent and she will make sure I am safe. But I must go back and clear your name."

"Why would you do that?" Florian asked.

"Because I care about you," Elorah was bold in her grief and from the safety of the circle of his arms.

"Care - as in love?" Florian mused. "That is a complication."

"I was sort of hoping you might care about me too," Elorah cried.

"I do, but at one stage I was scheduled to be your brother-in-law," Florian said. "Meanderer would never accept it."

"What has she to do with us?" Elorah was

rebellious.

"With your father injured, she is the one who has to approve," Florian sighed. "If you are determined, we had better get you home before you are missed!"

He tossed Elorah a sable cloak woven from the finest of spider webs and dyed with the ink of midnight. Elorah drew the cloak over her head and became nearly invisible. "Thanks, I ought to have thought of it myself."

"You are welcome," Florian gave her a peck on the cheek, with the promise of something better should they get their situation sorted out.

Elorah left the castle through isolated corridors and melted into a convenient tree. When she arrived home, the Releafian kingdom was still in an uproar. The faerie princess emerged from her room and strode towards the throne room where she expected to find Meanderer in charge.

***

Elorah was shocked to find Meanderer presiding over the muster of troops to be sent against the province of Angor. "But Father isn't dead yet!" she cried.

"Attacking a head of state is an act of war," Meanderer replied with thin lips. "And sister, you need to be mindful of your own future."

"What do you mean?" Elorah gasped.

"Get preparing for your wedding, we have received an offer for your hand," Meanderer declared. "Trystane and I will take care of things here."

"Who would want to marry me?" Elorah mouthed somewhat naively.

"Duke Mikolo of the South!" Meanderer sounded unconcerned. "It's a good match for you."

Suspiciously Elorah frowned. "He must be centuries older than me!"

"And you will be a step-mother, just think of that," Meanderer obviously saw the circumstance as a blessing. "I want you to pack your bags and journey south at once."

"Alright," Elorah agreed, somewhat to her sister's surprise. The young princess was determined to investigate her father's assassination, and all the signs pointed towards Mikolo. Going south would place her in the best position to uncover the truth. "Promise me one thing though, Meanderer? If Florian should not be responsible for our Father's murder, please do not invade Angor."

"I would obviously avoid an unnecessary war." Meanderer sounded amused. "I am grieving, but not insane."

"Thanks!" Elorah ran off to pack a trousseau. The tree faerie was determined not to marry Mikolo, but she would travel willingly into his duchy and go through the motions. A slither of concern wriggled around the back of her mind. Once Mikolo had his fiancé in his household, the only people between him and the throne of Releaf would be Meanderer and Trystane, who had not yet had a child.

***

After a three day journey, Elorah arrived in the southern province. When she looked deep into the swimming blue eyes of her stepdaughter, Vikara, her heart swelled with sympathy. Household tales of a fever spoke of the mother being struck down by a poison similar to the one that doomed Elorah's father.

"It will be alright," Elorah spoke determinedly, lifting the girl out of her curtsy.

"My lady," Vikara was confused.

Elorah turned to Mikolo. "I would like to throw a party to celebrate our betrothal."

"Surely a quick wedding would be more convenient?" Mikolo suggested.

Elorah shook her head. "No, it is not fitting for a princess to wed so hurriedly."

Mikolo would not gain political power from their engagement until it had been formalised into marriage. Elorah also hoped that by creating as much publicity as possible, news of her plight would be carried back to Florian. The Duke looked disappointed, but he hastened to follow Elorah's instruction to organise a grand reception.

"Why don't you show me around?" Elorah turned to Vikara. It would be pleasant to see the southern kingdom through the eyes of the younger faerie instead of the jaded mind of Duke Mikolo.

The Water Faerie looked flattered. "If you would like." She turned and led the way through the huge archway, up the stone steps from the courtyard into the castle. "This is the main hall, and the raised podium is the feasting area."

"Impressive," Elorah murmured. What the southern castle lacked in comfort and ornamentation, it gained in stone fortifications. The windows were mere arrow slits, and the foundations were sloped to make the walls difficult to climb. Elorah had already noticed the approach had been via a long stone bridge, easily isolated in the event of a siege. Battles here would be costly. She sincerely hoped that the situation could be resolved without military action. "Show me the private quarters."

Vikara led her through the corridors. "The kitchen and storerooms are that way—and the servants mostly live on this level," she said. They climbed a narrow staircase into a pleasant room Vikara referred to as "the solar", which appeared to double as the family sitting room. A series of bed chambers opened off the solar. "This one is yours. I'm sorry it is not fancier, but it does have its own garderobe."

"Very convenient," Eorah murmured. She did not need an ornate room. Crossing to the narrow, slit window, she looked out on a steep drop towards the Southern Ocean. "Where do you sleep?"

"A couple of rooms further on," Vikara said, her voice trembling. "Past the suite that used to be my mother's."

"Show me," Elorah instructed. She laid a gentle hand on Vikara's shoulder. The girl's mother had died earlier that year from a wasting illness; death was unusual among the faerie folk and considered incredibly shocking. "I may yet lose a father. We could cry together."

The southern castle had originally been built for winter occupation, back in the era when the trooping fairies migrated with the seasons. It was solidly designed to withstand rain, snow and strong wind; making it more mysterious than the summer palace, which was open and airy. The summer palace was surrounded by flowers and groves of trees; and nowadays it was kept warm all year round by magical means. The court no longer visited the south annually, with the result that the southern province had grown more isolated. Whatever the outcome of the situation, Elorah vowed to persuade Meanderer to pay more attention to the south than their father had. King Koenig had been too trusting, and prone to let his cousin Mikolo too much freedom to indulge pride.

"Is there anywhere I can be among trees?" Elorah asked.

Vikara looked thoughtful. "There are orchards, but they are some distance from the castle, and I would need to arrange an escort."

Elorah shook her head. "No good."

"There was one tree left inside the rear wall of the castle," Vikara ventured hesitantly. "It was a hardy mountain variety that the builders chose to work around instead of uproot."

"Excellent," Elorah cried. "Show me where!"

Vikara led the way back to the solar and downstairs towards the rear of the castle. The two young faeries passed dedicated workers hurrying to prepare a feast to celebrate the engagement of their lord. As Elorah was a trooping fey, her request for a show of pageantry was considered perfectly natural; and unlikely to be recognised as the delaying tactic it really was.

The rear of the castle included several wells, set hygienically apart from the waste plumbing copied from Roman forces who had occupied the mundane world some time earlier in history. Elorah stepped forward and touched the yew tree. It was ancient, but still held a spark of life, and through the trunk she could feel its roots connecting it to the other trees in the kingdom. A buzzing hum of vegetative communication joined with the oaks and hawthorns of the summer palace, and the birches surrounding Florian's residence.

Elorah would have to contrive to visit the tree alone to use it to travel, however. She sighed and looked up at the sun, which was travelling towards the west. "We ought to prepare ourselves for dinner."

"Oh yes!" Vikara looked enthusiastic. Every young faerie loved a party.

***

That evening at the celebration, Duke Mikolo began fondling Elorah's knee under the rough oak of the table. His touch made her flesh crawl, but she forced herself to smile pleasantly, and remove his hand with a modest expression. As her fiancé drank more ale, his expression became lecherous, alerting Elorah to a new danger. If the princess could not be hurried into marriage, the solitary fey could climb one step closer to the throne by planting his child in her womb. Then he could become regent on behalf of any offspring.

Elorah mused that maybe she ought to translocate to Florian's palace and get him to do the honours in that department to prevent any possibility of a child she bore being Duke Mikolo's. Elorah got quite feverish at the thought of Florian's kisses and began to flush. Duke Mikolo mistook her blush as enthusiasm and squeezed her buttock where it rested on the side of the chair.

Elorah slapped at the Duke's hand in shock. "Later my dear," she managed to snap.

"Is that a promise?" The drunken Duke leaned closer.

"Perhaps not tonight." Elorah managed an affected simper. She fanned herself with her hand. "I feel a little faint after my long journey."

The Duke muttered a few phrases of shallow concern and allowed Elorah to finish her meal in relative peace. After the feast, she greeted the southern dignitaries politely and excused herself on the pretext of requiring an early night. By this stage, Duke Mikolo appeared too intoxicated to constitute a threat, but Elorah invited her maid to share her bedchamber as a precaution.

***

It was almost midnight when something woke Elorah. She stilled her limbs under the quilt and attuned her fine ears to listen to the sounds in the dark of the night. There was a scrabbling at the door, and her heart lurched in terror. "Who is it?"

"Vikara," came the soft reply. "I'm sorry if I woke you…"

Elorah sat up. "What do you want? Is everything alright?"

"Earlier this evening, you said that you felt ill," Vikara explained innocently. "I brought my mother's medicine for you."

"Thank you," Elorah said. Her hand closed over an angular glass bottle. It felt cold and evil. "But Vicky darling, this medicine did not cure your mother."

"I know," Vikara's voice was choked with grief.

"I think it might be a little too strong for the heart," Elorah said. She fumbled in the beam of moonlight that entered through the slit window and set the bottle down carefully in the drawer of the bedside table. "That was very kind of you anyway, Vikara. Go back to your own bed now."

The maid gave a little snore and Vikara jumped in alarm. "Who is that?"

"My attendant, I felt safer with her by my side," Elorah admitted.

Vikara giggled. "It took me years to persuade Nan to stop sleeping in my room!"

"You are at home," Elorah said. "I'm in a strange place."

"I understand." Vikara faded from the room and padded softly down the stone passage until the sound melted into the darkness.

Elorah lay back with a sense of satisfaction. The princess was sure that she was now in possession of the poison that had killed Vikara's mother and was in the process of killing her father. She only needed the suit of armour to persuade Meanderer that Florian was innocent, and Mikolo guilty.

***

The next morning Duke Mikolo announced they would be participating in a hunt in honour of his engagement. The majority of the trooping faeries cheered because they loved a good hunt. Elorah shivered, as she was aware of the solitary Duke's reputation for actually shooting at the deer, unlike many others for whom the hunt was simply a ride. Moreover, she could tell by his expression that the Duke enjoyed killing and did not just slaughter in order to eat.

When the warriors were all lined up and ready to ride out through the portcullis, Elorah caught sight of a helmet that made her heart leap. It appeared that Florian had somehow joined the party! Urging her horse forward, she left the Duke's side and drew up beside the warrior wearing Florian's insignia. Her innocent greeting was met with a surly grunt, and Duke Mikolo placed a steadying hand upon the rein of Elorah's horse.

"You are wearing the wrong helm, Rufus!" Mikolo growled to his henchman, who began to apologise and backed his horse away. The man tethered his mount to a hasp in the wall and disappeared into the armoury, emerging a few moments later wearing a helmet that was a better match for his armour.

Elorah noted the entry to the armoury with sharp eyes. After the hunt, she meant to return and purloin that helmet as her final piece of evidence against Mikolo. Then she was forced to turn her back and ride out of the castle, pushing her horse hard all day to keep up with Mikolo, who liked to be at the front of the chase.

***

The party returned late in the afternoon, and the formal dinner became a supper, with the deer rotating on the spit for hours before the meal commenced. Duke Mikolo was full of self-importance and bestowed a couple of crushing kisses upon Elorah that she was unable to dodge. Elorah bore his brutish advances with as good humour as she could muster, making an excuse to slip away from the great hall into her room.

Safely in her room, Elorah changed into an unremarkable gown and donned the spider web cloak. She slipped the bottle of evil medicine down her bodice, where it lodged safely amongst her stays. The princess then slunk back through the corridors, down the stairs and to the armoury. Once hidden in the dark cavity of the weapon storage, she cautiously lit a candle and scanned the shelves for the helmet bearing Florian's insignia. The helm had been carelessly thrown among the spare equipment, and Elorah scooped it up, knotting it into the folds of her skirt.

Fearing someone might discover she was missing

from her room, Elorah hurried along the servant's route through the castle and out the back, where she was lucky to find herself alone among the wells and plumbing. She slid into the grotto housing the ancient yew tree and begged the trunk for sanctuary. Hearing angry shouts and cries from the front of the castle, Elorah shivered as she waited for the tree to open up and accommodate her. Once inside the yew, the faerie translocated into a scratchy hawthorn near the royal palace.

***

When she found Meanderer, her sister was crying because their father had finally been pronounced dead. Trystane was attempting in vain to comfort the older princess, who was showing signs of stress from the past few days.

Meandered looked at Elorah dully. "It was good of you to return for the funeral," she said.

Elorah held out the helm with Florian's insignia and the bottle of poison.

Meanderer recoiled. "Where did you get those awful things?"

"In Mikolo's castle," Elorah explained.

Trystane took the bottle of poison and the helmet

from Elorah. "We will have the guards examine them, but there is a good chance they belonged to your father's killer."

"I can hardly believe it," Meanderer choked. "One of our own."

"Mikolo has long been hungry for power," Trystane said. "I think you need to give up your campaign against Florian, my dear Meanderer."

***

There was a flurry of cloud, and Duke Mikolo arrived at the royal palace in a burst of thunder. The solitary fey no longer looked like a middle-aged drunkard; because he had spent energy on renewing his appearance. Taller and darker all of a sudden, he was clearly a malicious sprite. Mikolo had a sword in his hand and lunged at Meanderer.

"Give me back my fiancé," the Duke cried. "Through her, I mean to rule the Sidhe."

"Oh no you don't!" Trystane snatched a weapon off a rack on the wall and leapt to the defence of his wife.

Back and forth, the two men dodged and feinted. The Duke was the more experienced swordsman, and Trystane was hard pressed to keep the evil faerie away from Meanderer. There was the sound of horse hooves clattering along the open approach to the summer castle. Polite murmurs sounded as the attendants helped someone down from their mount and pointed them in the direction of the royal family.

Florian stepped through the door and saw Trystane fighting with Mikolo. The Prince of Angor had only come armed with Elorah's dagger, which he had meant to return, yet he valiantly entered the fray. Mikolo was gaining ground on Trystane, but he was forced to divide his attention to meet the new threat. Florian dodged the flailing sword arm and brought his dagger up under Mikolo's chin.

"Halt and desist!" Florian ordered. Mikolo shuddered and dropped his sword, as the sharp dagger pricked the soft skin of his throat.

Hearing the commotion, several guards followed Florian into the room. They took the disarmed Mikolo into custody and awaited further instruction from Meanderer.

"Duke Mikolo is the one who assassinated the King," Elorah announced into the confusion.

"That explains a lot," Florian surveyed her sternly. "But what is this I heard about you getting engaged to him?"

"You seem to have dealt with it appropriately!"

Elorah remarked cheekily.

Trystane laughed and Meanderer looked puzzled. "What's this all about?"

"I think your sister has a little crush," Trystane said.

"Oh no she doesn't!" Meanderer declared stubbornly. "Elorah has just been through one political engagement, and I won't be letting her enter any other relationships in a hurry."

***

Their father's funeral concluded, the two faerie princesses stood side by side. Meanderer was sedate as a flower, while Elorah was as restless as a tree in the wind. Faeries have an indeterminate life expectancy, and subsequently neither fey had expected their father to die. Until he had been stabbed by a poisoned dagger wielded by the hand of Duke Mikolo, that was.

"I'm afraid I am going to have to ask you to miss my coronation." Meanderer turned to Elorah.

"Oh, why?" Elorah was surprised.

"I need you to go south," Meanderer explained. "I am appointing you as guardian to the young Duchess Vikara."

"You intend to allow Vikara to rule the southern

province?" Elorah was relieved to hear the queen-elect did not intend punishing the daughter for the sins of her father.

"The alternative ruler would be Mikolo's brother Rollo, who is not at all acceptable," Meanderer declared. "Duke Mikolo poisoned his wife, so Vikara is as much a victim as we are!"

Elorah had secretly been hoping to commence a relationship with Florian and move to Angor. Meanderer had not given official permission, but the tree faerie expected the Queen-elect could be persuaded eventually. "I will go then."

"It is important that you arrive with pomp and ceremony," Meanderer said. "So, although I want you to arrive quickly, I'm going to have to ask you not to travel by tree."

Elorah nodded. Only the more talented among the fey could translocate, and they generally kept their ability to do so quiet. "I will go and organise a small retinue. I trust you can spare some guards?"

"Excellent thinking!" Meanderer agreed. "That way we increase our military force without actually invading one of our own provinces."

"Always a good thing." Elorah's tone was dry, but the irony was lost on the self-important Meanderer.

***

Elorah bid goodbye to Prince Florian, who intended to stay in Releaf until Meanderer's coronation was concluded. By this time, both had acknowledged that their bond was as tantalising as it was challenging.

"Meanderer has sent me south again," she whispered.

"Just as long as you don't go getting engaged this time," Florian joked.

"Earl Rollo is so not my type, but I am honorary step-mother to Vikara."

"So, do what you have to do!" Florian laughed.

***

When Elorah and her retinue arrived at the winter palace in the southern province, she was relieved to find Vikara was prepared to welcome her with open arms. The young water faerie apparently held no resentment over the broken engagement to her father. However, Elorah could tell at a glance that something was wrong.

"Uncle Rollo said that a girl could not rule," Vikara confided.

Elorah bristled. "Together we will show him.

Don't worry, the province is yours! You have earned it twice over, with your loyalty to the crown, and the loss of your mother."

"I am afraid that Uncle Rollo will try to take the Duchy for himself," Vikara whispered. "Or even try to break Father out of prison."

Elorah shook her head. "It won't do him any good."

She did not want to give any details, but as the faerie did not believe in capital punishment, they used a magical stasis system to keep their prisoners immobilised and unconscious for all of their extended lives. It would take powerful magic indeed, from a group of sprites willing to sacrifice something to break Mikolo out of containment. The solitary fey were not very good at teamwork, so Rollo was unlikely to gather a group of willing candidates.

"I will organise to have you sworn in as Duchess tomorrow," Elorah suggested. "In the meantime, I think you ought to hold an audience. Listen to your subjects and begin giving orders."

***

Vikara took her place on the podium in the great hall, with Elorah sitting to her left. Many of the requests were simple, and Vikara ruled in favour of some common fey who requested compensation for livestock lost to bandits.

"It seems these things are getting worse," Vikiara commented.

"Mikolo's dark leanings may have kept the malicious sprites at bay," Elorah suggested.

Vikara nodded uncomfortably. Although she had suffered at her father's hands, it was still difficult to listen to criticism of him.

"Send some of the guards I brought to patrol the borders." Elorah was confident the problem could be managed.

When Earl Rollo arrived, he looked displeased to see Vikara sitting at the centre of the council. "On whose authority did you start this?" he demanded.

"Mine! And through me, the Queen," Elorah pronounced, confident in the fact that Meanderer had been crowned by now.

"I guess you will be wanting advisers." Rollo was clearly looking for an alternate route to power.

Elorah had prepared Vikara for this possibility. "I value your opinion very much dear Uncle," the young water faerie returned. "But officially, I have appointed some of the noble fey as counsellors and a senior officer as my equerry."

Rollo looked unsatisfied, but there was nothing he could do in the face of Vikara's courtesy.

***

The next day, they received a report from one of the guard patrols that a coastal town was being terrorised by a morvach. It was unusual for a sea serpent to approach the coast unless it had been summoned, so Elorah was thoughtful. Earl Rollo, on the other hand, looked almost pleased; as if the presence of the monster represented a chance to demonstrate his prowess.

Elorah knew that Vikara was an excellent bows-woman, having been trained by her father, who had been an outstanding hunter, whatever else his faults. She discretely instructed the young Duchess to lead the defending party herself, instead of allowing Earl Rollo the glory of doing so, and the party set off.

They arrived at the village and paused to comfort the frightened fisher fey before going down to the shore. Then Vikara and several of the most skilled guards rowed out in a wooden boat to confront the morvach. Elorah stayed on the beach and crooned a soothing spell under her breath in order to counter any summoning that might be binding the sea serpent to the coast.

The morvach reared as if to strike the boat, and Vikara shot a powerful shot from her longbow, striking the monster just below the head. The guards all threw their spears, hitting the morvach in a concerted flurry. The blows did not kill the sea serpent, but they did thoroughly frighten it. The serpent swam away, towards the deeper water where it usually lived.

The onlookers all cheered.

The young Duchess Vikara had just proved her ability as a strike leader! Earl Rollo looked crestfallen but was forced to congratulate his relative. The troop rode back to the winter palace in triumph.

***

After the conclusion of dinner that evening, Elorah allowed herself to melt away from the crowd, and slink through the corridors to the solitary tree in the service yard. Reaching out to touch its bark, she felt the soothing affinity of the wood. Focusing her mind upon Florian's palace in Angor, she was transported there in no time.

Florian greeted her arrival with a friendly hug. "How's it going?"

"I think my task is almost done." Elorah gazed at

Florian expectantly, and he obligingly leaned in for a kiss. Their first, incredibly exciting kiss.

"What about Meanderer?" he queried.

"Forget Meanderer," Elorah whispered. "I'm sure she will agree to our relationship sooner or later."

"In the meantime, it would be exhilarating to continue seeing each other in secret," Florian mused.

"Very exhilarating," Elorah agreed.

CECELIA HOPKINS-DREWER is a speculative fiction writer, researcher and poet, who lives in Adelaide, South Australia. She has also written a Masters paper on H.P. Lovecraft, and a teenage vampire series consisting of three YA novellas: *Mystic Evermore, Saints and Sinners,* & *Autumn Secrets* (published under her own imprint "CGH Literacy Institute"). Cecelia also has speculative poetry published in *The Mentor* (a sci-fi fanzine edited by Ron Clarke) and *Spectral Realms* (edited by S.T. Joshi).

Bibliography
100 Word Zombie Bites, Reanimated Writers Press, 2019
Angels, Black Hare Press, 2019
Apocalypse, Black Hare Press, 2019
Beyond, Black Hare Press, 2019
Lovecraft Annual 11, Hippocamus Press, 2017
Lovecraft Annual 12, Hippocamus Press, 2018
Lovecraft Annual 13, Hippocamus Press, 2019
Lovecraft Studies 31, Hippocamus Press, 1994
Monster, Black Hare Press, 2019
Scary Snippets: Christmas Edition, Suicide house Publishing, 2019
Scary Snippets: Halloween Edition, Suicide House Publishing, 2019
The Australasian Record, Signs Publishing, 2007
Unravel, Black Hare Press, 2019
Worlds, Black Hare Press, 2019

Connect
Amazon: amazon.com/Cecelia-Hopkins-Drewer/e/B071G968NM/
Facebook: Cecelia-Hopkins-Drewer-Author-Page-1906791576107159/
Goodreads: goodreads.com/author/show/16975323.Cecelia_Hopkins_Drewer
Blog: creativearts2009-picturefiles.blogspot.com
Website: chopkin39.wixsite.com/website

THE WIZARD'S DRAGONS

By Dawn DeBraal

Convicted thieves Chardon Linken and Zabor Ash are given an opportunity to redeem themselves by their Wizard Falk when he gives them forty dragon eggs to hatch and train to protect their territories.

Chardon Linken and Zabor Ash walked the road to town every day searching for work. Occasionally, a rich man offered them some coins to do a job. Some days, they made enough to feed their families. Other days like today, they did not. There was a time when the men had been well-to-do landowners. That was before drought came to Adwinia. Heading home after a day's work, Chardon and Zabor noticed a young man walking briskly along the road with a few loaves of bread under his arm. They stopped the boy, asking him where he got the money to buy the loaves of bread.

"Sorry, I must continue on my way. My master and his men are waiting for their dinner." The young man nervously scurried away. Zabor and Chardon watched longingly at the disappearing loaves. It was difficult to face going home another night, letting their families down. It was then they devised the plan to steal from the lad.

It was Chardon who came up with the idea. The hide of the last cow he had slaughtered was still green, drying on a rack in the sun. Chardon told Zabor they could take the hide, drape it over themselves, pretending to be a lone cow in the field. When the boy walked by, he wouldn't be able to resist bringing home such a prize to his master. They would overtake the boy before he realised the cow was fake.

The two men worked on the disguise, rubbing mud on the dried skull to make it black. They sewed the hide so that both men would fit beneath, and Zabor made a twitching tail. The costume completed, they waited for the boy the following day.

The lone cow stood a short distance from the road, out in the dark field. From a distance, and in the dark, it was the perfect lure. Chardon convincingly made a lone cow sound as Zabor twitched the tail. When the lad came along with an armload of bread, he spied the cow in the field. Falling for the ruse, he ran out to grab the beast. Zabor and Chardon fell upon him, striking him unconscious and stealing the bread. They took everything with them, thinking they'd got away with their crime. They hadn't got away.

***

They were standing before the Tribunal Council. Zabor looking defeated, was ready to be sentenced.

"Zabor Ash, you have been found guilty of stealing a loaf of bread. Your punishment is to place your hand into a hole on the punishment board and draw your sentence." The Tribunal Counsel had made its decision.

A brightly painted board with several holes, large enough to fit a man's hand through, stood on the platform. Zabor trembled, trying to decide which hole to choose. The crowd waited anxiously to see what punishment Zabor would draw. Deciding, he inserted his hand, feeling for the parchment sentence. Instead of pulling out a paper, Zabor screamed and withdrew a bloodied stump where his hand used to be. He bent over, putting the hand to his body to stem the flow of blood as they led him away. The crowd murmured approval. Zabor stole from a boy and his hand had been taken. Zabor's punishment was just. The crowd died down as the reporter came out on the stage, unrolling the scroll, and in his sing-song voice, declared, "Chardon Linken, you have been accused of stealing a loaf of bread, how do you, plead?"

Chardon numbly walked up the stairway, looking at the punishment board, deciding he would sacrifice his right hand. He had always favoured his left hand over the right, but the menfolk forbade him to use that hand, making him strengthen the other. He would need the strongest hand to pick up his sword to defend his family. Chardon looked out to the crowd where his wife of many years, his two sons almost grown, and his daughter stood in horror. Many of his neighbours looked on, knowing the price of his thievery after Zabor's punishment. Chardon knew he needed to be brave for his family. Stealing to feed your family was one thing, not accepting punishment as a man was another. The reporter sang out again.

"Chardon Linken, how do you plead?"

Chardon's heart was in his throat when he shouted out to the crowd. "I did what I needed to do to feed my family. Any of you would have done the same. I am guilty." Chardon knew any place he stuck his hand would result in the same punishment. The Council wished to discourage thievery between the Adwinan's. Chardon prayed for the sword wielder to be accurate and swift. He lifted his hand, deciding to use the lower portion of the board so that the swordsman would take his hand on the downstroke. A murmur broke out in the crowd. People turned their attention to a large group of men riding up to the Council platform.

Upon seeing Falk the Wizard, Hegney, leader of the Council, called out, "Stop!"

Chardon's hand dropped to his side, and he fell to his knees in relief. Several men on horseback escorted Falk—who had been away for several months—back into their fold. When Falk's horse came to the Council's platform, he looked at Chardon kneeling before the punishment board then turned his eyes to Zabor, who was still bent over his bloody stump. Falk knew what was about to happen.

"Who has allowed this?" Falk looked straight at the head Councilman who shrank back in his seat.

"I did. It is chaos here. Thieves are taking food from boys. They must be punished."

Falk looked across the people of the town and saw their misery. Dismounting, he walked to Zabor, who still held the stump to his stomach. The wizard pulled

Zabor's arm away from his body.

"Bring me his hand," Falk called out. The swordsman came from behind the board carrying the severed hand in a basket. The wizard took the bloodied stump and held it to Zabor's wrist. With an incantation of magic, he restored Zabor's hand. The crowd gasped, stepping away from the wizard. What would Falk do to them for their disobedience while he was away? Hegney looked uncomfortable. It was up to him to keep the law in the territory. Falk had just undermined that in front of everyone. Hegney could feel his anger coming to the surface and unsuccessfully tried to hide his displeasure.

Hegney began to disburse the crowd with a crust of bread—payment for attending the Tribunal Council meeting, but Falk called the people back before they went too far.

"I have several wagons of food coming from Talkien. They have agreed to see us through the drought, and in exchange, Adwinia will become their ally. The carts will be here tomorrow with food and livestock.

"We don't have water!" some of the villagers shouted.

"I will take care of that," Falk replied before turning to the men on the platform.

"Zabor, Chardon, I need to speak with you." Zabor looked at his reattached appendage in awe. He would have done anything that Falk asked of him.

***

The wizard walked with both men back to a wagon in his caravan. Pulling the sheet back on the cart, Falk revealed several containers.

"I need the two of you to help with this plan." Zabor and Chardon looked at the baskets. There were several large eggs in each one.

"Dragon eggs?" Zabor said under his breath. "What are we to do with these?"

Falk asked the man driving the wagon to step down, motioning to Zabor and Chardon to climb up onto the cart seat. "You two will hatch the dragons and train them," he explained.

"We have no water to raise the dragons," Chardon said. Falk brought out two small sacks from the folds of his robes, handing one to each man.

"Here, put these in your wells. Water will come back quickly. I know dragons need a lot of water."

Neither man had any experience with egg incubation or raising dragons. The baskets contained instructions from the Talkiens on how to mature the eggs along with the help of the Wizard. Chardon looked at Falk, lowering his gaze. "It was your manservant we stole from, Wizard." he said, quietly. Zabor nodded in agreement also ashamed for what they had done to the boy.

"This is why I chose you for this task. Because you are both honest men. I knew your crimes before you admitted them to me. You and Zabor are forgiven."

Both men were astonished. They took the wagon, and their families, leaving town before the wizard changed his mind.

Chardon was first to put the magic bag down his well. He waited for a few moments, and then the earth rumbled and shook as if an earthquake had happened. Water started to rise, spilling over onto the ground into the small dry stream bed near him. He realised that Falk was a mighty wizard, but someone would have to pay for his changing of the universe. Chardon wondered who that would be.

Chardon and his son took half the baskets and put them in his barn before shaking Zabor's hand and wishing him luck. As he watched the wagon roll out of sight, there was a stir in the clouds and the skies darkened, thunder rolling in the distance. Chardon knelt, thanking the gods for bringing Falk back to them in the nick of time, for delivering the rain, and the knowledge they would have food from the Talkiens the following day. Chardon's livelihood was spared, and he was provided with the opportunity to raise the dragons for Falk—a wizard he had betrayed. He was ashamed, yet so very honoured. It had been an emotional day for everyone.

***

Hegney was jealous; Falk had undermined his authority *and* rewarded the thieves by honouring them with the task of hatching dragons. Hegney's bruised pride forced him to go to Falk's tower.

Falk's home was a vast stone tower built before any of the people living in the village were born. Hegney pounded on the door, and it was answered by Falk's manservant—the boy who had been robbed by Zabor and Chardon.

"I need to speak with the Wizard," Hegney shouted. The boy asked Hegney to wait at the entrance, coming back to him a short time later.

"My master will speak with you another day. He has retired for the evening, exhausted from his long journey."

Hegney pushed the servant out of the way, but armed guards stepped in front of him, discouraging his entrance into the tower. Resigned, Hegney left for his cottage. He would still speak with the wizard to re-establish his rightful place as the head Councilman of Adwinia. This inherited position came with rights and privileges, which would not be taken away by the return of Falk, he would see to it.

Hegney headed across the open field, and as thunder rumbled and the sky darkened, he started to trot back toward his cottage.

The drought is over! He had a mixture of joy and concern when he saw water from the almost dried-up river come rushing down its banks at high speed. The skies opened, the rain came down. Hegney couldn't see through the wall of water that fell around him. As the riverbed rose, Hegney searched for higher ground, amazed at how quickly the empty bed had filled its banks. Hegney put his cloak over his head and hurried through the storm that tried to beat him back, the wind and rain were against him as lightning struck the ground around him. He walked the dike above the stream, moving as fast as he could. The torrential water pushing against the dried-up levee started to carry away the path beneath Hegney's feet. Stones and earth moved down the stream at an alarming rate, and Hegney started to panic. What had he done? Had he brought the wrath of Falk down on himself? He stood at the top of the earthen dam, screaming to the sky.

"You have won, Wizard! Spare me! I am your servant!" The rain let up a bit, the water slowed beneath him.

Hegney was never so happy as he was to see his home that night. He knew how close he had come to sacrificing himself for Falk's powers. He would not allow that to happen again.

The woman who cared for Hegney's house threw open the door. She had a warmed blanket which she draped over him as he sat down in the nearest chair. Every pot he had in the house was set outside the door to collect the falling rain. Hegney had the feeling, now that Falk was back, they wouldn't need the containers, but praised the housekeeper for her cleverness just the same.

Once the fear—but not the frustration—of the day left Hegney, he set out on a plan to put the wizard in his place. Hegney had many men who respected his power of the Council, and they would do his bidding. He went to bed that night thinking of the things he would do to his adversary.

Hegney would not stand by and watch his power be taken away.

***

The people of Adwinia rejoiced that they had water again. And, when wagons of food, as promised, rolled into their village, there was plenty for everyone. The Talkien leader, Beckett, gave a speech, ensuring the people of Adwinia, including Hegney, understood this gift came with strings. Hegney and Beckett had a long-standing dislike of one another stemming from their fathers and grandfathers before them. Beckett agreed to help the Adwinians because the wizard offered to help the Talkiens raise the dragon eggs they'd found in nearby caves. In exchange for the help with the eggs, Beckett's territory came with food and livestock.

Falk told the people of Adwinia to bring their rakes and hoes to him. The wizard put them under a spell so they would work faster, producing a significant amount of food in a short period time.

After all the people had received their rations of food, there were still wagons of supplies leftover. Every farmer went home with a sack of grain to plant. Cows and horses, one of each, were given to each family, along with sacks of feed to last until the crops grew. The townspeople thanked Falk and his men for bringing life back to Adwinia, and they thanked Beckett and the Talkiens. Hegney watched the whole scene with disdain for Beckett and the people he ruled over. For his people now grovelled at Beckett's feet. Hegney was no longer the man in charge at that moment, but a mere figurehead.

***

The grass appeared a little greener after the rains. In a few weeks, no one remembered how barren the landscape had been. The magic hoes and rakes made the planted food grow twice as fast. The Adwinians had their cattle and horses bred to multiply their stock. People of Adwinia were on the rebound. Everyone was happy, except for Hegney who still burned with anger toward the wizard. Falk's interference made the townspeople no longer fear him. Hegney knew Falk had expended all his energy by using sorcery to make the rain come to Adwinia. Falk would be weak. It would take several moon cycles to build Falk's power back up. Hegney was confident this was the reason Falk refused to see him the night of his return to Adwinia just a few weeks before. The wizard was weak and vulnerable.

There was to be a celebration in the village that night. The celebration, planned by Hegney, had been a ploy to get Falk's guards away from the tower.

Hegney's men, those who felt they owed him their lives, would sneak into the tower and take the wizard by surprise. In his weakened state, Falk would not be able to defend himself, and Falk's guards would be cavorting in the town square, unaware of Hegney's deception. Hegney led his group of men, under cover of darkness, to the tower after the townspeople started to dance in the streets. He pounded on the wizard's door. As he suspected, the manservant was the only person with Falk.

"I demand to see the wizard," Falk shouted at the boy who tried to shut the door but was too late. The horde of men pushed through the opening in search of the wizard. The manservant attempted to warn his master but was stricken down, trampled by the angry mob, before he could get his warning out. Hegney's men stepped over the bleeding boy as they ran to the top of the tower.

A wooden door, cloaked in a spell, blocked their way to the wizard. This is what Hegney guessed would happen. He had consulted an old witch before his attack on the wizard—she wasn't very forthcoming with her information, but after days of torture, she told Hegney what he needed to know and about the potion. The Councilman, satisfied the witch had told him the truth, took the potion from her and ordered his men to finish the job. The witch shouted incantations at Hegney as his men cut off her head.

Hegney knew he needed the blood of an innocent man to make the potion the old witch had given him work. The men he had with him were far from innocent. He thought of the boy who lay unconscious in the entryway. Hegney ordered two men to go and fetch the servant. To his other men, he explained they could not break through the door because it had been bewitched by the wizard's spell. Hegney could hear the boy crying and begging for his life with each step as he was dragged up the tower stairs. One of the men asked for mercy for the servant—the boy was his wife's nephew—but Hegney stabbed the offensive man in the stomach with his dagger. Those around the dead man stepped back, allowing room for the two men to drag the boy in front of the magic door. Hegney took the already bloodied dagger and cut the servant's neck, filling the potion bottle with the blood of the innocent man. Pouring it on the lock, the chains broke away from the wooden door. The men fell upon the wizard, binding him. Hegney came into the room laughing at the helpless wizard.

"You see, you are not so strong after all, Wizard. You will see no more."

Knowing he couldn't kill Falk, Hegney cut out the

wizard's eyes and left him trussed up on his bed. The men left quickly, but one man, fearing the wizard, plucked the eyes from the floor. He cut away the ropes from Falk's hands and feet, and begged for his life.

"Please, take pity on me, Wizard. If I did not come tonight, Hegney would have killed my wife. I owed him this favour." He placed the eyeballs into Falk's hands, thinking Hegney a fool. Hadn't he seen what Falk could do with a severed hand? Would eyes be any harder?

When the guards came back from the celebration and saw what had been done to Falk and his servant, they wanted to retaliate, but Falk told them revenge was his to extract, and that he would take care of Hegney in due time.

***

Adwinia was renewed in the few short months after the rains fell, and Chardon and Zabor continued to tend to the eggs, keeping them moist and turning them every day.

Chardon entered the barn when he heard his horse whinnying and trying to break down its stall. As he calmed the mare, he realised the dragon eggs were starting to change; the shells had become opaque. He took the horse out of the barn, away from the eggs, and she calmed down once outside.

Chardon looked at the thinning shells, calling his eldest son, who stood at his side. Tempel asked his father if they needed to do anything, but Chardon did not know what to tell him. The only instruction were to keep the eggs moist.

He felt the dragons were ancient—they probably knew what they'd need when the time came.

Tempel and Chardon stayed in the barn, watching the eggs for the whole day, waiting for the hatching. They had twenty eggs they were responsible for. He sent his younger son Chad to Zabor's farm to let him know what was happening, and Chad returned bearing the same news from the Ash farm—soon, the two men and their families would be tending to forty dragons.

As if by magic, Falk arrived on horseback to oversee the hatching of Chardon's dragons. His head was bandaged for his eyesight was still healing from the attack, and one of his men had to lead him to the barn. Luckily, the spell the witch put on Hegney made everything he touched unsuccessful; Hegney had only temporarily maimed the wizard. Falk entered the barn feeling that the eggs were ready. He put his hand on Chardon's back to congratulate him. The dragons required no further care to hatch.

Chardon was uncertain what to feed hatchlings. Falk, standing far away from the dragons so that they wouldn't imprint on him, reassured the farmer that, once the dragons imprinted on Chardon, he would be able to take them out into the field. The dragons would instinctively know what they could eat; be it small rodents and insects or buds and fruits, depending on the kind of dragons they were. As Falk talked, the dragons moved about in their shells to the rhythm of his voice; they seemed to know him.

Falk left Chardon and was led to the Ash farm where he told Zabor and his son, Zeb, the same things. By the end of the evening, forty dragons lived in Adwinia, imprinting on two thieves who had been turned into dragon trainers!

***

The small dragons looked like birds as they followed Chardon out into the field. The first one pounced on a dragonfly, eating it with one gulp. At the smell of the dragonfly's death, all the little dragons ran to the first successful dragon, trying to get what he had already swallowed. The next dragon caught on and captured a small vole. Soon the dragons ran through the fields, scooping up bugs and slugs and small mammals, although some of the dragons were content with flowers and wild fruits. Chardon was amazed by how quickly they caught on.

As Chardon and Tempel poured water into trays for the dragons to drink, Chardon yelled out shaking his hand. "Bloody bastard just bit me. But oh, that rascal is a cute one."

"Father, it's so strange…his colour…none of the others look like him," Tempel pointed out.

"He is the alpha male. He will be their leader," Chardon answered. Father and son watched the dragon's antics, laughing and feeling excited about their success.

It takes many years to raise a dragon and to train it. A dragon's instinct is to fly away—they are independent creatures after all—but the imprinting had taken for Chardon and Zabor and their families. The dragons followed their humans around as if they were family. Chardon and Zabor could no longer go into town; their dragons could be aggressive and would bite anything that stood in the way—except for the Ash and the Linken family members. After several weeks, Beckett and the Talkiens arrived at the Ash Farm looking for repayment of their aid.

Falk was expecting this from the Talkiens. The soldiers took Zabor and his twenty dragons, along with

Zabor's family. Zabor and Zeb could not be separated from the dragons—they attacked Beckett's men when they tried to take them away—but Zabor agreed to go with them peacefully. The Talkiens had only allowed the dragon's eggs out of Talkien because the wizard had the knowledge and power needed to make the eggs grow. Zabor loaded his family, along with the dragons, in the wagon, stopping at Chardon's farm on his way to their new home. The two men were heartbroken; they would most likely never see one another again. With heavy hearts, Zabor turned his cart in the direction of Talkien, followed by their soldiers, and Chardon watched the cart disappear before he turned back to his work. He would miss his friend.

Zabor felt moving was the least he could do to have his hand restored. At nightfall, Zabor recounted the dragons in his wagon, coming up with twenty-one for a second time. How could that be? After several counts, Zabor suspected one of Chardon's dragons had come along for the ride. It was too far to go back now. Zabor trusted his friend would understand.

When Chardon put the dragons in the barn that night, he came up one dragon shy. He counted several times and searched until dark for the missing dragon. He deduced that one of the dragons, the one he had named Linken—the alpha male—had seen the wagon leaving his farm and thought he was being separated from his group. When Chardon met with Falk, he admitted to missing a dragon. Falk let him know that things happen for a reason, and Chardon was not to worry about the lost dragon.

***

As the dragons grew, they were no longer content in a barn. Chardon and Tempel scoured the nearby cliffs and, upon finding suitable caves, Chardon had the dragons follow him to the cliffs. Daily, Chardon or Tempel checked on them. Chardon knew, as he grew older, that Tempel and his son, Percy, needed to take on the task of dragon training. Dragons didn't fly until they were fifty years old—by that time, Chardon would be gone. He knew that Percy would need to produce an heir to continue with the task given to him. Falk never seemed to grow any older and was constant with his support. Falk knew they would need the dragons someday, to save their territory.

Years later, Chardon received word that Zabor had died after losing his son, Zeb. Zocor, Zabor's grandson, and his son ,Jaden, had taken over the dragon raising in Talkien. Saddened that he never would get the chance to see his friend again, Chardon realised his days on

Earth were also short—he was already in his nineties, unable to get out to the cliffs to check on the dragons. Tempel, Percy, and Percy's daughter, Shallee, tended the dragons now. The creatures trusted Percy and Shallee as they had Chardon and Tempel. Imprinting lasted through generations.

Chardon was sitting on a chair, enjoying the warm sun, when he spied it flying overhead. It was one of his dragons. They had learned to fly! He did not think he would be so graced to see this before his death, but there it was, circling him before clumsily landing. The dragon righted himself slowly, and recognising his master, walked over and put his head down so Chardon could pet him. Chardon identified the dragon as Altruer and called him by name, laughing with joy. Altruer accepted his praises, then flew away. Chardon had done it. With the help of his son and family, Adwinia would have nineteen dragons to help defend their territory. Tempel and Percy came running across the field in excitement, only to find a lifeless Chardon still sitting his chair with a smile upon his face. He had left this world a happy man.

***

Zocor Ash, grandson of Zabor, had several men

helping him train the dragons after the death of his father, and then the death of his grandfather. It was devastating to lose the two men who had shaped his life in such a short time. Zocor's nephew, Tarth, took over his duties when Zocor went to find other work. The Talkiens did not help the Ashes financially as much as they had promised.

The dragons were old enough to fly and support the weight of a human on their backs and Zocor's son, Jaden, was the person the dragons responded to most as he had played with the dragons as a child. It was he who called his father back to work with the dragons after Tarth had put them in cages.

Zabor's grandnephew, Tarth, and Beckett the third, felt they should have all the dragons for helping Adwinia years ago during the drought. At Tarth's suggestion, the dragons were put in cages to keep them from flying off. One day, the dragons grew strong enough to break out of their pens and flew to the nearby caves. It took the Ash family a long time to re-establish trust with their wards. Their dragons had gone wild. The Talkien's were pushing on Zocor to ready the dragons to attack Adwinia. They wanted to claim all the dragons for their own. Zocor had never met the Linken clan, but stories handed down to him told them they were friends and not enemies. It bothered Zocor, and Jaden, that they were being told to rise against his grandfather's people. There were plenty of dragons to go around, and now that their dragons were of mating age, they would have small dragons coming soon. It had taken a significant amount of time to get his dragons to trust him again. He should have never allowed his nephew to take over while he was away. Zocor was ashamed that Tarth cared for his dragons by caging them. A dragon's heart was purer than the heart of a man—dragons had no business being in cages. For them to fly, dragons needed to be free. Zocor and Jaden were able to get all the dragons back on their side, except one. The dragon they called Linken—the overly large dragon, who was a different colour than all the other dragons—was the alpha male who was at constant odds with the other males in his pride. Zocor always suspected this dragon was the one who joined his grandfather's wagon when he left Adwinia; Linken had not imprinted on the Ash family. He was the dragon Zocor and Jaden would need to keep a close watch over.

The captain of the Talkien army came to the farm to check on Zocor's progress. There had been reports of seeing the dragons flying around. Zocor proudly confirmed that his dragons were starting to fly. The captain asked how long before they could support a man on their backs. Zocor was not sure but felt it shouldn't be too much longer. The dragons were flying with the straps used to harness a man, but flying was still new to them. To put the additional weight of a man on them so quickly, would make them rebel. Zocor asked that the captain pick some men to work with the dragons so that they would eventually accept their weight. The captain sent twenty men and supplies later that week. The soldiers camped near the caves, visiting their selected mounts daily. Zocor and Jaden explained the need to respect and trust their dragons.

The wizard, Falk came to the Linken farm, he had urgent matters with Percy Linken and his daughter Shallee. Falk came with the news that the Talkiens' had their army learning to ride their dragons and that they were preparing to fight to come and take Adwinia's dragons. Tempel, now an old man, had turned the dragons over to his son Percy. None of the male dragons had stepped up to be the alpha male. The dragons had already determined their leader upon hatching. Percy worried that the dragons, in not picking a new leader, would not fight as one unit. Percy wondered what would happen when the time of confrontation came. Would his dragons be faithful to the Adwinians'? Or, would they recognise and follow their alpha dragon when he showed himself to them?

Percy agreed with the wizard that they needed to start the process having the dragons trust their riders. Falk sent out several army members who volunteered to ride the dragons. Shallee, instructed the men daily on how to get the dragon to trust them. Shallee was the one person, the dragon's allowed on their backs. The soldiers' hand-fed their mounts special treats depending on their breath gifts. The fire-breathing dragons preferred meat, while the healer breathing dragons preferred honey.

Shallee, was respected by the soldiers of Adwinia who knew the dragons could kill them if provoked. It was the honour of her family that kept those dragons from killing them. As the tensions mounted on both sides, the Talkiens and the Adwinians started to build up their defences. Falk was saddened at how a confrontation started from greed. The Talkiens and Adwinians should have been close allies. Their leaders, who were braggarts, wanted more than their neighbours, and they started to push back at one another. Hegney's grandson, also named Hegney, assumed the Tribunal Council lead when he became of age. His counterpart, Beckett, grandson to the Beckett who ruled during the drought and rescue of Adwinia, was equally stubborn and greedy. The two leaders had become enemies and started the overtures of war.

Zocor and Jaden worked with their men—teaching them how to fly on the dragons in Talkien—while Shallee and Percy worked with their men. The safety of their villages and their livelihoods hung in the balance.

Without a clearly defined alpha male, Percy's dragons floundered a bit. But they knew what their job was, and they took the soldiers on their backs and learned how to fly with them. They worked together in harmony. Each relationship between the dragon and its rider was unique and special. The giant female dragon, Sydon, was Shallee's favourite. She had played with this dragon since she was a small child. Gideon, her pilot, was kind to Sydon giving her special honey treats he had made on his own time. They had a special bond. Other soldiers, seeing Gideon's relationship with the dragon, made them want follow suit. They quickly became a tighter group.

The day came when the Talkiens declared war. It was unthinkable to Adwinia, who had never been forced to defend their territory before. More unthinkable that they attack the region who saved them years ago. All this, over the dragons.

Percy pushed his men and his dragons. They learned how to dive and pull up quickly. They mock-fought amongst themselves, preparing for the day that real war would begin. Gideon and another soldier dived off the cliff in a nosedive, both pulling up at the last minute, but Gideon had not tied himself to Sydon properly.

On the upswing, Gideon fell from his mount. Sydon, tried to save her pilot by diving under him, but the velocity at which Gideon fell made him unable to hang on to her. He crashed into the ground, breaking most of the bones in his body. The reality of the precariousness of dragon flying was instilled in the soldiers that day.

Shallee spent time with Sydon, who was inconsolable. It wasn't Sydon's fault that Gideon had not attached himself according to regulations. They both suffered the consequences for it.

***

Falk rode out on his horse, warning Percy that the Talkiens were on their way. It was official now that war was declared. The territory of Adwinia rose up in a battle cry, arming themselves with every weapon and tool they had. The Adwinians marched to the border of their lands, as did the Talkiens. The dragon troops held back, allowing the foot soldiers to make it to the border lands first. A dragon could fly so fast they would cover the distance in a short time compared to the days of walking on foot. The confrontation would take place at the river where their lands met. The Talkiens wanted the entire dragon force. Adwinia would not give her dragons up.

Percy paced in front of his dragons, back and forth. With the death of Gideon, they were now two dragons short of the Talkiens' count. Without the alpha male, the dragons, had never congealed into a tight-knit unit as he would have hoped they would. Percy watched a slight soldier cross the field and seat themselves on Sydon. It was Shallee. Percy would not sacrifice his only child for this foolish war.

"Shallee, I forbid this," Percy said as he approached her. His daughter, so young and innocent, looked at her father.

"Father, Sydon is the alpha female. This pride of dragons would be without a leader. No one knows Sydon better than I. We are already down one dragon to the Talkiens' twenty-one. Without their alpha leader, this pride of dragons will not fight together as one."

Percy knew that his daughter was right. He hugged her fiercely. With tears in his eyes, he watched as the commander of the dragon troops gave signal to fly.

Such a sight the few remaining people in Adwinia beheld. Nineteen dragons in shining colours, reflected in the sun, flew over the village, some with their flags and streamers proudly displayed. They met up with the foot soldiers sent to the border lands ahead of them, ready to do battle. On both sides of the river stood the soldiers, waiting for the command from their leaders, Hegney and Beckett.

On the horizon, Shallee could see the Talkien dragon force coming to the fray. They looked magnificent. Shallee noticed one dragon among the others who stood out. His colour was different, and he was quite a bit larger than the others. She knew in her heart that the dragon was Linken, the alpha male to her great grandfather's dragons, and perhaps to all the dragons in the fight today.

The territories fought below the dragon riders with hoes and clubs. Blood was drawn between the territories as the soldiers did their leaders' bidding. Shallee watched Linken go after the archers who shot at the dragons. Linken breathed fire on the archers, who ran away in flames screaming. The healer dragons from both sides flew down and breathed healing breath on the injured and burned. Shallee marvelled at the instinct her dragon's displayed. They knew what needed to be done and how to make that happen. Shallee circled on Sydon, passing over the Talkiens. Sydon, a healing dragon, breathed on the injured, too. As Sydon circled again, Shallee caught a glimpse of Linken.

Shallee called Linken's name. Linken turned quickly upon hearing Shallee's voice, almost losing his pilot. Linken remembered his imprinting. He knew this woman was of Chardon's clan. He had known all along that his fate was to save his pride the day he jumped into Zabor's wagon. The Wizard Falk had put that knowledge in him as a young fledgling. Linken flew upside down, close to the ground, until his rider fell off. He then turned on the Talkiens and breathed fire on many of them as they fled back to their side of the river. Linken went after his former captor, Tarth; the man did not deserve to live. The beasts in Linken's natural pride recognised their leader. The dragons raised with Linken were suddenly confused, watching their strongest male turn himself over to the Adwinians side. The Ash pride of dragons had lost their leader.

Fires on the ground blazed, almost out of control— the soldiers of Talkien and the Adwinian were more concerned with putting the flames out. Both sides used their buckets, running to the river, filling them and dousing the fires.

Shallee and Sydon landed on the Adwinian side of the river. Linken and Jaden landed near Shallee. Linken moved over to his mate, Sydon. Dragons mate for life, they had never forgotten one another.

Shallee found a bucket and ran for the river where she met Jaden. Together with the other soldiers, they helped put out the fires on both sides. Smoke rose up in the air from the extinguished fires. The weary people sat on the banks of the river overlooking a field of their dead. They never wanted war, only Hegney and Beckett wanted it. Against their leaders wishes, both sides refused to fight any more. It was time to bury their dead.

Jaden asked Shallee how she had gotten Linken to turn over to her side. They realised Linken was Shallee's great grandfather's lost dragon, and that they were the heirs of Zabor and Chardon.

"I had always suspected he was the one, so different from the rest." Jaden reflected.

The armies on both sides stood on the riverbanks. The dragons pulled at their harnesses, freeing themselves. The pride, minus their pilots flew off, leaving the humans to look at what they had destroyed. Now, neither territory had dragons. How foolish they felt. Zocor and Jaden would not return to the Talkien Territory. Punishment would be severe for not completing their task. They wanted to return to the land of their grandfather and great grandfather, Adwinia.

The dragons followed their leader, Linken. Where the dragons went, no one knew. The Adwinians and the

Talkiens remained allies, vowing never to go to war against one another.

***

Falk rode his horse along the road of memory, followed by an entourage of guards and their families. He was tired, having ridden for days. Hegney and Beckett, whose hands were bound, stumbled at the end of their ropes tied to Falk's saddle. Something beckoned the Wizard, knowing he would follow its ancient call. Falk spied the castle in the distance, through healed eyes—the stone building rose from the Lost Mountains. Falk was light-hearted upon seeing his boyhood home still standing after centuries. Around its tower, several dragons circled, being led by one large dragon with odd colouration. The dragon recognising Falk, swooped down to welcome him home. Falk's heart swelled.

The Wizard knew peace would last between Adwinia and Talkien now that the dragon pride was hidden from their view. In a thousand years, they would only be a legend, all but forgotten. The marriage between Jaden and Shallee assured harmony in the land between dragons, humans, and their progeny.

And what of Hegney and Becket? Their living hell

had just begun. Hegney and Beckett's daily sacrifices would supply Falk with renewed energy for many years to come.

DAWN DEBRAAL is an American fiction author of several genres in both short stories and poetry. She lives in rural Wisconsin with her husband Red, two rat terriers and a cat. She is the mother of two adult children and two grandchildren. Her stories have been featured in many online magazines and over forty published anthologies. She discovered her love of writing after her retirement from the real world, and now lives in a fantasy world of her own design.

Bibliography

100 Words of Horror, KJK Publishing, 2019
Bad Romance, Black Hare Press, 2020
Curses & Cauldrons, Blood Song Books, 2019
Dark Drabble Books 1-10, Black Hare Press, 2019
Dark Series, Eleanor Merry Publishing, 2019
Explorer One, Zimbell House Publishing, 2020
Gleam, Poetica, Glamour, Portal, Clarendon House Publishing, 2019 & 2020
Isolation, The Element Series, Fantasia Divinity, 2019 & 2020
Jibberknocky, Black Hare Press, 2020
Monsterthology 2, Zombieworks Publications, 2019
PRIDE, LUST, SLOTH, Black Hare Press, 2020
Samhain Secrets, Irish Horse Productions, 2019
Storming Area 51, Black Hare Press, 2019
The Dead Game, Zimbell House Publishing, 2020
The Marshall, Zimbell House Publishing, 2019
Twenty Twenty, Black Hare Press, 2020
Under Her Dark Wings, Kandisha Press 2020
Zombie Bites 1 and 2, Reanimated Writers, 2019

Connect
Amazon: amazon.com/Dawn-DeBraal/e/B07STL8DLX

A CURSE OF BLOOD & GOLD

By Zoey Xolton

Rosa has always known she was different—she can feel the forest, and runs like the wind—but it's not until she becomes entangled with a cursed bear that she truly realises just how deeply magic is rooted in her life...and the lives of those around her.

Ragna, the Queen of Storskold stood from her throne, her great crown adding to her stretching shadow as the sun set beyond the Black Keep. "It pains me to do this," she said through pursed lips and clenched teeth. "You are my child, and deep in my heart, I do yet hold love for you. But this," she said, gesturing to her wounded eldest son, the First Prince of Storskold, "is unforgivable!"

Berengar, her second, and youngest son, awaited his sentence in silence, wearing a smooth mask of indifference. This, it seemed, served only to aggravate his mother further.

"You are a fool to think you could have succeeded at claiming the throne in such a callous manner. Have you no honour?" She paused to compose herself, her usually pale face flushed with colour. "It matters not. For the attempted murder of your brother, the rightful and future King of Storskold, you are henceforth banished from these lands. You leave today, with less than you were born. I revoke your titles, your wealth, your holdings, and your arranged marriage will be made null and void. I daresay the King and Queen of Adelrhun will not want blood on the hands of their innocent daughter."

With a wave of her hand, the Royal Sorcerer—the Queen's closest counsel—stepped forward. "Farvald," she said, summoning him.

Berengar met the dwarf's gaze evenly. *He should have known.*

"Upon you, my second son, I place a curse. For the love of gold and power, you would see your beloved brother dead, and for this, you will be made to suffer.

No longer will you walk among us a man; for a man you are not. Your actions are those of a beast of greed! And so, it is with all the might of the Crown, that I condemn you to the life of such a creature. I only hope that in time, you will learn that there are more important things in this world than the glitter of gold, my dear son. Until that day, my ruling shall remain. Farewell, Berengar. I think you'll find the nature of your form, most befitting."

With that, the queen sat, and the dwarf, holding his gnarled oaken staff, walked down the dais toward Berengar. Wielding it in his direction, he called out for all present at court to hear:

"Upon two legs, you shall no longer go,

Upon four, will you walk through forest and snow.

With eyes of coal, and teeth so strong,

To fur and cave, you shall belong!"

Berengar winced, his hand clutching at his gut, as a stabbing pain knifed him in the belly. The pain radiated outward, debilitating him. He'd been wounded in campaigns before, but never like this. He doubled over, dropping to his knees. He growled, the sound escaping his snarling lips.

"Any last words, brother?" came his elder brother's voice.

With great effort, Berengar dragged his eyes from

the floor. "I will see you again, Einar," he said through gritted teeth as bones broke within him, growing, and stretching, with dark magic.

Einar nodded. "I hope so, little brother. Come that day, should you break the curse upon you, I will forgive you for your treason, and for the breaking of the bonds of brotherhood."

Berengar's handsome face contorted in indescribable, silent agony as his bright blue eyes turned black as coal, and his blonde hair darkened to a muddy brown. A shimmering, swirling cloud settled over him, obscuring him from vision. The lords and ladies gathered, collectively taking a step back, as the young prince's blood-curdling screams became wild, terrifying roars. As his body could no longer accommodate it, the clatter of armour on the stone floor could be heard.

Then, nothing but heavy breathing permeated the otherwise deathly silence that fell over the throne room. When the magical haze dispersed, an imposing brown bear stood hunched on all fours, in place of the would-be usurper.

One of the ladies of the court dared speak out as his frightening splendour was revealed. "Your majesty, what have you done?" she said in a forced whisper, her splayed fingers over her mouth.

In response, Queen Ragna announced, "Citizens of Storskold, I give you Berengar the Damned."

Berengar raised his heavy head to meet his mother's gaze and roared, spittle flying as he unleashed his rage. The look in his eyes echoed the lady's sentiments.

Mother, what have you done?

"Be gone, beast," she ordered, a slender finger pointed directly at the immense, ornate double doors. "You are no longer welcome here."

Berengar moved one large padded paw forward, eliciting a low growl as he did so.

"I think not, *Once-Prince*," spat Farvald. "Be gone from the sight of the Royal House. Be gone from the Lands of the Kingdom of Storskold! You are in exile. Be gone, now—on pain of death! Until such a time as your heart truly cares for another, more than for yourself, you will remain a beast. I imagine we won't be seeing you again."

Berengar glowered at the short-statured sorcerer. *We will meet again*, he swore in his mind. *And when we do, you will regret acting as the Hand of Fate. Mark my words.*

The dwarf shifted his weight uneasily, as if he had heard his thoughts.

Berengar, lowered his head, bowing to his queen

mother. He hoped that it was received as mockingly as it was intended. *So be it.* Raising himself up onto his two hind legs, great clawed paws low by his sides, he bellowed so mightily that the stained-glass windows of the cathedral-like throne room shook within their frames.

The Queen's Guard stepped aside as Berengar the Damned took his leave, charging out of the throne room, beyond the city and its cobblestone streets, and into the wilds that lay beyond the mapped borders of Storskold.

***

Three years later…

"Girls! Have you hung out your pinafores?" called Thora as she tipped the dish water out of the kitchen window and into the herb garden below. "Albina? Rosa?"

The girls tore into the kitchen, a flurry of ice and fire. "Yes, mother!" they sang in unison as they chased each other around their humble wooden table.

"Girls! Honestly. You are getting much too old for this kind of behaviour."

Albina stopped dead in her tracks, her pale cheeks flared with colour. "Too old? We are not yet even sixteen, mother!" she protested.

Rosa agreed, bumping into her twin sister. "What would you have us do? Knit blankets and cook supper?"

Thora huffed in good-natured exasperation. "It would be a good place to start," she said. "You'll be of marriageable age in six moon's time. I think it's time to put your childish fancies to bed and begin focusing on the duties of womanhood. Who will marry a dirty little wench, covered in tree-sap and mud, hair askew? I ask you, earnestly."

"A good man?" they said together.

"Why should we be measured by how well we keep a house?" asked Rosa. "Any woman can maintain a home."

"We may yet marry wealthy lords," quipped Albina. "And we can be ladies of luxury, doing with our time as we please."

"What kind of lord would allow his bride to run wild?" asked their mother.

"Lords with a good sense of adventure!" said Albina, her bright blue eyes sparkling with mirth as she flicked her long, white-blonde hair aside.

"Lords who appreciate that their wives have more to offer than the fruit of their loins!" chimed Rosa, a devious smile on her pale, freckled face.

"Rosa! I won't hear any more of this. You *will* give me grandchildren young lady! I won't be a lonely widow. I want a cottage full of small feet, and shrill laughter."

The twins rolled their eyes at each other with a mutual grin.

"Mother, we've hung our clothes and already cut wood for the fire. Can we please go out?" asked Albina, fluttering her white lashes.

"The forest calls to us!" pleaded Rosa, mischief in her tone.

Thora sighed. She knew when she was beat. "Alright," she agreed.

The girls knocked one another as they wrestled for the door.

"But—" their mother called. "You *will* be home, clean and ready for supper at moon rise."

"Yes, Mother!" they called, letting the cottage's wooden door clatter closed behind them.

"Woe is me," said Thora, shaking her head, hands on her hips. "If those two forest sprites find husbands, I'll be a merry ma'am!"

***

"Come on, Albina!" sang Rosa as she ran through

the verdant forest. Hiking up her skirts, she leapt fallen logs and bounded over decaying stumps as easily as if she had wings. The forest was alive to her in ways she couldn't begin to describe to their mother. *She felt connected;* as if the very pulse of the forest thrummed in her veins, to the beat of her own heart.

Albina, her twin—the ice to her fire—understood better than their mother. She enjoyed the forest for its beauty and curiosities; but she didn't *feel* it the way Rosa did. In this, despite sharing almost everything with her sister, she was alone.

"Wait up!" Albina puffed as she chased after her. "You are a demon!" she called out. "You run faster than any hare in the forest! How do you do it?"

Rosa checked her pace, a wry smile upon her face as she allowed her sister to draw level with her. "I do not know," she said earnestly. "I feel as if my skin is all that holds me back from joining the wind!"

Before long, the girls arrived at their favourite spot, a quiet glade, protected by the Black Forest's tall, dark trees, with their thick, moss-covered, almost ebon trunks. Albina collapsed, exhausted, beside the silver pool at its centre. Pulling her hair over one shoulder she leaned over the clear water and splashed her face, before drinking her fill.

Rosa climbed an outcropping of ancient stones,

their rough grey surface peppered with pale green lichen. Plopping herself down, legs overhanging the edge, she closed her eyes and revelled in the warming beams of sunlight that pierced the heavy canopy. She always felt more alive outdoors than she did cooped up in their small cottage.

The Black Forest felt like home. She understood the chatter of the native red squirrels and spiny-quilled hedgehogs; the twitter of the bee-eaters, and common black birds. And if she sat in silence, attuning herself to the wilderness, she could even hear breathy whispers that she could never quite make out, and distant songs carried upon the breeze.

She often wondered if there was something peculiar about herself, something not quite normal. Albina could not hear the voices of the forest, nor could she understand, and converse with the beasts of it, as she did. *Am I mad?* she wondered. *If I am*, she decided. *I am quite glad! I could not imagine living without feeling, as I do.*

"Rosa! *Rosa!*"

Rosa blinked, as if startled awake, and looked to Albina who was standing below her.

"Where have you been, sister? Off with the elves?" she teased. "I've called you five times and you didn't answer. I was beginning to think you were having another turn."

Another turn, thought Rosa with an internal eye-roll. That was what Albina said when she got lost in her communion with nature. Though they were as close as sisters could be, deep down, she suspected that her snow-fair sister was envious of her strange, and unusual gifts. She'd never give voice to such a thing, she was far too polite, much like their mother, to speak ill of anyone, or give unpleasantness any creed; but Rosa saw it written in her body language, and on her face—when she thought no one else was looking. And what was worse, is that Rosa *sensed* it, too.

In private, late one night, she'd asked her mother about her uncanny empathy, and her ability to know how others felt. Thora assured her that she was merely a Sensitive—a normal soul blessed with divine knowledge—but Rosa felt that her mother was hiding something from her. A secret haunted behind her mother's eyes like a bodiless spectre, but what it was, she could only guess.

"Forgive me, sister," said Rosa with an apologetic smile. "I was just—never mind. What is it?"

"I want to explore deeper," she said, surprising her sister.

Rosa climbed down from her rocky ledge and dropped down beside Albina. "Really? In which direction?"

"Let's follow the stream, north!"

Rosa's brows shot up. "Colour me intrigued, sister. I thought you might want to return to your books."

Albina grimaced. "It's true, I do love to read in the comfort of our home, but I enjoy a good adventure, every bit as much as you do!"

"Your nose is perpetually buried in books!" snorted Rosa. "I practically have to drag you outside half of the time!"

Albina scrunched up her nose and made a face. "Fine, I love to read *more* than I enjoy being out here in the wild, dark forest…but today, I simply feel like an outing."

Rosa flicked her sister's long white-blonde hair, dancing playfully out of reach. "Very well then. An adventure north, it is. Do try to keep up, though!" she teased.

Albina sighed. "Why don't you give me a head start? It's the least you could do for all the mischief you get us into," she reasoned.

Rosa's laughter rang out through the dark forest. "Me? Mischief? Never."

Albina cocked an unforgiving eyebrow at her, one that said: *Are you kidding me?*

"So be it, then," Rosa said as she casually leaned against an ancient oak. "I will give you to the count of a hundred."

Albina grinned. "Do not count too fast. I know you! You are as tricksy as a pixie, sister of mine!"

Rosa acquiesced with a flourished hand motion. "I will count slow, and steady, just for you, 'Bina. Either way, I will catch you up, and you know it."

"We shall see about that!"

Amused, Rosa watched her twin disappear into the forest, and then began her count. As she reached the count of fifty, the sound of snapping twigs drew her attention. She smiled, rolling her eyes. "Albina, you are going to have to be a lot more delicate than that if you intend to try and sneak up on me!" She spun around, ready to jump at her sister, when she came face to face with an enormous, brown bear.

Her breath caught in her throat as she froze. It regarded her with coal-dark eyes, scenting the air with a twitching black nose. It stood not several paces away, and every fibre in her being thrummed with the instinct to take flight. *Could I outrun a bear?* she wondered.

The bear cocked its head, as if observing her. Rosa swallowed her fear and took one slow, careful step backward, only to find the tree she had been leaning against blocking her escape. *Stay calm, do not provoke it*, she told herself. *I am fast, faster than my sister by twice, at least. If I could just...* Arms low, and wide to either side, she slid against the rough bark to her left. The bear growled, and in the space of a single heartbeat, it bounded forward, its face literally a hands breadth from her own.

Its hot breath blew the red tendrils of hair from her face as it huffed, sniffing at her. She squeezed her eyes shut, clinging to the tree's girth. *This is it, then,* she thought, forlornly. *If only I had been able to say goodbye to Albina, and mother.*

The bear's wet nose nudged her cheek and she whimpered, turning her face away. *Make it fast*, she prayed. *At least, I die here, in the wild, able and free, rather than in my dotage, married off to some pompous or cruel landholder.* She waited with bated breath—but death never came. Her chest rising and falling, she dared to open her eyes. The bear regarded her but made no move to strike, nor did it seem aggressive.

What in Frigga's name... Face to face with the beast, she could not believe her eyes. All around him, there shimmered a deep purple-black haze. It traced around the bear's entire form, enveloping him entirely, like a shroud of darkness. Somehow, she knew what it was, despite having never being taught of such things. *Black magic! Sorcery!* she gasped. *What manner of beast are you, that you should be cursed like this?* she marvelled to herself.

I was not always a beast, came a cultured male voice, interrupting her thoughts.

Rosa's eyes grew wide as she stared back at the bear. Taking several moments to compose herself, she licked her lips. "Did you just speak to me?" she ventured.

I did, came the bear's reply. *And what manner of creature are you, that you should be able to speak with me, mind to mind?*

Steeling her nerve, she relaxed ever so slightly. "I believe I asked you that same question first."

The bear sat back on its haunches, giving her some space, before she heard a chuckle in her mind. *You are bold, for such a young girl.*

"I am already woman," she retorted. "I am in my sixteenth year and will be of marriageable age, soon."

Are you now?

Rosa stood forward from the tree. "I speak the truth," she said.

Very well, I will answer your question. I am—or rather, was—a prince of Storskold. My name is Berengar, and I am Queen Ragna's second son.

"Are you speaking the truth?" she countered. "Are you not one of the scorned elf kin?"

I am, beneath this curse, he assured her, *a mortal man.*

"I cannot believe it," she said. "I had heard rumour that one of the queen's sons had been banished, but this—this is…how could she? What did you do!?"

I will not answer until you have answered me. What manner of creature are you? he repeated.

"What do you mean? I am simply myself. My name is Rosa, and I am nothing more than I am, the daughter of a widow, a sister—and a peasant."

And yet, you can converse with an enchanted bear?

"I do not know how I came to have this gift," she answered. "I have never spoken with an animal before. At least, not like this."

Go on.

"I have always been able to hear the forest," she began. "I can feel it. I can't quite explain it, but I feel as though I am connected to it, as any flower, tree, bird or beast, is. I can feel its life, its decay. When I sing, or speak to the animals, they seem calm, and unafraid of my presence."

And you can run, said Berengar. *Twice as fast as your sister.*

"Oh, you heard that? I can, yes. When I run, I feel at one with the wind. At my fastest, I feel almost as if—"

As if you had wings?

Rosa smiled. "Yes! Precisely. I feel like I could fly if I could just run fast enough."

And you never suspected that you were elven?

Rosa laughed, her voice a magic of its own. "Elven? Do not jest with me, prince," she said, pushing her auburn red curls aside. "My mother is a woman, a mortal."

And your father?

"My father is dead."

Is he?

"Mother told us all about him. He was fair, with blue eyes like Albina. He was killed in a hunting accident. Mother said he was gored by a wild boar, and there was no saving him. She has been a widow ever since and raised us alone."

He certainly fits the description of the light elves.

Rosa shook her head in disbelief. "Are you truly attempting to imply that my mother had a dalliance with an elf, and that she lied to us about it?"

I am not merely implying it, Rosa. You are most certainly Halfling. Mindspeech is not a mortal gift.

Rosa put her hand to her forehead, her mind racing. "I cannot be," she said in disbelief.

Why?

"One's mother does not simply fall pregnant to an

elf and keep it a secret for sixteen years!"

It is more rare an occurrence than it once was, but Halflings of all races exist. Surely you can see the truth of my words? You can feel it. You said as much, yourself. You have always felt different—always heard the voice of the forest.

"Even if it were true, what does it mean? My sister, as far as I know, is not like me in this way."

It means you could have more in life than you do. You have unsung magic within you. You could learn to use it, harness it, to better your life. It seems to me that your sister acquired the physical traits of the elves, but your mother's mortality; while you take after your mother's beauty but have the gifts of the elves.

Rosa threw her hands in the air. "So now I am part elven, and I am talking to a bear—a cursed prince of Storskold, no less! Either I am dreaming, or I ate some of those spotted red mushrooms mother told us to stay away from…"

You are awake, and you are as of sound mind as I am.

"Well that is comforting," said Rosa, eyebrow cocked. "Sane as a talking bear."

Your sister comes, said Berengar, suddenly alert. *If you wish to meet again, and speak with me, I will be here again, three days from now. I must go. It was a pleasure to meet you, Rosa Half-elven.*

Before Rosa could protest, he disappeared back into the growing shadows of the forest. Knowing he would hear, she smiled to herself. *Goodbye for now, prince.*

***

Did you tell your twin about me? asked Berengar.

"No, at least—I haven't yet."

May I ask why?

Rosa bit her lip, her cheeks flushing a becoming shade of pink, highlighting her freckles. "I just wanted the chance to get to know you better, myself."

Berengar smiled internally.

"Forgive me, but the question has been burning in my mind since first we met... What did you do, that the queen has punished her own son, so?"

Berengar's entire demeanour, even in his bear form, changed. His shoulders slumped, his head dropped, and he refused to meet her eye.

"You can trust me," she prompted.

I am afraid that if I share the crimes of my past with you, that you will not come back to see me anymore.

Rosa studied Berengar, before finally speaking.

"No one is innocent," she began. "And we all make mistakes, but mistakes can be forgiven, if the heart has truly changed and is remorseful. If no one was given second chances, there would be very few souls left upon the earth."

You believe in redemption?

"Of course! I could not bear to live in a world where we could not be redeemed of our follies. There is always hope, Berengar. And, for what it is worth, I promise that I will hear what you have to say, without passing judgement."

Very well, he said taking a deep breath. *As you know, I am my mother's second son—the proverbial 'spare' as it were. My whole life, I have lived in my brother's shadow. He has always been the golden child; the future king of Storskold. There has never been a great deal of love between my brother and I. As he was made to learn and pursue the virtues of a ruler, there was naught for me but to pursue acclaim through battle and conquest. Yet, still, no matter what I achieved, nor how much territory or riches I claimed in the name of our kingdom, my mother deigned not to waste her affections on me.*

"That's terrible," exclaimed Rosa, aghast. "My sister and I are equals in all things. There are no favourites in family—at least, there should not be."

I feel that there should not be, either...but the inner workings and politics of royalty and the nobility is a complex beast, steeped in timeless generations of tradition. It is not easily changed or challenged.

"I am sorry to have interrupted, it just struck me as disturbing, and wrong. Please continue with your tale."

As the distance between my brother and I, and my mother and I, grew, a great bitterness was birthed within me. I felt myself loathing them, for the love and admiration they received from our peers, and they had for one another...I felt like an outcast in my own home. On my nineteenth birthday, after returning home from a six month campaign, I got drunk; I tried to drown my sorrows. Truth be told, I had every intention of drinking myself into the grave that night... Instead, I found myself visiting my brother in his quarters.

Berengar stood, pacing the forest clearing on all fours, as if he could physically distance himself from the pain. Rosa sat in silence, knees tucked up to her chest, her skirts pooling at her boots as she waited.

We had a fight. He told me that we both had our place, and that neither of us could change the course of fate. That he was born first, and so the burden of the crown was his. He implied that my burden was freedom, itself—that I should count my blessings that I was free to do as I wilt with my life. That it was he that was the prisoner, and not I. I remember seeing red. Einar couldn't understand what it was like to live in his shadow, to always be the second choice. He turned his back on me, and...

Berengar met Rosa's already welling eyes with shame. *I drew the dagger from my boot and I stabbed him in the back, Rosa.*

Rosa looked away, her gaze on distant trees as she wiped her eyes with her long sleeve. "I am sorry...I cannot imagine," she whispered.

As noble as your intention not to pass judgement, Rosa, I am a guilty man. I will not hold how you truly feel against you. I deserve it, I understand that now.

"Your brother, Einar, he did not die?"

No, he lives. I am—was—the General Major of the army of Storskold... I know well how to strike to kill a man, but I struck my brother in anger... He could have died, it is true, had my mother's pet, the dwarf sorcerer, not healed him; but it was not a directly fatal blow. However, the outcome would have ultimately been the same without intervention, so I was in no position to argue semantics before the court. And for my crime, my mother had Farvald place a curse upon me. I am doomed to live out my days as a beast of the forest.

"Is there a way to break it? The curse, I mean."

Magic is a fickle creature. It has rules of its own,

and the caster's intentions affect its use and result. There was a caveat, but it's been three years and with each passing year, it feels as though I am losing a little more of who I am; like I am becoming the bear, truly.

"Think, Berengar!" Rosa insisted. "If we are to find a way to save you, it seems this knowledge is crucial."

We?

Rosa blushed, her eyes downcast, before she recovered with a more serious expression. "No one else can understand you, and our paths have crossed—do you think such a thing would happen without reason? I know it in my bones. I am meant to help you, prince."

Berengar nudged Rosa's arms with his big, wet nose, his dark eyes full of sorrow. *I do not think anyone has cared for me so much as you*, he said.

Rosa bristled. "Then you cannot have known very good people." Rosa reached out with a tentative hand and gently scratched Berengar behind one large, furry ear. "Think on it, Berengar. Think hard. The spell that was cast may hold the key to unlocking the curse."

I will do my best, he assured her.

"Return to me when you have the words," she made him promise. "My home is not far from here. Come to me, no matter the time or season, and we will find a way to break this horrid curse of blood and gold."

***

The months passed, as did the autumn. The air grew more brisk, and the first snows of winter began to fall. Rosa sat silently by the window near the hearth, her eyes trained upon some point in the distant dark.

"Rosa," said Albina, coming to sit beside her, a look of concern on her pale features. "I worry for you. Something burdens your thoughts, and you have been more distant than I have ever known you to be. What is on your mind? You can tell me, anything."

Rosa turned to her sister, sadness in her eyes. "Can you truly keep a secret?" she asked.

"Of course, sister! You have my confidence and my word."

Rosa sighed as she wrung her hands. "I am concerned for a friend," she began.

"A friend?"

"Of sorts," said her crimson-haired sister.

"I do not understand," said Albina. "Aside from when we journey into market with mother, we do not see another soul. Who is this friend?"

Rosa's eyes drifted to the darkness once more. "He—"

"He!" gasped Albina.

"Hush!" said Rosa.

"You have met a man?" Albina gasped again, her ice-blue eyes full of light and mischief. "Is that why you were disappearing into the forest? Rosa! Have you—? You have not... You're still a—?"

"Oh, goodness, 'Bina!"

"You cannot blame me for asking," Albina responded, an impish grin upon her face. "We are young women, after all. We have both had our moontide for four years, already."

"It is not like that," Rosa assured her. "My friend, he is...a bear."

Albina's expression contorted into a comical mask of confusion as she scrunched up her nose. "A bear, Rosa? Have you quite lost your mind? Is this some sort of joke?"

"It is no joke," said Rosa.

"So, I am to believe that you have been meeting in secret with a real bear all these months? A dangerous, man-eating, wild bear!?"

"He is not like that at all," said Rosa defensively. "He was once a man!"

Albina's eyes bulged and her hand came to her mouth. "Rosa...I love you, but this is absurd. Our years of fairy tales are gone by. We are almost of marriageable age, now. The time for children's fancies is behind us. I thought we were speaking plainly with one another."

Rosa caught Albina's hand as she made to rise. "Sister, I swear it. I am speaking the truth. Please, sit, and I will explain."

Albina stared at her sister, one eyebrow raised. "I could be sleeping," she responded.

The wooden door of their humble home rattled, and their eyes flew to the entrance way. "The wind?" said Albina.

The door rattled in its frame again, and Rosa swallowed. "It must be."

Rosa?

Rosa gasped. "It's him!" she whispered.

"What? Him—as in, the bear?"

Rosa rushed to answer the door, but Albina threw herself between it and her twin.

"Are you mad, Rosa? If there really is a bear beyond this door, you cannot let it in!"

"Albina, you must trust me. The bear outside is no ordinary beast. He is enchanted, and he needs my help! Please, move aside."

Should I go? I am sorry to intrude, but I have recalled the sorcerer's words.

"No! Don't go," she said aloud.

"Are you talking to the bear?" said Albina in

astonishment.

"Sister, please."

"No!"

"Albina, I will show you the truth—but for me to do that, you must step aside."

"I will not. I will not lose you! You have lost your mind! Mother! Mother!"

Rosa's heart dropped. She had no choice. "I am sorry, Albina." Summoning the dormant strength within her, she seized her sister by the shoulders and cast her aside. Albina collided with the wooden kitchen table before falling to the floor. Rosa winced apologetically, surprised by her own strength, before unlatching the heavy door, allowing it to swing open with the winter wind. "Quickly!" she urged. "Come inside, Berengar."

Berengar padded inside and lay down beside the fire. Rosa secured the door, then all but flew across the room, throwing herself onto the cursed prince. She clutched at fistfuls of his thick, damp fur and sobbed. "I've been so worried about you," she said into his hide.

Albina rose from the kitchen floor, her mouth agape. "Did you say Berengar?"

Rosa nodded.

"The younger prince of Storskold?"

"The same."

Edging closer, Albina observed the bear warily. "If you really are the prince, tap on the floor, thrice."

His midnight eyes upon her, Berengar rapped three times upon the wooden, straw-strewn floor with his fore-claw.

Albina gasped. "Rosa…is it true?"

Rosa smiled, her eyes brimming with unshed tears. "It is true," she said. "He has been cursed by a dwarven sorcerer at the queen's behest. I want to help him, Albina. It is written in the stars, I know it. It was my fate to meet him."

Swallowing her reservations and fear, she came to sit on the floor, a few paces from Berengar. Looking to Rosa, then the bear once more, she smiled sheepishly. "Forgive me," she said. "I have never encountered magic, nor have I ever spoken to a bear. It is a pleasure to make your acquaintance, prince."

Berengar reached out a solitary paw in her direction, a gesture of peace, and trust.

Albina pursed her lips, then tentatively laid her hand upon his paw.

Rosa moved to sit beside Berengar, closer to his face, so she could stroke the space between his ears. It felt good to be so close. His presence gave her comfort. "You said you remembered the spell," she prompted.

I did. Would you like me to recite it?

"Yes, please do."

Upon two legs, you shall no longer go,
Upon four, will you walk through forest and snow.
With eyes of coal, and teeth so strong,
To fur and cave, you shall belong.

"Is that all?" asked Rosa, perplexed. "There seems to be no caveat, or hope, there."

The sorcerer, Farvald, said no more, though my mother did. While it was not a part of the curse, itself, which is why I mentioned the importance of intent, when understanding magic. It was upon her desires that Farvald formed and cast the curse.

"Then tell us what your mother said."

Upon you, my second son, I place a curse. For the love of gold and power, you would see your beloved brother dead, and for this, you will be made to suffer. No longer will you walk among us a man; for a man you are not. Your actions are those of a beast of greed! And so, it is with all the might of the Crown, that I condemn you to the life of such a creature. I only hope that in time, you will learn that there are more important things in this world than the glitter of gold, my dear son. Until that day, my ruling shall remain. Berengar paused a moment before adding, *When Farvald bid me gone, he also added: Until such a time as your heart truly cares for another, more than for yourself, you will remain a beast.*

Rosa repeated the speech word for word, aloud, for her sister's benefit.

"Well that is it, then!" said Albina suddenly, rising to her feet in excitement. She began to pace back and forth.

"What is it, sister?"

"It is as plain as day, do you not see? Ragna cursed you for your pride, and your love of station and wealth, as much as for the crime committed against your brother! Until you learn that there are more important things in life than the glitter of gold, you will remain cursed."

"You are saying that he needs to value the truly important things in life?" asked Rosa.

"Precisely! Family, friends, togetherness—love!"

Berengar sighed. *It has been over three years since I was first condemned to this form. Over three years spent pondering my fat, and what I have lost. I feel I had already come to these conclusions, yet I am still a bear...*

"Perhaps, there is another way?" said Rosa, hopefully, attempting to buoy Berengar's spirit. She placed her hand upon his great cheek and smiled sadly. "No matter how long it takes, or how hard it may be, I will help you, you have my word. I-I care for you, and if it is within my power to restore you to your true form, I will."

Berengar bowed his head against her. *I do not deserve your devotion, Rosa, though I am glad for it. I care for you too. I wanted so many times to come to you—to profess how I feel, but I did not want to seem too forward, or frighten you. I am no more a prince than I am a man, and I have naught to offer you.*

The tears she had been holding back since spring, fell, etching their way down her face by the warm, orange glow of the hearth.

"I beg your pardon," said Albina, eyes averted. She headed upstairs, leaving the prince and her twin sister alone, together.

"I do not want anything from you," said Rosa, wiping away her tears. "I only want you."

Berengar nuzzled her, and she embraced him. *I love you, Rosa. I want only the best for you. You are brave, and kind—a rare, beautiful soul. I count myself blessed by Freya to have met you.*

"Then stay with me," she whispered, resting her forehead against his. "Our home, is your home." Rosa then nestled into Berengar's thick pelt and closed her eyes.

Berengar curled up protectively around her, and

together, succumbed to sleep.

***

"Father?" said Rosa, her mind swimming as she shielded her eyes against the brilliant, blinding light. When the illumination dimmed, a tall, devastatingly handsome elf lord stood before her. Cloaked in gold, a crown that resembled a tangle of briar thorns atop his familiar white-blonde hair, he radiated magnificence. The grove in which she found herself was breathtakingly beautiful, and a strange, distant music, like pipes, drifted on the breeze.

"My daughter," said the lord.

"I do not understand—am I not sleeping? Where am I, and how did I come to be here?"

"You are dreamwalking, Rosa; it is a gift of our people."

"What is your name, father? And why am I here?"

"My name, my common name, that which your mother knows me by, is Adalric. And you are here because I know of your plight, my dear. I have watched over you always, from afar, and it has come to my attention that you intend to pledge yourself to a cursed mortal."

Rosa blushed. "I think I love him, father."

"I know you do," said Adalric. "Your love for him glows. To full-blooded light elves, it is visible to us as an aura of rainbow light that surrounds you. Your love is true, and you are pure in a way that most of our kin are not. There is no fickleness in your nature, no penchant for deceit. You are honest, and caring, just like your mother; which is why I have summoned you."

Rosa approached her father, until they were face to face. His resemblance to Albina was uncanny.

"I mean to help you, Rosa."

"How?"

"By showing you how to use the magic that lives within you, here." Adalric reached out, and taking her hand, guided it to rest over her heart. "Elf magic is true magic. It does not require tools, or worded spells. It requires only intention and emotion. Magic comes from the heart, but you must give it shape with your mind."

"Even with magic, how can I break another's curse?" she asked.

"Berengar loves you. I can hear his thoughts. He has thought of you without rest these past few months, and has guarded your home. He knows that love, companionship and life are more important than riches, but he needs you to help him recognise the truth of it. It is one thing to know, and another to truly believe."

"So, all I need to do is show him that my love is genuine—that real love is without caveats and conditions?"

Adalric inclined his head with a smile, and the grove began to shimmer and distort.

"Father, will I ever see you again?" said Rosa, panic striking her heart.

"I am never far, daughter. You need only call my name in your sleep, and I will come."

"Will I ever meet you in the flesh?" she hastened.

"You are a princess of Álfheim, Rosa. You will see me again, and walk the glittering halls of your kingdom, I have foreseen it. You will find the way. For now, goodbye, daughter. The light within you is bright. Let it shine and illuminate your path."

"Thank you," she said, reaching out for his face as the dream fell away and she awoke; once more in her home, the fire crackling, and the wrath of the storm beyond, shivering the windows in their icy frames.

***

All winter long, Berengar came to the home of the twins, and was eventually introduced to the girls' mother, Thora. The cursed prince was welcome in their humble cottage, and together, they grew as close and familiar as a family ought.

Despite the burning desire within Rosa to share her dream meeting with their father, she kept her secret, and used the cold months to practise her elven magic. When the snow drifts melted, and the land turned green with spring once more, the twins celebrated their birthday—they were now of marriageable age—and Rosa felt it was time to enact her wishes and make her feelings known to the prince.

Rosa sat quietly in the glade where they met, where she and Albina had spent so much of their childhood playing. The dappled sunlight streamed through the canopy above, causing the stream and pool to sparkle, lending it its very own air of enchantment and beauty. The gentle touch of Berengar's mind let her know that he was not far. Not long after, she heard his heavy footfalls on the grass, her heightened half-elven sense of smell picking up the fresh scent of crushed grass as he approached.

"Hail, Berengar," she said as he came to sit down beside her. She put her arms around his neck and squeezed tight.

Good afternoon, my lady, he said, before looking to his reflection in the glittering waters.

Rosa laid her hand upon his paw. She could see the pain there, the forlorn suffering in his gaze, and she could endure it no more. "Berengar, I have been keeping a secret from you since the beginning of winter, but if you will allow me, I would like to share it with you now."

Berengar's immense head tilted to the side in query. *Of course*, he said. *I will hear you.*

Rosa signed in relief, glad that he was not upset or offended. "That first night that you came to our home and stayed…I met our father. Not in the flesh, but in a dream, where we spoke with one another, mind to mind. Dreamwalking, our people call it," she explained. "He summoned me, and we talked, as if in another place. He knew of our peculiar situation—of your curse, and of our feelings for each other. He wanted to help us."

Go on, said the prince.

"He enlightened me as to how elven magic works, and since that night, I have been practising this gift in secret, so that I could use it well, when the time came. I believe that time is now, Berengar."

I do not quite understand, he responded.

Rosa smiled. "I need only for you to calm your mind and be open to what I am about to show you. This is…for us."

Berengar blinked his large eyes. *I trust you*, he said. *I will do as you ask.*

Rosa knelt before the prince, and placing her hands upon the sides of his face, closed her eyes and rested her forehead against his. With a deep breath, she focused on projecting a stream of images—memories—directly into Berengar's mind.

Berengar shivered beneath his fur as the memory of their first meeting, from Rosa's point of view, unfolded within his mind. He could feel her emotions—her fear, which melted into trepidation before relaxing into curiosity. He saw himself through her eyes as the scene changed.

They were romping in the forest together. Her laughter was like music to his ears as she playfully used her half-elven speed to run rings around him. He felt her joy, unbridled, like a stallion running free. She was happy and desired to spend more and more time with him. Many more balmy, beautiful days in the forest played in his mind, before finally, Rosa could ignore his predicament no longer. She confronted him, beseeching him to return to her only when he had recalled the words of the curse and the caveats surrounding its casting.

He felt her sadness and her loneliness as she isolated herself from her mother and sister. She spent hours just sitting by the window, hoping for him to emerge from the tree line with the answers she sought.

The months passed slowly for her, like honey dribbling down tree bark. She missed him, and pined after his company and the familiar touch of his mind. He heard her sing in the darkness to herself, wishing for a cure—a way to break the curse—so that he would be free, and they might be together.

The memories kept coming, and he felt his heart twist. Her love was so pure, he ached for the beauty of it. That he could have won her heart—that she thought he deserved her affections—hit him like a blow to the chest. How had he been so blind to the magnitude of what they shared? The scene changed several more times, memories of their nights spent together through the winter, camped by the hearth, her face buried in his fur. Her scent, during those long nights, had become so familiar, that he could not imagine a life without it.

The cosy cottage faded away and he found himself in an ethereal grove. It thrummed with magic. He watched as Rosa's father materialised before her, living the moment as if he was there. As the meeting unfolded, his heart raced. Rosa was not just a rare Halfling, she was the bastard daughter of Adalric, the King of Álfheim, himself. He had legitimised her claim to the lands of her kin and announced her a princess of the realm.

Then the grove and the stream of memories

tumbled away until there was nothing but peace between them—a quiet, restful sense of two kindred souls united. A deep pain suddenly lanced through his chest, and he roared. His eyes flew open, and he internally flinched as Rosa raised an arm to shield herself as she scrambled backwards across the grass.

Rosa watched in fascinated horror as Berengar rose into the air before her, suspended by the dark magic that held him captive. He twisted and writhed in pain, and then there came the sickening snap of breaking bones as his great muscular limbs hung at excruciatingly odd angles. His roar was almost more than she could handle, and she covered her mouth with her hands to stop the choked sobs that threatened to escape her. A shimmering swirling mist took form around him, obscuring him from view.

"Berengar!" she called out in fear. She heard a *thud* upon the grass, and then the maelstrom dissipated as quickly as it had appeared. There, lying in a pool of matted fur and blood, lay prince Berengar, in mortal form once more. Rosa gasped and flung herself forward without reservation. Pushing the immense bear pelt aside, she placed a hand upon his bare and bloody chest, and then lowered her ear to his mouth. She felt a soft exhalation of hot breath against her ear, and then there was no holding back the tears. She rested her face upon his chest and wept. "Berengar, my love, we did it! We broke the curse!"

"Rosa," he ventured as his eyes fluttered open, squinting to see her against the afternoon light. "You're glowing," he said, a small smile spreading across his lips. "I don't know how, but I can see it. Your light…it's beautiful."

Rosa touched her forehead to his and smiled in return. "I love you, Berengar," she said.

The prince reached up with a red-stained hand to touch her face tenderly. "And I love you, Rosa." Struggling to his knees, with her help, he knelt before her, and took her hand. *Even covered head to sole in gore, naked as the day he was born—he is beautiful*, she thought.

Hearing her thoughts, Berengar smiled. "I do not know what I have to offer at this time. I do not know if my titles or station will be restored, but will you take me as I am, Rosa? A man, once a cursed bear, who loves you with all his heart? Will you do me the honour of giving me your hand in marriage?"

Rosa laughed, her cheeks flaring a lovely shade of rose pink. "I will," she said. "I love you! I will!"

Berengar stood, his strength returning. He joined in her laughter as he picked her up and spun her around in the desecrated forest clearing. Then, setting her down gently, he ran his hand through her lovely crimson locks and kissed her.

Rosa melted into his embrace, savouring the feel of his lips against hers.

***

Dressed in their best, Thora, her two daughters and the prince, arrived at the Black Castle of Storskold; Thora having spent her meagre savings to pay for a simple coach to bear them hence.

"I will repay you for your kindness," said Berengar to Thora with an earnest smile as he sat side by side with Rosa, their fingers entwined.

"Please, do not speak of gold, it matters not! Seeing my rose-red beauty *alight*, and so full of joy— to have you for a son is truly more than I could wish for." She turned to Albina and petted her on the leg. "If only there were a handsome lord for my snow-white darling, too!"

"Mother, please," said Albina, grimacing in good-natured humour.

At the Black Gate, their coach came to a halt and Berengar, in a simple pair of breeches and a shirt sewn lovingly by Rosa, herself, leaned out the window to speak to the watchmen. "Master Wagner," he said.

"Would you kindly open the gate? I have company."

The armoured watchman's mouth fell open, and he looked to his fellow in disbelief. "Do my eyes deceive me? Is it really you, Prince Berengar? You are returned!"

"Indeed it is, friend. I bring my mother and brother good tidings."

"Of course, your majesty," he said, before sounding for the small passage gate within the Black Gate to be opened. "It is good to see you, my prince. After the—I never thought I would live to see the day. I am glad to have been wrong."

Berengar smiled. "No more glad than I, I can assure you," he said, and bid the watchmen farewell. Word raced ahead of them as trumpets sounded down the way, toward the castle, announcing a royal arrival.

**

In the throne room where his dark, and twisted journey began, Berengar stood before Queen Ragna, and Prince Einar.

"It surprises me to see you here, a man, once more," said the queen, eternally garbed in the black of mourning. It had been ten years since the king had passed, and still, she maintained her solitary vigil.

Berengar held his head high, though his eyes found the floor. *I could not imagine losing my Rosa, he thought to himself*—a rare moment of empathy for his mother. Several paces behind him, Rosa, Albina and Thora waited. He felt the soft, reassuring touch of Rosa's mind. She had heard him.

"Mother!" interrupted Einar. "We can do away with this pageantry. My brother is returned to us! He has broken the curse, which tells us everything we need to know." He bounded down the stairs of the dais and clapped a hand over Berengar's shoulder, his bright green eyes hopeful. "You are a changed man, brother. I see it in your very bearing. We are glad to have you home."

Berengar smiled, closing his hand over Einar's. "Forgive me, brother, for my folly. I was blind to the blessings I already have."

Einar returned his brother's smile. "All is forgiven, little brother," he said, playfully tousling Berengar's blonde hair. "It seems you have gained further blessings, Beren?" he said, looking pointedly over his shoulder.

Berengar stepped aside, gesturing towards his company. "Mother, brother? May I introduce Thora Mendler of the Black Forest, and her twin daughters— Rosa and Albina." All three of the women curtseyed gracefully in unison. "This family welcomed me with open arms, despite my accursed form. They have been gracious, caring and more virtuous than I could ever deserve. Rosa?"

Rosa approached, and Berengar took her hand, squeezing it gently.

"Mother, Rosa's steadfast loyalty, friendship and love over this past year has been my saving grace. Were it not for her, I have no doubt that I would still be doomed to walk the forests as a bear for the rest of my days. Her integrity and light have changed me, and I am a better man for it. I love her and have asked for her hand in marriage. We would seek your blessing of our union."

Queen Ragna observed the pair, united in their common attire, before the whole court. "You must be a rare woman indeed, Rosa, to have seen goodness within the dark heart of a beast. It seems you were the key to unlocking the curse."

Rosa inclined her head. "Thank you, your grace," she said, offering the queen a small, intrepid smile.

"I am glad to have both my sons once more, and for this, I have you to thank. The Crown is in your debt. It is my pleasure to extend welcome to you and your family. You have my blessing. Preparations for a royal wedding will begin forthwith."

Berengar grinned from ear to ear and Rosa mirrored his joy.

The unmistakable sound of a throat being cleared made the couple turn. Einar winked, raising his brows suggestively, beyond them. Rosa's eyes widened in shocked delight, and Berengar laughed.

"Albina?" said Berengar as they walked over. "It would give me great pleasure to introduce to you my older brother, Einar, the Crown Prince of Storskold."

Albina's pale cheeks flushed pink, and she extended her hand. Einar placed a lingering kiss upon it, his eyes never leaving her fair face.

"Charmed," said Albina with a coy smile.

Thora could no longer contain herself. Rushing forward, she laughed, tears streaking her face as she embraced her daughters; her delight heart-warmingly evident for all to see.

***

Berengar wrapped his arm around Rosa as they travelled by royal carriage through the spring-green, lush countryside of Storskold. "How does it feel to be a princess of two kingdoms? Nay, two realms?" he asked.

Rosa raised her brows, a mischievous look upon

her face. "I might ask you a similar question," she said cryptically.

"Rosa…where are we going?"

"You'll see!" she sang.

As the afternoon began to fade to dusk, and the Black Forest was bathed in the dying, golden rays of the sun, Berengar and Rosa saw the carriage off.

"Are we paying your mother a surprise visit?" he asked.

"Not today," said Rosa. "Come, run with me!" Hiking up her skirts, she took her husband by the hand and led him into the Black Forest.

"What are we doing?" he laughed, struggling to keep his footing as Rosa revelled in her elvish speed.

"How would you like to be a prince of two realms?" she called back. "We are going to visit my family in Álfheim!"

Before Berengar could respond, Rosa focused her intention, and in a blinding flash of light, together they vanished from the mortal realm.

ZOEY XOLTON is an Australian Speculative Fiction writer, primarily of Dark Fantasy, Paranormal Romance, and Horror. She is also a proud mother of two and is married to her soul mate. Outside of her family, writing is her greatest passion. She has featured in dozens of anthologies to date and has recently celebrated the release of her debut short story collection 'Darkly Ever After'. You can find further details regarding her various publications, including her short eBook series, the 'Fast Fiction Collection', on her website!

Bibliography

Bad Romance, Black Hare Press, 2020
Coffins & Dragons, Dragon Soul Press, 2019
Curses & Cauldrons, Blood Song Books, 2019
DARK DRABBLES Books 1-10, Black Hare Press, 2019
Darkly Ever After, Blood Song Books, 2020
Deep Sea, Black Hare Press, 2020
Deep Space, Black Hare Press, 2019
Divinity, Iron Faerie Publishing, 2019
Fable, Iron Faerie Publishing, 2019
First Love, Dragon Soul Press, 2019
Forest of Fear, Blood Song Books, 2019
Key to the Kingdom, Black Hare Press, 2020
LUST, Black Hare Press, 2020
PRIDE, Black Hare Press, 2020
Sea of Secrets, Dragon Soul Press, 2019
SLOTH, Black Hare Press, 2020
Storming Area 51, Black Hare Press, 2019
Twenty Twenty, Black Hare Press, 2020
What If?, Black Hare Press, 2019

Connect

Website: www.zoeyxolton.com
Amazon: www.amazon.com/author/zoeyxolton

THE WITCH WHO WOULD BE QUEEN

By D.J. Elton

A disturbed dark witch schemes to marry King Henry VIII, with mayhem breaking loose as the Ancient Fae and two rogue druids gather forces to stabilise the kingdom.

A young dark-haired woman sits comfortably in her ancient chair, her thick skirts folded around her legs. With a focus born from years of concentration, she rubs her palms together generating heat. A small glass ball in her lap starts to glow and there is a crackle, high pitched and electrical. It's time to meet with the Great Fae Saras, where destiny meets magic.

"Are you there? Saras?" Anna is edgy, as walls have ears. She holds a timely plan for establishing a new order in England, possibly beyond the seas. Saras is the one who will help, sharing her mastery and skills. The lady, Anna Boleyn, is a novice in comparison. She fidgets impatiently.

Saras is as luxurious and luminous as one may wish to imagine her. Some have seen her as the Good Virgin, others as Kali or Medusa. No matter, she has The Power and uses it to best advantage.

More crackling and the room glows bright red. "Ah. You're here." The Lady Anna is pleased beyond doubt. She would never dare treat Saras as she sometimes treats her maidservants—scolding or blaming. Anna lifts the ball and holds it close to her nose. A tiny dancing figure in green, with long red hair streaked in white, comes closer into orbit. "I can see you now. D'you hear me?"

A laugh like metallic bowls is tinkling in the red glow. "Dear Anna, you look well. Your voice is clear. What is your request, Lady?" Like the Great Fae, Anna does not waste time with words. There is no need for small talk, unlike at the court which is full of gossip and false news. Anna hones into the magical orbit, grasping the round crystal, and speaking with a heavy voice.

"We need to work. The king is becoming fonder of me each day, and I'm certain he will marry me if I move wisely. My father, Lord Thomas, is also helping to bring this to a deal and conclusion."

The Great Fae's question was straight to the matter. "Does the king remain uninfluenced by others?"

Anna lowered her voice. This talk of the king's advisers could be seen as treason. "Wolsey is failing, but Cramner is rising. He will help in securing this marriage. Yet, I do not trust him."

Saras did not hesitate with a spell. "Then we shall use the dust. Put in on the king's pillow for when he sleeps, and he will become totally yours. Wait for the white bird to bring it." Saras moved her hands in an elegant way, as if stroking an animal. She was leaving.

"Don't fear, Anna. The new realm will come to be." The ball became so hot and cloudy that Anna could not hold it anymore. She placed it on a silk pad on her desk, feeling a tight bond of love for Saras and her selfless assistance. After Saras' abrupt departure, a feeling of self-doubt tried to slip into Anna's thoughts. Just then she heard the *caw caw* sound coming from an open small window. A large white crow jumped excitedly up and down, as if jigging, on the inner wooden ledge.

"Already!" Anna gasped. *There is no delay with Saras' magic. Would mine be so strong one day?* However, it was useless to ponder this idea. Although Anna knew some of the Arts, she had been birthed by parents of the human variety, unlike Saras, who had been fathered by the wind itself. Anna sighed, screwing up her nose at the unnecessary comparison.

The giant crow had a small bag full of pink dust attached to one of its legs. Anna removed it carefully, gently stroking the bird's head. "Thank you. So fast. You did well." Of course, as it was a magical crow, it cocked its head, and before flying off, winked mischievously at Anna, fully appreciating the situation that the pink dust would entail.

***

Unlike Lady Anna, the witch Magillika was able to transcend the boundaries of time and space. She could go forward or backward in time, a most useful activity. Consequently, she chose where she spent her days, running amok and creating havoc as the Magillika bloodline did best. Wherever she went she kept her several robot armies nearby, ready for battle.

"It's the day, Helix. It's coming soon." She gleefully grabbed and swung the metre-long tail of her cat. Helix was in a grump, so just spat and hissed in return. "I'm going to wed King Henry. We will be such a power couple." She sighed lustily, rubbing a patch of gold painted warts on her cheek, while visioning herself and the king holding court. "He is the most splendid specimen of a king ever there was, and I want him for my own!"

Magillika, although she was one of the three most powerful dark witches of the north, had a lot of weakness in the area of discerning people and situations. As you would imagine, this was quite problematic at the best of times. So, when she became infatuated with the good King Hank, she also became quite delusional about his anticipated response. She was slowly starting to unravel, and that was not a good moment for the stars, the gods, the fae, or any other living being or creature that was part of Hank's current timeline as King of England.

Mayhem was about to hit the fan.

***

It was a splendid autumn afternoon. King Hank, the Lady Anna, and the king's beloved fool, Will Summers, were dallying along the path to the Jasmine Garden. Anna was feeling like the cat who had dived into the cream. Things were going well so far, and the pink dust was working most effectively. King Hank held Anna's blue-gloved hand as Will led the way through the fragrant entanglements. They reached a small well-lit grotto with several exquisitely carved wooden chairs.

"This is so lovely." Anna was delighted, clapping her hands.

"This is the king's most secret outdoor spot." Will spoke proudly, pinching his nose several times. "A little dusty today." Anna smiled, wondering if the pink dust were affecting Will too. She liked this entertaining man with his long red ringlets and bright clothes.

Hank was quiet, enchanted, with moist cow-like eyes for Anna alone.

"My Lord King." Will bowed emphatically. "I have news. My brother and his companion are travelling to London. They bring a maidservant with them." Hank half heard his fool. He gazed endearingly at Anna and held both of her hands.

"Oh! You have family then, Will?" Anna was intrigued. *Could there be more like him?*

"Yes, my Lady, I do. My brother, Rino, and his patron, the Faz."

"Well, they must stay here then, my man!" Hank was generous and hospitable as ever. "Close to your rooms."

"Ahem." Will cleared his throat, bowing even lower. "They have a little business to do." He glanced curiously at Anna as he said this. She had a vision of two elderly monks, druids perhaps, in strange wonderful garb, each resting their hands on the fingertips of the Great Fae Saras. The scene went as quickly as it came, but Anna trusted her sight well and knew that things were hotting up.

***

In mid-2020, the two aged monks, Rino and the Faz, were planning to leave their winter home at the Blue Castle with a view to go time-tripping for a little light adventure. Rino was meticulously cleaning his miniature tigers-eye wand.

"What about Scotland, Faz?" They had already decided on the time, thinking that the sixteenth century would be interesting. And they would prefer to keep out of Europe.

"Ach, lad." The Faz laughed, staring through his larger telescope, gripping its sides with his knobbly fingers. He pointed at Rino, his friend from birth, and spoke rhyming lines.

"Patterns and pictures. Time to go. Taking a trip.

We fly with the crow." He plonked himself into a favourite armchair.

"Magillika's got her armies in Scotland." The Faz looked deep into his portable telescope where a scene of kilted robots wielding swords and hatchets came into view. Magillika's army.

"Where's that Braveheart when you need him?" The Faz was never too serious.

A tinkling lightness entered the room. Rino felt heat rise up his spine. He broke into a large smile as the Great Fae Saras appeared. Her long white hair with its red flames elegantly tied above her ears. She made a stunning entrance as always.

"Good morning, dearest comrades! There's an invitation from your clan-brother Will." Her smile made Rino feel alert and ready for action.

"Will Summers? That's it, Faz!" Rino did a little jig across the room, almost tripping on the corner of the Turkish rug. "Let's go to the court of Henry the King!" He gathered his long cream shawl as he bowed respectfully towards the fae.

"Number eight. The eighth Henry." The Faz was still pre-occupied with his telescope and the scenes it was revealing. Now he could see an evil and dangerous foe, the witch Magillika. Here she was, usually the most mean, dancing and singing with glee. How odd.

Magillika was singing! He strained to hear her words. That voice made one think of toads and rats.

"I'm going to marry the king. Great King Henry. What a beautiful pair we'll make."

Saras tapped the Faz on the shoulder. "My dear friend, we must away soon, time is essential. The Lady Anna Boleyn is to marry the King of England and will gain the rights to bring a new better order to the place. This is her great quest. The king will marry her...eventually. But the witch Magillika is also planning to overthrow the Lady Anna and marry the king herself."

The trio reflected for a brief moment on what troubles this would cause. With a mutual shudder, honed from years of combined experience, they came together in a circle. The three commanders of the army of magical circumstances. Lightly they touched fingertips, generating a strong energy. As is the old way, they focused their very clear thought into London circa 1533, into King Henry the Eighth's royal household.

***

Magillika leapt for joy. As excessively badass as she was in most things, she could still manage to squeal and jump like a five-year-old when her happy hormones got touched, and today they were throbbing.

The Scottish Highlands is a wonderful place for a witch. Magillika reflected on how she had stalked the King Macbeth, hoping to marry him. Yet it had not worked out, as three other crones got there first. Now was her Big New Chance as the gorgeous King Hank was up for grabs. Well almost. She just needed to get rid of that gormless female, Anna Boleyn, and bewitch the king into marrying herself. Easy enough to do in theory, but it would take some sharp practical skill. Unfortunately, Magillika wasn't at all savvy with her discerning abilities, unlike Saras and the Faz.

***

Fourteen full moons later, an elegant ceremony was to be seen in the grand old rooms near the chapel of Henry's palace. The royal pair were spectacular in their matching white robes lined with gold damask, adorned with pearls of gold and cream; Anna, now queen, and King Hank, bursting with pride at the christening of his only child, a girl named Elizabeth.

"So magnificent." Rino's eyes fluttered, absorbing the beauty and pomp. The king and queen walked together, with Queen Anna holding the newborn

Elizabeth.

"I am so happy," Anna whispered to Hank. His smile was glittering with love. It was the best he could provide, as some deeper darker turmoil was brewing in his heart. Hank rubbed his fingers in a circular motion with his free hand. A habit when he worried.

It was bad enough that it hadn't been a son. He so wanted a boy. Then there was the problem of the first wife, Spanish Katherine, refusing to be dowager princess. And Mary, the older daughter, so haughty, disobedient and fierce. These women in his life brought so many problems. Hank would rather be out riding, hunting, fighting, and cavorting. He glanced up, and it was then he saw the faerie, Saras. *How she looks like the maidservant of those two monks Will has as guests.* The Great Fae was stunning in her green summer dress and cloak, her face full of magic.

Henry, being human, was not able to grasp the subtle idea of a magical being, so he just stared at Saras with his mouth wide open. Most odd for the king. He found himself locked into her face, her eyes. *Extraordinary.* It was as if huge burdens were tumbling from his soul. He could breathe normally again. His perception had changed. *All is well. Most well.* The kingdom was being taken care of safely. Protection was right here in the atmosphere.

Anna waved to Saras, lifting her gloved hand to the Faerie Godmother of the Princess Elizabeth, her daughter, who, when queen, would forever remain a virgin.

Rino and the Faz bowed low to the king, Queen and royal child with great respect as the ceremony began.

Then the voice of Magillika came softly to Hank's ear. "Your wife, Anna, is an adulteress and she will never bear you a son, O King." Magillika had come in an invisible form.

Hank wriggled as if a snake had slid down his back.

"Whose words are these?" He stepped forward and grasped his throne, sitting down heavily with an unceremonious *plonk*. No-one seemed to notice, they were all gazing with dewy eyes at the child, as if enchanted. Only Saras saw Hank react.

Saras also knew Magillika was here and set to cause trouble. It had started. She caught the king's eye, speaking to him with her crystal-clear mind. "There is an evil witch in the palace, King Henry. She is plotting to overthrow the queen."

"Treason," Hank muttered, unsure of the goings-on between his two ears. It was bad enough that this marriage had taken so long to fulfil, now it was becoming messy. He glanced at his wife, paler and thinner since childbirth, and had a creeping thought: *Would she ever give him a beloved son?*

***

So it came to pass that many things became undone whilst Magillika tried one spell after another in her attempts to bewitch the king and get rid of Anna. You would think that the combined magical powers of the Faz, Saras, and even Queen Anna, would destabilise the effects of Magillika's bad magic. But not so. Although she was a very powerful witch, Magillika's two main faults were in becoming highly emotional, usually angry. Secondly, in having a lack of clarity.

This is how Magillika's magic played out.

One day, Will Summers lost all his wonderful long red locks. Another time, Rino's tigers-eye wand got stuck up his left nostril, where it could be seen. Poor Rino retired to his room for a few harrowing days. Queen Anna grew another fingernail on her right hand, which was supposedly a sign of witching. The Princess Elizabeth seemed to be forever sneezing and coughing, and the king had constant headaches. Even the Faz developed an itch on the back of both his ears. Most peculiar, all of these incidents. Only Saras was certain who was responsible and unfortunately, could only protect herself from the curses of Magillika. Even King Hank started to lose his clothes. Small pieces at a time, which caused some embarrassment as well as entertainment, in and out of the court circles.

Anna met Saras in the private rooms of Rino and the Faz. She was perplexed.

"There are strange goings-on and I fear for myself."

The Faz was looking through his scope.

"It's Magillika. Her magic is messed up."

Anna groaned. "But what is she trying to achieve?"

Rino looked hard at the Faz. "Tell us."

"She has a plan to marry the king." The Faz shook his head, chuckling. "Ridiculous."

"Impossible!" Anna was horrified. "What does Saras say?"

"The main thing, Anna, is not to be afraid. Your fear will fire up Magillika's cause." Saras rubbed her hands together, creating shooting beams of pinkish yellow light. "This will help for now." Flicking her hands gracefully around Anna's head, she hummed softly.

"Your new order will come from this. Elizabeth

will be a great queen."

Then Saras disappeared. *Pop!* Anna also disappeared. Another *pop!*

"O Lordie. Faz. Do let's have a drink." Rino wiped his forehead. With a sigh, he moved closer to his friend, who was still looking into his telescope. "Too much goings-on."

"They've gone to Nardis, Rino." The Faz always smiled when he mentioned Nardis.

Nardis was the great region past the field of physical matter. It was a timeless, spaceless place, and only fae and those with a completely clear intent could visit. Saras went to replenish herself and had taken Anna along so as to further initiate the new order.

***

King Henry was most displeased. Firstly, the queen had vanished for almost twenty hours. Then she had returned having an overabundance of energy that was quite disconcerting. She also seemed to have acquired some bumpiness to her complexion which he found highly unattractive.

The false Queen Anna-Magillika came bursting into the king's inner rooms with an enthusiasm that betrayed her, but only to the Faz, who was always highly attuned to magic spells and their results. Rino and the Faz were playing cards with Hank, whilst Will Summers was picking at a large plate full of nuts, fruits and tantalizing sweetmeats. He coughed on his mouthful as the queen came over in the most uncharacteristic pushy manner and leaned heavily on his left shoulder.

"I'll have some of those." A gloved hand snatched a hazelnut sweet from Will's plate and shoved it into her mouth. *Only a witch like Magillika would have such bad manners,* the Faz observed quietly to himself. He could see past Magillika's magic to realise that this was indeed herself, and she was fooling everyone in sight to believe that she was Anna the Queen. *Holy Roly!* The Faz felt like laughing out loud at the spectacle, however decided it best to shut up and stay low temporarily. *Let's wait until Saras returns.*

"Ah. My dearest," King Hank mooned, temporarily distracted from his card game. He beamed lovingly at his wife, although something did seem a little odd with the queen. Henry wondered if she were unwell, or even pregnant again.

Anna-Magillika sat brazenly next to the king, taking hold of his arm and looking into his mildly puzzled face, all the while looking just like Queen Anna but without her grace and manners.

"*Such horror*," the Faz muttered to himself. He hoped that Magillika would not realise that he could see who she really was. That would have meant a total downfall. He knew Magillika's robot armies were never far away from their mistress. He had the dreadful thought there could be one in the nearby woods. If there were conflict of that level, Anna would never get her new order established. *All would perish!*

The Faz excused himself, taking off quickly to the royal washrooms. Anna-Magillika was busy patting and touching Hank's arm, neck, and face with such a shamelessness that he needed to leave. Will, also embarrassed, called Rino to come along to the kitchens and find some fresh apple wine. Leaning breathlessly against the solid wooden door of the washroom, the Faz closed his eyes and used his mind to speak to Saras, requesting she return *immediately* from Nardis, but there was no response.

Most unusual. What dreaded omens are these? The Faz drew the telescope from his carpet bag, tapping it gently three times, glancing into the dark glass.

"Oh, damn fog! Saras! Come, speak, Lady." She still did not respond for some reason. *Maybe this is her response?* Faz was feeling a tad frantic. He reluctantly put away the scope, but it was starting to warm up and he couldn't fit it into the bag.

He looked again into the lens. Voices were getting louder. Men and women of the court. Elegant people scheming. Whispering and gossiping about the queen. *"The Queen Anna, tart more like it. She sleeps with her musician. And her brother! That Lord...Henry Norris. Mark Smeaton. Sir Francis. Wicked witch. She should burn!"* The Faz shuddered. Everything was suddenly chilly in his bones. They were discussing Anna the true queen. Rumours were spreading about her through the court. This was high treason.

The Faz sighed deeply. There was nothing he could do about it—it was outside of magic. It couldn't be changed. He thought of the beautiful headstrong Anna and his heart missed a beat. Dear child, she had so much good in her to propose this change to the old religious ways for the common people, by making the books known and spreading them throughout the realm. And Henry had been so helpful in getting the old order changed. How could these courtiers curse her so? *What karma she had!*

***

Nardis, being a timeless place, did not keep the Great Fae Saras, or the Queen Anna in its hold for too long. They had returned refreshed and rejuvenated to the south of England.

Saras and Anna walked through an old gate, past bright green overgrown trees and shrubs. It was a divinely beautiful garden they had come to, at the nunnery of St Elron near Bournemouth, on the sea.

"I love this place." Anna laughed. "It's so fresh and wild."

True, it was nothing like the clipped gardens of Henry's palaces. This was a place of old magic, ripe with stories of power, love, conflicts and victory.

Saras looked ethereal, totally attuned. "You'll enjoy your time here before you retire, Anna. You'll be comfortable, your own person."

Anna felt enthralled. The time spent in Nardis had opened up to more ideas as to how to proceed with the new order. Now it seemed the witch Magillika had taken her place in Henry's life. *What gall!* Otherwise, what a great result, as she would never have been able to leave Henry in any other way. Saras was godmother to Elizabeth. No more need be said about her success in the future. Anna felt most happy. She grabbed Saras' hand, and they danced a wild faerie dance in the daylight, in the garden. Fate and fortune were co-operating together well.

***

However, circumstances were never the same in Henry's main palace, Hampton Court. The king himself was often seen chewing his nails, slapping the heads of his manservants and scowling more than ever.

"He's like an old strumpet who's lost her favourite pair of shoes," remarked Will Summers to Rino and the Faz. They sat comfortably together in Will's small sitting room, sipping on pear wine and munching on daisy cakes.

"Ssssshh! Will! You speak treason." Rino suspiciously looked over both his shoulders and rolled his eyes skyward. He hadn't felt quite the same since that witch's curse had placed his tigers-eye wand up his left nostril. In fact, he was not sleeping well at all, starting to worry about small and ridiculous things. Anxiety had edged in.

"I wish we could leave," he whispered to the Faz when Will had turned to tidying his over stacked sweets and biscuits cupboard.

"Don't be such a wuss, Rino." Although lately, it seemed to Rino that the Faz was acutely preoccupied with staring into that *wretched* telescope—catching hold of too many stories and rumours—he was still verbally sharp as a tack.

"Rino, I know your power lessened since the wand got up your nose." The Faz snickered. "I also know you are desperately missing the good lady Saras…but really, man, all is happening *as it should*. All is good."

"You do know that Magillika has betwitched the court, don't you?" The Faz wondered how this had escaped Rino's usual observations.

Poor Rino. He must be in a bad way. It's high time Saras should return from her gadding about.

Just then, the Great Fae herself appeared, bright as ever, hair long white and splashed with red streaks. She gleefully sent whispers of excitement through the fog of the Faz' telescope.

"Dear Faz. No worry, I'm with the Queen Anna. Not the false queen, Magillika the witch." She giggled and tinkling bells filled the room. It was catching, most infectious really, that Great Fae laughter. Will and Rino were both consumed by it, and soon all three of them were groaning, snorting, and cackling loudly. All very hilarious, this saga of Magillika turning into Queen Anna. Who would have thought?

The Faz was briefly interrupted by Saras' departing words. "The true Queen Anna got to a nunnery. A magnificent place near Bournemouth. We're here now. The new order, it's already begun."

She slipped out of the Faz's vision and the scope went foggy. Time to tune out.

***

The new Queen Anna-Magillika sat alone on her bedroom chair, staring into an ornate mirror. Hank had gone riding with two visiting lords, the Seymours. *Phhhwtt!* She spat into a small silver bowl. *How dare he not ask me to accompany them*!

Everything she touched on her dressing table felt sticky and poisonous. Her fingertips felt like glue. As she thought of Rino and the Faz, a deep seething rush of prickly heat began swishing and swirling through her veins. This ill feeling had taken its hold in the past day and was becoming more oppressive. She needed an outlet.

"Those two eejits!" She visualized Rino and the Faz sitting in their parlour in their home, the Blue Castle which had *once* been hers. "How they bother me!" Her black and orange cat, Helix, rubbed itself against Magillika's spindly legs. She stood, gripping the sides of her 'high intensity' cauldron, watching the hot, dark water hissing and whirling.

"That Faz! Such a slothful old bastard!" She spat into the rippling waters, throwing in some brittle dried flies and two dead mice, recently delivered by a proud Helix, for good measure.

Magillika concentrated as well as she could. Considering the turmoil hovering around her, she thought she saw her enemy, the Faz, appearing in the dark water. However, it was Rino. But as her eyesight had dimmed somewhat from all the nocturnal activities with the King Hank, she saw the assistant instead. "Such a waste of space, that Faz, useless as they come." She grimaced and glared into her cauldron with vicious glee in her voice. "I'm going to make him ill and send him to his bed for two weeks. Then I can start plan B."

Helix purred and growled, nodding. Magillika was a loyal, although moody mistress. Many a time, one of her robots had whipped him up by the tail and thrown him onto the witch's washing cart. An almost fatal experience, even for a cat. Still, there were lots of mice, insects and other treats here, and nowhere else appealed.

Magillika cackled…once, twice, thrice. She threw mugwort, basil, and fingernails by the handful into 'high intensity', muttering foul angry curses towards the Faz. Then she collapsed into her chair, breathless, sweaty. Her hatred was settling back into its usual place for the moment. An invisible barbed arrow of her direct malice was spearheading towards the unknowing Rino.

***

King Henry sat back on his heavily cushioned couch, picking at a tapestry pillow underneath his heavy knees. His hands were hot, throbbing. Unable to keep still. Will Summers was dutifully massaging Hank's large, taut calves, then dipping his long fingers into a fragrant herbal concoction, provided by the queen herself. It was a quiet moment between the king and servant. Hank appreciated this loyal entertaining fool who had been many years in his service.

The king addressed his angst. "Will, do you know what they are saying about Queen Anna?"

Will always pretended to hear and see nothing. An extremely useful attitude in keeping best relations with His Royal Majesty.

"No, my Lord. Do say?" Will was intrigued.

Hank sighed. "They say that the queen has others in her bed. *Five others in fact.*"

The king groaned as if in agony. The impact on his masculinity was overpowering his ability to think rationally. A small soggy tear ran down each cheek.

Will's strong hands continued their work on the king's knees, but his mind was confused. *How could this be possible? It's all heresay.*

"Is there proof, my Lord King?" Will spoke.

"Yes, Will." Henry sniffed. "My man Cramner is certain and has begun proceedings already. These men shall confess. It's treason."

Will shifted uncomfortably on his stool. He looked long at the king's fat white toes.

"Does the queen know all this?"

Henry winced, throwing the tapestry pillow across the room. Then he roared, "Wretched woman! She will not see me again! She has killed my love."

He was going to send her to the Tower.

***

The true Queen Anna awoke to a brilliant blue-sky morning. Shards of clear light streamed through large open windows. *Ah freedom!* The next bed was empty, and she was not surprised. Saras hardly slept at all, not needing to rest. The Great Fae would be out in the woods already, consolidating in and beyond the realm with nature, the elements, and the future.

King Hank certainly knew how to keep married life moving. No sooner had he relinquished his second queen, Anna-Magillika to the Tower, he had his heart set on marrying the Seymour girl, one of Anna's ladies-in-waiting.

A small party of six left the king's rooms for the garden. They used the secret entrance, hidden behind stone walls that could tell many stories.

"Give me your lovely hand, sweet Jane." Hank's childlike eyes were gleaming. The Faz observed that he was touching Jane's paw as if it were a delicate bird that may fly away any moment.

He's lost in lust, Rino was thinking. *This simple Jane is to become the new queen, and King Henry is mad for her.*

Will Summers, disliked by the Seymour brothers, wondered how he would fare from the deal of royal politics and a king's heart, and still keep his dignity intact.

The small group sat under a red and cream fringed canopy. Fragrant flowers surrounded their large table. A fountain sprayed blue water, and soft music played. This charming place was for the king's private occasions.

Hank was larger than life, having become more animated in the absence of Anna-Magillika, and so totally attentive to his new lady. He responded to Cramner with a flick of his right wrist, displaying his ruby and emerald rings, glinting in the fading light.

Cramner bent low, before his dismissal, to hear the

king's whisper.

"No talk of the witch today, man. I celebrate here with my true love." Hank's eyes fluttered like a besotted dove. He stared fondly at Jane, thinking her so chaste.

Plain Jane, Cramner thought, but was quiet; always tactful and reserved. He whispered to the king. "My Lord, the French sword arrives by nightfall."

"My darling." Hank towered over Jane. "I give you this gift as a symbol of my affection." He held out his large hand and dropped a neckpiece the size of a small plate into Jane's free hand. Jane giggled. Will Summers coughed. The piece of jewellery which had once belonged to Spanish Kate, the good queen, bore lilies and Tudor roses entwined with hearts and cherubs. A skilled artisan had redesigned the 'K' for Katherine to a 'J' for Jane.

This is how he treats his wives. What would be Jane Seymour's fate? Rino shuddered, seeing the future.

Hank sat in an elegant chair with Jane on his knee. Now free from scandal, with an adoring woman who would finally give him sons. All seemed well.

***

It wasn't so bad in the Tower. Anna-Magillika had availed herself to her surroundings. But she didn't like being held there, *alone to redeem*, as had been stated at her Inquiry. She used her expert skills in bribery, manipulation, and magic to get some creature comforts for her room. Helix had come and was relishing in a game of rat-catching. The cat wisely kept well out of Magillika's way as she was extremely volatile. Her small cauldron was ready for use, but her head was in such a fuddle that she was unlikely to think of how to use it.

She had been told that, on the morrow, she would be executed.

Magillika knew that it would be impossible for her to die, being the witch she was. So, escape was not in her plan. She would continue in this role as the queen to the end.

Saras, the Great Fae was also working behind the scenes with her fine magic, assisting Anna with the new order, so the dark witch needed to be distracted by this event. King Henry had sent for a silver sword from France, so as not to upset her swan-like neck in the event. Was Hank feeling guilty? Queen Anna had a long beautiful neck, and the sword would be far better than an axe.

"Small mercy," Magillika grumbled at Helix,

tripping over his long tail stretching like a lazy snake across the floor.

A kindly priest had been allowed to enter the room. "Lady Anna. Do you wish to confess?" She no longer held the title of Queen of England.

"No! Go away!" Magillika was seething. *How dare these religious bigots think I have anything to tell them.* She spoke venomously, "I cannot die, you eejit. My bloodline lasts forever."

"My lady, you are under false illusion. Do this confession. Please," he begged. "For your soul." The priest was bold and unwavering.

Magillika looked hard at the man, staring deep into his eyes. For a fleeting moment, he got the full energy of her evil motives—no longer seeing a queen about to die before him, but a hellish witch. He fainted. Then, whilst having a heart attack, he died on the spot.

"Win some, lose some," Magillika remarked coldly to Helix as she sat down to contemplate the depleting moon.

***

Some days later, Rino and the Faz returned back in time to 2020, home to the much-missed Blue Castle.

"What's for lunch, Rino?" The Faz stepped back

from his larger telescope where he had been watching the scenes of Queen Anna-Magillika's end.

A sad, ugly scene indeed, to the human eye, but his sight gave him an alternative perception. *All part of the bigger picture.*

"How is King Henry?" Rino was keen to know news of the old kingdom. He piled baked savoury rolls onto his plate, eyeing the sauces, salads and fruits. It seemed that they hadn't eaten for days. Food was a most important requirement for Rino. Food meant sustenance, love.

The Faz, at the same time, could forget to eat and go for days on just nuts and bottles of fizzy drink. He chuckled. "King Hank is marrying his third wife, Jane Seymour. He just can't help himself! He's driven to get a son to keep the Tudor line going," he said, thoughtfully. "This king is but a pawn in a system."

"The Lady Anna is most well! She does great work giving support through the realm, getting all these new books printed for the people to read—those who can—and taking up the new order. No one recognises her now. But chaos is coming. Bloody Mary, Henry's first daughter, will rule before Elizabeth comes to the throne. A lot of blood will flow, and witches will burn."

He sat down to choose his meal. "Thank you, Rino. Always considerate."

Rino didn't need to ask of the Great Fae Saras. Both knew she would be well, in and out of Nardis, preparing for what next, letting down her hair, casting her magic and spreading her laughter.

"What of Magillika? Is she gone then?" Rino was hopeful. He was scared of the witch and her offhand spells.

"No." The Faz kept on eating and drinking for several minutes. "A witch like Magillika cannot die by the sword. True, she lost her head—those who saw were under the impression it was the true Queen Anna—but Magillika takes birth again with more evil intent. Give it five Earth years until the child grows. She will be back."

***

So, the two old monks enjoyed their lunch, philosophically anticipating their further dealings with Magillika—the dark witch who would be queen—and the Great Fae Saras, who were, in reality, both sides of the same coin.

D.J. ELTON is a speculative fiction writer of short stories and micro-fiction who lives in Melbourne. Her themes include historical fantasy, robots and horror with humour. She has work published in several Black Hare Press anthologies, Eleanor Merry Publishing, and a novella, The Merlin Girl. When not playing with a pen, she loves to get out to the country, meditates often, and works in healthcare.

Bibliography
ANGELS, Black Hare Press, 2019
APOCALYPSE, Black Hare Press, 2019
BEYOND, Black Hare Press, 2019
DARK VALENTINE, Eleanor Merry Publishing, 2020
DARK X-MAS, Eleanor Merry Publishing, 2019
HATE, Black Hare Press, 2020
LOVE, Black Hare Press, 2020
LUST, Black Hare Press, 2020
PRIDE, Black Hare Press, 2020
THE MERLIN GIRL, Balboa Press, 2018
TWENTY TWENTY, Black Hare Press, 2020
UNRAVEL, Black Hare Press, 2019

Connect
Website: djeltonwrites.wordpress.com
Amazon: www.amazon.co.uk/-/e/B07YK9TJ5F
Twitter: @DJEltonwrites
Facebook: djeltonwrites

THE CHALICE OF ETHELRED

By Stephen Herczeg

At the desperate height of the battle of Stalingrad, an idealistic Russian bomber pilot finds herself at the mercy of a force far older and darker than war. Can she outwit the legendary Baba Yaga and stave off inevitable defeat at the same time?

King Edmund sat patiently listening to the troubles of another farmer from an outer-lying region of Midtonia. He sat bolt upright, his neck muscles tensed to ensure his head didn't droop forward and signify to the vassal that he wasn't paying attention.

Pedric, Edmund's chief advisor, stood nearby

389

keeping his gaze on both Edmund and the farmer. Every time he noticed the king's eyelids droop, he stamped the ceremonial mace he held. The sound of it striking the stone floor reverberated around the audience chamber. As he asked for the last statement to be repeated, the king would snap back to full awareness to concentrate on the words of the man before him.

Finally, the farmer finished his request and dropped to one knee. Edmund turned and called Pedric to him.

"What say you, Pedric?" he whispered in his advisor's ear.

"Farmer. A bit of a dry winter. Crops are down. Sheep aren't breeding. I suggest a simple tax reduction strategy," he said.

"Good, good, thank you," said the king. He turned to the kneeling man and bid him to stand. "My dear man, your plight is worthy, and I sympathise with you. Your tax payment for this year will be deferred until next season when you shall be back on your feet and flush with funds," he said.

The man's eyes lit up. He bowed and said, "Oh, thank you, your highness, thank you."

"Very good," said Edmund, waving a hand at Pedric. "My chamberlain will escort you to the cofferer to take note of my request. Good luck to you and yours for the coming season."

Pedric motioned for the man to join him. They left the king alone in the chamber.

The king visibly deflated on his throne, his body slumped and threatened to pour out of the great chair.

Pedric returned moments later. A small smile crossed his lips as he noticed his king's demeanour. From outside, various grumbles and murmurs wafted into the chamber, followed by the sound of wooden chairs dragged across stone and footsteps leading away.

"I have called a halt to the audiences for today."

Edmund gazed at his Chamberlain and nodded. "Wonderful," he said. "Listening to these trivial problems simply wears me down. I'm afraid I grow wearier each day."

"I'm wondering if your fatigue is not somehow linked to the dramas that have afflicted our vassals and farmers of late," Pedric said, his voice thick with sympathy.

"Yes, as the legends say, the king is one with the land and the land is one with the king. When I am healthy the land thrives, when not, it suffers," he said. "And of late, it suffers from my weariness and in turn I suffer. An endless cycle may begin that will destroy the land and me with it."

"Sire, I have studied the histories of the land and there are stories of an ancient artefact that could relieve your pain," he said.

The king brightened. "Say more, my friend, say more."

"According to our history, four hundred summers ago Ethelred the Brave, acquired a goblet that could restore life and vitality to the drinker. It became known as the Chalice of Ethelred and gave him life for a further one hundred summers."

"And where is the chalice now?"

Pedric paused for a moment, a slightly dour look crossing his face.

"Ah, now that is where the problem lies. The great wyrm Galeru attacked the former Northern capital of Bengraman and laid waste to all, including Ethelred. The chalice was lost and is presumed with the dragon in its lair in the Gellilydarn mountains."

The king visibly slumped.

"Then all is lost."

"Perhaps not."

"How shall we retrieve this prize from within the dragon's domain?"

"We have a hero," said Pedric.

***

Several days later, the king stood on the audience chamber's balcony and stared out at the countryside. The trees were leafless, the grass brown. It was early autumn, but an iciness permeated the air and chilled him to the bone. He stepped inside, seeking the warmth of the chamber.

Winter has come far too early. The land bleeds because of me.

The chamber doors were thrown wide open, and a large shadowy figure stood within the arched doorway. Edmund glanced at the stature of the outlined shaped and smiled.

He has come.

He turned and hobbled to the throne, ready to face his visitor.

Pedric appeared next to the man and spoke quietly to him. The figure nodded, then followed the chamberlain as he strode towards the king.

"Your Majesty, I present Sir Tharion of Gunderland," he said.

Tharion knelt before the throne and said, "Your majesty."

"I know well of Sir Tharion," Edmund said. "Arise Sir, you have no need to bow before me, your deeds are famous, your reputation precedes you."

The knight rose.

"Your Majesty, I received word that you seek my assistance. What is your will?"

The king took in Tharion's entire appearance. He stood a good head and shoulders above Pedric. His chest was broad and muscular, his arms bulged as if filled with walnuts. His blonde hair flowed down his shoulders. There was no mistaking this powerful man just by his mere presence in the room.

"My good knight. I am afflicted with illness and old age. By the laws of the land, my health and the health of my country are one. I cannot reverse my age, but there is a legendary artefact that may relieve my pain. I need you to retrieve it for me."

"Just tell me what and where and I will return successfully forthwith," Tharion said.

"Do you know of the land of Gellilydarn?" asked Pedric.

"Gellilydarn? The old wives tell of a dragon that inhabits those mountains," he said. "Is that you quest? That I must face and defeat this dragon?"

"I only need one part of the dragon's horde. You may not even need to kill the beast," said the king.

Tharion smiled. "What would be the point then?"

"Good. We have chosen well," said Edmund. A sudden series of wracking coughs erupted, leaving him exhausted when finished.

With a whispered, croaking voice, Edmund said, "Only one other thing, good knight. You must pledge fealty to the kingdom. The artefact is of incredible importance and priceless. I know you owe us nothing, but I must insist."

Without hesitation, Tharion unsheathed his sword and dropped to one knee. He held the sword out before him.

"I pledge my allegiance to the Kingdom of Midtonia. I will do as she asks and promise to return successful."

The king smiled then grimaced as a bolt of pain shot across his chest. He closed his eyes and breathed slowly to ease it.

Pedric took the opportunity and led Tharion away.

"I will tell you all you need to know."

The king managed to wave them away with a final croaked, "Good luck, Sir Knight," before they left the chamber.

***

Pedric led Tharion deep into the castle basement. They came to a solid wooden door, and Pedric knocked several times. The door swung open with a creak, and a raspy voice echoed out from the smoky interior.

"Come in, Chamberlain and Hero."

They both ducked to avoid the low lintel of the doorway and found themselves in a large smoke-filled room. Straw, parchment and books littered the stone floor. A figure dressed in rags, stood stooped over a table where several pots of various coloured liquids bubbled away.

"Be with you momentarily," it said. "If I don't mix this gently, we'll all be blown to pieces."

The figure raised a beaker with a pair of tongs and slowly poured it into a round receptacle. Once finished, it pushed a cork bung into the hole and sighed.

The hooded person finally turned, and Tharion beheld the oldest man he had ever seen. A pair of watery grey eyes stared at him, nestled amongst wrinkles and folds of skin that seemed to slough off the bones beneath.

"Kaith, this is Sir Tharion. The king has tasked him with the retrieval," said Pedric.

The ancient mage smiled, showing a severe lack of teeth. He cackled and shuffled across to another workbench, on which lay a large antique volume opened to a page with an ornate drawing of a golden goblet.

Kaith motioned for them to join him and pointed at the drawing.

"That is your quest, my good knight. The Chalice of Ethelred. Its magics can prolong life and cure all ills," Kaith said.

Tharion's eyes lit up. Even in the simple drawing, the beauty of the bejewelled goblet would have bewitched any mortal man or woman, but given its purported magical abilities, it was priceless.

"You'll also need this," Kaith gave Tharion a piece of folded paper. He found a copy of the original drawing with a roughly drawn out map on the back, showing the supposed location of the dragon's lair.

The old mage stroked his chin as he looked at Tharion's sword. A small smile came to his lips. "You won't be doing much damage with that, I'll tell ya."

"This is the mighty sword Altherion, known throughout the land," said Tharion, a hint of offence on his breath.

"Yeah, good for it, but steel and iron ain't gonna hurt a full-grown dragon, now is it?"

Tharion looked confused.

The mage smiled and walked across to a large safe. He shuffled back and handed a small cloth-wrapped bundle to Tharion.

Within was a dagger in a leather scabbard. Tharion removed the knife, flooding the room with brilliant, white light.

"The dagger of Escardarus," said Kaith. "Made from pure diamond that has captured the rays of the sun. Sharpest blade known to man. Now put it away before you blind me."

Tharion sheathed the dagger, sending the room back to semi-darkness.

The mage moved up next to Tharion and put a finger to his throat. "Now, the only place ya can kill a dragon is the neck. You'll need to be real quiet and creep up on the sleeping beast. Slip the blade between the scales under its chin and when you've found a gap, tease it in further until you can push it all the way in and up into its brain."

He stepped back and clicked his fingers.

"Dead in a second."

"What if there's no gap?"

"The blade's sharp, you'll find a gap," Kaith said.

Pedric butted in to ease Tharion's suspicions. "Do you have any other magical weapons that our brave knight might use on this quest?"

Kaith's eyes lit up at the suggestion, he moved across to his workbench. "Oh, yes, I've been hoping someone would be able to test, er I mean, use these."

He brought back a leather satchel and pulled out several small coloured spherical objects. He held out a blue one to show Tharion.

"These are my own invention," he said, pointing to a small knob on top, "Push this all the way in until it cracks, then wait two seconds and throw it. The blue ones will freeze anything near them, the red ones will blow it apart. They aren't powerful enough to hurt the dragon's skin, but at least they might stop anything else you come across."

Kaith put the balls back in the satchel and handed it to Tharion.

"Now, whatever you do, don't drop the bag. The spheres aren't very tough, and they might all go off at once," he said.

Tharion's eyes lit up in horror.

The old mage cackled. "Ah, you'll be right. I trust ya."

Even Pedric didn't seem reassured.

***

Tharion, with his page Daniel, set out on their three-hundred-league journey. Across the Kingdom of Midtonia at every inn and homely house, they were welcomed with open arms. Treated to all the food and drink they could wish for, and in Tharion's case, to more from the young ladies of the towns. Legend has it that months later, many a strong babe was born in those towns, much to the surprise of the locals.

As they crossed the borderlands of Midtonia the king's plight became more apparent. Lush green lands gave way to dry, dusty plains where nothing grew. Farmsteads stood empty, as the vassals of that area took heed and withdrew into the heart of the country to seek more profitable lands.

As they trotted on, Daniel turned to Tharion and remarked, "This land dies as the king dies. Does that mean if we are not successful then the whole country may die as well?"

Tharion nodded. "Aye, Pedric took me into his confidence. The king's life hangs by a thread. The best healers in the land have been brought before him, none can temper the flow of the life force that leaves him like a torrent. Magic is his only hope now. The magic that the chalice possesses."

"Then we must do everything in our power to gain the chalice. Even if I have to lay down my life, I will do it," said the young page.

Tharion chuckled at Daniel's comments. "I hope it will not come to that," he said. Inwardly, a knot of concern grew, not just over his young protégé's fate, but also his own.

***

Three weeks after departing, the intrepid pair found themselves high in the mountains of Gellilydarn. Daniel scrounged the barren hills for wood and built a fire by which they both warmed their bones. They ate a meagre meal of bread and dried meat, donated by a farmer and his wife almost a week previously.

Tharion chewed unconsciously on a thick piece of jerky, trying to ignore the salty taste, and studied the map that Kaith had given to him.

"The dragon's lair should be somewhere around here," he said.

Intrigued, Daniel leant over and studied the map held in his master's hand. It showed the mountain range, with a rough guide of fifty leagues from the border of Midtonia. Since entering the mountains, their progress had stalled to barely ten leagues a day. Their last habitable stop had been forty leagues inside the border which put them just about at the lair's entrance.

"It should be somewhere nearby," he said.

"Yes," said Tharion. "In the morning we will need to search for the entrance. Kaith told me we could find it simply from the sulphurous smell of the dragon's breath."

"Breath or something else?" said Daniel, an immature smirk on his face.

Tharion noticed and smiled himself.

"Yes, and probably from that," he said, getting to his feet. He walked over to his horse and retrieved a small goatskin from the saddlebag. He returned and offered it to Daniel.

"A small toast to our success so far."

Daniel's eyes widened. He grabbed the skin with glee and quickly sprayed wine into his mouth.

"Woah, steady on there. I need you fit and able in the morning, not hungover for the first time in your life," said Tharion, taking the skin back and slaking his own thirst.

"Sorry, you've just never shared with me before," Daniel said.

"Till now I considered you too young, but I believe this adventure will be the making of you," he said.

Tharion grew tense as the sound of rocks slipping down a steep slope nearby filtered through. He dropped the goat skin and pulled his sword free.

Daniel stood and said, "What is it?"

Tharion threw up a hand to quieten his page. He listened intently.

He turned and slashed at the air as a growl and flash of brown greeted him. The sword rang true and a brown fur covered body fell into the flames, sending sparks and coals across the ground.

"Goblin," Daniel cried and quickly drew his own sword.

More growls rang out from the darkness. A surge of small bodies leapt into the light, several attacked Tharion, more headed towards Daniel.

Tharion's sword flashed in the dying light of the fire. The blade's bright orange sheen quickly mottled with the black blood of the defeated goblins, their bodies littered the ground at the hero's feet.

Nearby, Daniel held his own battle. His smaller sword, swinging through the darkness, split many a goblin asunder, but he was no match in strength. The goblins ganged up, forcing him backwards; their claws nicked his skin and drew blood; their foul, fetid breath cloyed his nostrils and lungs.

He lunged at a body, spearing it between the ribs and stopping its attack. Two more replaced it and slashed at his face. Rivulets opened on his cheeks and forehead, clouding his sight and diverting his attention. He swung madly, luckily slicing across the throat of one, sending up gouts of black blood as it crashed to the ground.

Two more joined forces and rushed him. He brought up his sword just in time to counter their claws and stepped back. His foot found nothing but air. Gravity dragged him down.

Tharion turned as the terrified shriek rang out across their camp. His last sight of Daniel was the young page's head disappearing over the edge of the cliff. His scream lasted for mere seconds before a sickening thud replaced it.

"Daniel," he yelled.

His fury exploded. He sliced through the remaining goblins with a sudden strength fashioned from vengeance. The goblins peering over the edge of the abyss were rent apart with one blow from Tharion's great sword. Their bodies followed Daniel, sending up lighter sounds as they smacked into the rocks below.

***

Tharion picked his way carefully down the sheer cliff face. If there was any chance that Daniel could be saved, he would fight tooth and nail to achieve it.

The cliff levelled out to a small platform, barely ten yards across. There lying in a pool of his own blood and surrounded by the torn bodies of his assailants, lay the young squire. Tharion quickly rushed to his side and knelt.

"Daniel," he said, caressing his brow.

The young boy stirred.

"Sire, the goblins, behind you," he said in a dazed

voice, his eyes flickering slightly behind their lids. "I can't feel my legs or arms," he said, his voice thin.

Tharion's face grew more concerned.

I have seen this before. His neck or back, broken perhaps.

"It is the cold, you're numb. Rest here. I will make you comfortable," the hero said, dashing back up the cliff face.

He returned moments later with bedding and tinder to make a fire. He placed a blanket over Daniel and carefully lifted his head upon a small pillow. When the heat of a small fire bathed Daniel with its glow, he knelt down again and spoke quietly to the boy until the sun broke over the nearby mountains.

I'll never be able to move him from this place without damaging him further. The chalice is his only hope.

"Daniel." The boy stirred, and his eyes flickered open to gaze on Tharion.

"My lord?"

"Daniel, you've damaged your back. I don't want to move you in case I hurt you even more. I need to bring the chalice to you. Its healing power is all the hope we have."

The boy's eyes showed agreement and understanding. He tried to nod, but even that movement was denied him.

Tharion built the fire up further. He knelt and gave the boy a drink from his water bottle before saying goodbye.

"I'm going now. You need to sleep and recover. I shan't be long; the dragon's lair must be nearby. I will retrieve the chalice and be back before sundown. That I promise," he said.

The boy simply closed his eyes and drifted off.

***

The day broke bright and clear without a hint of breeze. Tharion marked their camping spot and built a small cairn to show the way down to Daniel's resting place. Packing his essentials, he mounted his steed and trotted off into the mountains.

Within an hour he spied a pillar of grey smoke drifting straight up. He climbed a nearby hill to gain a better look.

The line of smoke drifted out of a wide-open cave, nestled in a small valley not far away. The entrance shone with a glass-like radiance, as if the living rock had been melted into slag then solidified. The putrid smell of sulphur hung in the air.

This is it.

Scattered around the area were dozens of skeletons. Most with their skulls speared onto long thin pikes. The horrid display was intended as a warning to any erstwhile adventurers such as he.

This wasn't the dragon. The goblins set this as a warning.

Paying no heed, he drew his sword and stepped inside.

The smell was overwhelming. A mix of sulphur, decay and manure adhered to his nostrils. The atmosphere was dense and thick with smoke. Several times he had to resist the temptation to sneeze. He maintained hope that he still had surprise on his side.

Tharion followed the tunnel as it gently sloped down into the bowels of the mountain. After several hundred yards, the passage widened out and presented Tharion with a glimpse of the extent of the dragon's lair.

The legends of dragons told of their hunger and greed for gold, silver, jewels, any type of treasure. They amassed as much as physically possible during their lifetimes, with no care to the actual value. Simple accumulation; their goal and desire, the protection of their horde was legendary.

Even the legends hadn't prepared Tharion for what lay before him. Galeru's lair stretched for hundreds of yards in each direction. The ceiling was almost lost to sight. The cavern took up the entire interior of the massive mountain above. Every section of vacant ground was covered with treasure. Piles of it. Coins. Goblets. Plates. Swords. Shields. Armour.

Light filtered in from above. Creating a dazzling display in what should have been a darkened pit. The treasure gleamed and reflected beams of brightness across the cave.

Suddenly, in the middle of the cavern, a shower of coins rained down from the top of a large mound. Tharion peered across.

The dragon.

It slumbered beneath a massive pile of treasure.

He pulled the dagger from its sheath and gently stepped onto the golden floor. The ground shifted beneath his feet, threatening to topple him at any moment, but he picked his way through the piles of gold and approached the sleeping drake.

The beast was huge and bloated, possibly from lack of activity which boded well for Tharion. Its skin consisted of pearlescent scales that reflected the surrounding golden treasure.

Tharion circled the creature and laid eyes on the great head. It slept behind closed eyelids and its chest rose and fell in a long, slow rhythm.

Tharion sheathed his sword, instead holding the small dagger in his favoured right hand, and he slowly made his way towards the beast's neck.

As luck would have it, the head rested at such an angle as to reveal the delicate area beneath the chin Kaith had mentioned. Tharion stepped through the gap between the creature's front legs and knelt down, ready to deliver the killing blow.

He chose a spot and pressed the tip of the diamond blade between two scales. Placing both hands on the hilt of the dagger he pushed with all his might.

Nothing. The blade stubbornly refused to pierce the dragon's skin. He moved it to another spot and repeated the action. Trying several more times, his heartbeat raced in response to each successive failure.

Suddenly, a deep booming voice growled out of the stillness of the cavern.

"Oi, can you stop that? It tickles and it's quite annoying."

Tharion's eyes grew wide in fear. An emotion he rarely felt. He stepped back quickly, switching the little dagger to his left hand and unsheathing his sword.

The dragon's eyelid fluttered and gently opened revealing a huge yellow iris that slowly adjusting to the light. The creature picked his head up, showering the floor with a cascade of gold coins and treasure. He opened his cavernous mouth wide and yawned away the stupor. Finally, turning to face Tharion, he blinked a few more times while his eyes grew accustomed to the light and focused on the hero.

"And who the hell would you be?"

"I am Sir Tharion of Gunderland, also known as Tharion the strong."

The dragon smacked his lips several times and glanced around the chamber for a moment before continuing.

"Well good for you, it's always nice to have titles. Now how the hell'd you get in here? Nobody's managed to get in here for centuries. What were those useless goblins doing? Sleeping, I guess."

He cocked an eyebrow at the knight.

"You didn't kill them, did you?"

A sly grin came to the dragon's lips.

"Yeah, you've got spots of black blood on ya. Bugger, they took years to train. Can't get good help all the way out here. Nobody wants to live in the mountains, and I can't stay alert all the time. Goblins is all I could find."

The dragon looked off into the distance for a moment.

"Might have to try orcs next time. They've always had the added quality of greed. I can tempt them with gold, I suppose."

The dragon conversed with himself rather than Tharion. The knight jumped when the great head swung back to face him.

"Now, back to you, what are you here for?"

"I have been sent on a quest by King Edmund the benevolent, ruler of Great Cornadia and all of Midtonia," Tharion said, his hand tightening on his sword.

The dragon smiled, an unnatural sight in Tharion's mind.

"My you humans don't half give yourselves impressive titles do you?"

He shuffled around on the great pile of treasure, sending a cascading fall of gold in every direction. He crossed his arms in front of him and placed his head down, staring directly at Tharion and waited a moment.

"So, this king, what was it…Benny the Ball? Sent you here? For?"

The dragon let the last word string out for a while.

Tharion maintained a stoic stance and said, "It's Edmund the Benevolent. I was sent to find a relic of magical properties to alleviate the king's sickness."

"Oh, yes? Can't remember any magical relics but do go on."

"It is called the Chalice of Ethelred the brave."

The dragon lifted his head and let out a loud raucous laugh.

"Ethelred the brave? Ethelred the brave? That's the best one yet."

He laughed long and hard before unconsciously snorting and sending a scouring surge of flame towards the roof of the cavern.

"Oh, excuse me, I can't control myself sometimes."

A wide grin remained on his face as he dropped his head back and glared at Tharion.

"Ethelred the Brave." He chuckled. "The only Ethelred I know was a king in that cesspool of a country called…now let me think…ah yeah, Benjamin."

"Bengraman," corrected Tharion.

"What?"

"It was called Bengraman."

"Who gives a rat's? If it's the same king, there was nothing brave about him. He soiled his armour when he saw me. Tried to hide behind his knights, then when I'd killed them, his queen."

The dragon's eyes drifted towards the ceiling, as if in ecstasy as he remembered the event.

"I ate her, then faced off against him. By the time he'd finished being a complete and utter coward, I didn't want to be near him, so I just vaporised him.

Smelly bugger."

He chuckled again, venting small puffs of smoke from his nostrils.

"Brave. Not!"

The dragon focused back on Tharion.

"So, this king sent you to find something magical that used to belong to the not so brave Ethelred? What was it? A goblet?"

"Chalice?"

"What'd it look like?"

"Gold."

"Not much of that round here," the dragon chuckled.

"About one cubit high. Eight-sided base. Four large rubies around the top."

The dragon's eyes lit up.

"Yeah. I know that thing."

Suddenly, the dragon whirled around, Tharion ducked to avoid the great slashing tail. Galeru scrambled off into the depths of the cavern, mumbling and chuckling to himself. Left alone, Tharion searched for escape, unsure how to proceed now that his element of surprise had vaporised and his only attack useless.

He eyed the exit and took one step towards it then stopped still. A clatter of treasure echoed from the bowels of the cavern growing louder as the dragon raced back towards him. He held a gold chalice in his hand, making it look like a child's toy. Galeru stopped with a skid, sending a shower of coins towards Tharion, who held up his arm to protect himself.

"Oooh, sorry about that, I get excited sometimes." He opened his hand and showed the chalice to Tharion. "Is this it?"

The hero peered at the golden cup. He reached into a pocket and pulled out Kaith's parchment. The rough drawing mirrored the object in Galeru's hand.

He nodded, "Yes."

"Oh, well, at least your journey wasn't in vain. They sent you to the right place."

"I can have it?" asked Tharion, a slight hint of elation growing in his mind.

This might be easier than I first thought.

"What you got to trade?"

"I have this," answered Tharion pulling out the diamond dagger and holding it up to the light. It glowed with an inner fire as the diamond absorbed the sunlight and cast it back through a thousand facets.

"Ooh, now that's pretty."

"Do we have a deal?"

The dragon's eyes never left the blade. Finally, after several moments a grin crossed his lips.

"Yeah, nuh," he said.

"What?" said Tharion, suddenly fearful.

"I don't need to make deals. I'm a dragon. I want it all. I mean, I just take what I want, when I want. Just cause you've got some pretty knife, doesn't mean I'm gonna cut a deal, okay. I've got my reputation to uphold. If I make some deal with you, you'll go home to wherever it is you came from, give the chalice to Eddie-baby, and tell everybody. Next thing I know, I got heroes knocking at my door and trying to bargain with me, or worse, steal my stuff."

The dragon flicked the chalice to one side. It bounced end over end and disappeared behind a huge mound of treasure. Tharion watched and memorised the direction.

"Now, let's get back to the real business. You came into my lair. Tried to kill me with that little pig-sticker and steal my stuff. That sort of thing has consequences, doesn't it? I wouldn't be a dragon if I didn't exact some sort of punishment on you, now would I."

Tharion tensed.

The dragon didn't even wait for an answer. Talking had finished. He spun, quicker than Tharion believed possible, and lashed out with his great barbed tail.

Tharion unsheathed his sword and brought it up in

front as the tail connected. He flew several yards into the air and crashed down on a pile of coins, spraying gold all around. Thankfully, the loose mound cushioned his landing. He slid to the bottom of the pile and stayed still.

"Now, I just want to re-iterate, this is nothing personal, okay? I've got appearances to keep up, and besides I'll need a bit of time to recruit another gang of gatekeepers, since you despatched my last set."

Tharion rolled over on his stomach. The sharp edges of coins, necklaces and plates dug into his bare skin. He ignored the discomfort and listened for the approaching dragon.

A sudden shower of coins rained down on him. He looked up into the dragon's grinning face.

"Hello sunshine, you ready to die?"

Tharion tensed, grasped the dagger tightly in one hand and his sword in the other. In one swift move, he stood and vaulted up the side of the treasure mound. At the top he leapt towards the dragon, swinging his sword around in a wide arc and bringing the dagger upwards in the same movement.

Tharion was strong. Tharion was quick, but Galeru was quicker. The dragon lashed out with his hand and caught Tharion in mid-air, sending him crashing into the base of another pile of gold.

"Nice try mate, really nice try. The bards would say valiant effort, but they're only going to be singing your eulogy, I'm afraid."

Tharion picked himself up and regained his feet. Coins and gold pieces dropped to the floor as they became dislodged from his skin. He pointed his sword at the dragon and glared into his face.

"Come on, Dragon. Let's finish this."

"Oh, you are a brave bugger, aren't ya. Foolish, but brave."

The dragon clambered across the floor, knocking piles of treasure out of the way. Tharion drew his sword back, ready to slash at the beast's face.

Galeru planted his feet, slipping forward as he came to a stop.

"No, I don't think so."

The great beast drew breath, pursed his lips and quickly blew a finger of fire towards Tharion's sword hand. Tharion tried to drag it away but was too slow. The flame enveloped sword and hand, holding both within the inferno.

Tharion screamed. The sword turned white and disappeared, running down to encase his hand in molten steel slag.

Galeru stopped the tongue of fire and observed the knight.

Tharion let go of the dagger and grabbed his right wrist. The stench of burnt flesh stung his nostrils, bringing tears to his eyes on top of those from the intense pain.

He dropped to his knees.

It's over. No sword hand. I'm nothing now, but useless.

"I reckon I know what you're thinking. Oh, woe is me, I'm a warrior without a sword hand. Yeah. Yeah. I can sympathise with you there, mate, but don't worry nobody else is gonna know."

Tharion peered up at the wide grin on the dragon's face. Galeru knew he had won. It was only a matter of time. Tharion peered at the cooling metal encasing his claim to fame. His shoulders slumped and his other hand dropped away and brushed against the leather purse hanging by his side.

His eyes grew wide.

Kaith's spheres.

He slowly slipped his hand under the flap and eased out one of the spheres. It felt cool. He sighed in relief.

Fire isn't going to stop the beast. Ice may work.

"Now, if you don't mind, I've got a lot to do. You've left quite a mess, and of course, once I've finished with you, I'll have to clean up the blood."

Tharion heard the dragon creep closer.

"Now just hold still. This is gonna hurt you a lot more than me," he chuckled, opening his mouth wide. Long fangs slid forward, ready to spear Tharion before consuming him whole. As the dragon prepared to attack, Tharion pressed the small bump on top of the orb. He counted to two, then threw the sphere into the gaping maw of the dragon. He dived sideways, out of the way.

The effect was immediate and incredible.

The small blue orb exploded inside the dragon's mouth. Galeru's entire head turned white as it froze with a permanently surprised look.

Tharion simply stared for a moment until a broad smile crossed his face.

"Well, that shut you up."

He pulled a red globe from the bag, eeighed it in his hand, then pressed the bump on top. He waited for a count of two, then lobbed it into the wide-open mouth of the frozen dragon before diving behind a treasure pile. A moment later, a catastrophic explosion rocked the cavern, with chunks of frozen and raw dragon meat peppering the area around him.

Finally, Tharion stood and surveyed the result.

The great beast's body remained where it stood moments before. The long neck finished in a raw and bloody mess of gristle, bone and jelly. The smirking grin of the dragon permanently erased by Kaith's invention.

"I think these orbs work then."

***

Hampered by his damaged hand, Tharion picked his way down the rocky slope. His only goal was to save Daniel. The lack of feeling in his hand, told him life would never be the same. He was no longer a warrior. All he could do was help his page and take the chalice to the king.

He finally reached the small cliff and spied Daniel. The fire was just ashes. The area cold in the fading light. He moved quickly to the boy's side and knelt down.

His hopes faded.

Daniel was a sickly shade of grey that Tharion had seen many times before; mostly as the sun rose over the bodies on the many battlefields he'd had the misfortune to tread.

He felt the boy's forehead.

Cold. I'm too late.

He dropped his head and shed a tear for the boy.

In his mind's eye he saw the face of Daniel's

father, both proud that his son would be the squire to a knight, but showing the fear and worry that such a thought attracted.

Tharion promised to protect the boy and over time had grown to see the boy almost like his own son.

He looked at the boy's innocent face.

"I'm sorry I couldn't shield you. I'm sorry I couldn't return quickly enough to revive you," he said, falling silent for a moment before venting his anger in one final blast aimed at himself rather than the boy, "I'm sorry I took you on this stupid quest in the first place."

Tharion looked up the steep grade, then at his injured hand and back at the poor boy's body.

"I can't carry you," he said to the corpse, "All I can do is give you a decent burial and send someone to retrieve you."

He built the fire up to give him enough light to work by, then found a flat area and using branches, rocks and the metallic blob of his right hand, dug a small shallow trench in the hard, rocky ground. He laid Daniel's blanket in the depression then as gently and respectfully as he could, moved his squire into the shallow grave.

He placed another blanket over the body and carefully placed stones and rocks over him in a hope that any predators would be deterred and leave the boy's corpse alone until it could be brought back to Gunderland. At the boy's head, he built a small cairn of stones. Kneeling before the grave, he gave a silent prayer to protect the boy in the afterlife. Exhausted by the day's events, Tharion lay on the ground near the fire and fell into a fitful sleep.

***

Dawn broke across the blasted rocks of the Gellilydarn mountains, the light causing Tharion's eyes to flicker open. As he sat up, his gaze fell on the pile of stones covering the body of his page. Dropping them, he saw the metal encased stump that was once the greatest sword hand across all the lands.

It wasn't a dream.

He looked up the steep cliff and sighed. Packing away his bedding and weapons, as best he could one-handed, he shouldered his load, took one last look at Daniel's resting place and set off up the mountain.

It took him several days to reach the first small village on the edge of Midtonia, the place they had spent their last night in civilisation.

Tharion sought out the local smith. He needed to know the condition of his hand, even though he knew a lost cause when he saw one.

Marlon, the blacksmith, remembered when Tharion had passed through. He took an instant interest in the fabled sword Altherion and was overjoyed when Tharion let him hold it. His shoulders slumped as he looked at the remains of the sword now covering Tharion's right hand.

"I can gets it off for ya, but I thinks it's gonna hurt like buggery," he said.

"I can't feel anything anymore, so it doesn't really matter."

"Brace yourself then." The blacksmith took a hot iron and heated the edge of the metal. The smell of burning flesh scoured both their nostrils. Marlon pulled away, but Tharion urged him on.

The smith placed small tongs on either side of the spot and peeled the metal back. The sight below almost brought Marlon to vomiting. A thick pool of mucus and pus covered the blackened skin. Tharion willed himself to hold fast. The pain sapped his strength, and his stomach rolled and threatened to void itself at any moment.

"Finish it."

Marlon peeled the metal away, revealing the whole of Tharion's palm. The knight twisted his hand from side to side, the skin sloughing off and sticking to its metal shroud.

"Hold it down," he told Marlon, who clamped the top part of the metal with a larger set of tongs.

Tharion grit his teeth and pulled with all his might. The pain intensified, but finally his hand released its hold and slid free of its metal cage.

It was a mess. Tharion's resolve finally caved in. He turned aside and ejected the entire contents of his stomach across the dirt floor. Once finished, he apologised to Marlon and wiped his mouth with the back of his left sleeve.

Both of them stared at the charred, blackened claw. The flesh gone leaving bare bones covered with scraps of blackened skin. Marlon coughed and held a kerchief to his mouth.

Tharion took a deep breath and let it out slowly. His worst fears had been confirmed. He tried to move the fingers, but nothing remained to operate the hand.

"Do you have a glove?" asked Tharion.

"Of course, my Lord." Marlon disappeared into the bowels of his house, returning with a selection of gloves. He helped Tharion ease a thick leather glove onto the claw. Both winced as the burnt tendons and ligaments cracked and snapped when pressure was applied. When done, Tharion reached into his saddlebag, extracted a large gold coin and gave it to the blacksmith.

"My lord, that is a veritable fortune. I could not accept such a reward."

Tharion waved away his concerns, "Don't tell anyone where this came from, melt it down and sell off the gold."

Marlon bowed, "Thank you, Sir Knight, thank you. My family will be well fed for many a moon after this."

"Good. Thank you for your service and for your silence. I bid you goodbye," Tharion said as he left the smith clutching the coin to his chest.

***

Tharion stared into his tankard of beer, ignoring all the sights and sounds around him and the furtive glances directed his way.

A figure walked up to his table, dragged out the stool opposite and plonked down.

"Hello there, stranger," they said.

Tharion looked up. The face was familiar. A face from another time. She had a wide smile, pretty blue eyes and blonde hair that fell around her face in curling tresses.

"What's the matter? Don't you remember me? Of

course not, you're a famous knight, you wouldn't remember a young filly like Jennyfer would ya?" she said.

Tharion's mind flicked through memories of the trip between Great Cornadia and Gellilydarn. The name and pretty face jogged his recollections.

"We have met before," he said, "In this tavern."

She smiled wider.

"Good, yeah, we certainly met, if you know what I mean," she said winking at him.

"Of course," he said, kicking himself internally. His eyes widened with a touch of fear and shock.

She smiled, "Don't worry yourself love, you didn't knock me up or anyfing, I'm careful me."

Later, in Tharion's room, the couple disrobed. Jennyfer let her dress drop to the ground, revealing all the Gods intended. Instead of the reaction she had hoped, she found Tharion struggling to unclasp his armour with only his left hand.

"Have you hurt your hand?" she asked.

"Yes, it was injured on my quest," he said.

"Then let me help."

Jennyfer helped him with his armour, coat and shirt. When she started on his trousers, she accidentally knocked the glove and dislodged it. She let out a small squeal of horror as her eyes fell on the hand beneath.

Tharion grabbed the glove and tried to prize it back over his claw. After a few moments he gave up, let it fall, sat on the bed and sighed.

"Please don't tell anyone about this," he said, "I only have my reputation to protect me while I journey back to Great Cornadia."

Jennyfer looked at the hand, then the sorrow-filled face of the hero. She remembered their last meeting.

"Hang on, weren't you after some magical thingy that would heal your king or somefing?"

"Yes, the Chalice of Ethelred. But I daren't use something that is meant solely to help the king."

"Bugger that, what's more important right now? You or him?"

He peered at the sincere look on her face, smiled and nodded.

"True, if I can't protect myself then I may not be able to return the Chalice, anyway."

He moved to his saddlebag and withdrew the cup. The girl gasped at the wonder of the goblet.

"S'beautiful. How's it work?"

Tharion shook his head, "I have no idea. I assume you drink from it."

Jennyfer grabbed the chalice, filled it from the water jug and brought it back to Tharion.

"Here, drink then."

He took the chalice and drank deeply, draining the cup. They both stared at his deformed hand.

Nothing happened.

After several moments, Jennyfer said, "Do it again?"

Tharion shook his head.

"Maybe pour water over the hand from the cup?" she said.

She urged Tharion to his feet, then pulled him over to the basin, filled the cup with more water and slowly poured it over the claw.

Again, nothing happened.

"Stupid cup. What's the point of a magic healing cup if it doesn't work?"

Tharion chuckled at her enthusiasm and disappointment. He brought the dripping claw up to eye level and said, "I have no idea how to work the cup. It may need special water or even wine, it may need an invocation cast over it. Leave it for now, instead can you take me to a healer? I need to be rid of this, and I don't want anyone else to see it," he said.

She nodded and helped him dress again.

***

They made their way to a small hovel on the edge

of town. Jennyfer knocked, and the door opened, revealing an ancient crone. Her watery grey eyes stared up from a wizened face flanked by wisps of grey hair.

"Ah, the knight," she said and invited them in.

As the old crone pottered about preparing ointments and poultices, Tharion stared at the lifeless claw, slowly turning it to examine every side. A tear formed at his eye and ran down his cheek.

Finally, the healer stopped and moved before him. Tharion recomposed himself and faced the old woman with a heightened level of stoicism.

"I am Sandoran. I have seen this many a time before. The dragon does not always kill. He finds pleasure in maiming. Uses it to spread his legend to the four winds," she said.

"He won't be spreading any legends from now on," Tharion said.

Sandoran looked surprised and delighted. "You killed him?"

Tharion nodded.

She continued to stare into his eyes.

"But he has killed you, I think," she said.

Tharion dropped his head in response.

Sandoran gently took Tharion's hand in her own. She moved it around to study the damage from all sides.

"There's nothing to be done with it, I'm afraid," she said. "The dragon's breath is fatal to all it touches."

"I gathered that. Can you remove it and leave a stump? I should be able to get Marlon to fashion a false hand or hook to replace it," Tharion said.

Sandoran placed the hand down and stared into Tharion's eyes for a long moment.

"Yes, I can remove it. I can even fix the stump so you have no further problems. What I can't do is fix what's inside you," she said.

"What do you mean?" he asked.

"You are a mighty warrior," she said.

"Were," suggested Tharion.

She nodded in correction. "Were. Though you may not have the hands of one, you still have the heart of a knight. Your quest now is to solve the hurt inside you. To find a new purpose in life."

"I've never known any other life than that of a warrior," he said.

She stared deep into his eyes. He felt as though she were staring deep into his soul.

"You will find a new life. One that will make you even greater than before. It is written inside you," she said.

Tharion opened his mouth to ask what she meant, but she moved away and returned with a large-bladed saw and a small block of leather.

She handed him the leather block, "Bite down on this. I have to remove all the dead flesh and leave none behind."

Tharion popped the block into his mouth and held it in place with his teeth.

Many of the occupants of houses nearby were awakened by the screams emanating from the healer's house. Most turned over and went back to sleep. They had heard it all before.

***

Using more of the dragon's gold, Marlon took a few days to cast a golden hand for Tharion. The heavy fake dragged the knight's arm down from time to time, but Marlon had fashioned a series of leather straps and buckles that Tharion could easily manoeuvre with just his left hand. To a casual observer, it appeared that Tharion wore a golden glove over his right hand.

The knight rewarded the blacksmith with more coins, hardly putting a dent in the stash he had secured in his saddlebag. With his career in disarray, he'd had the foresight to ensure his ongoing years would be comfortable regardless of how he was received back at court.

After many days, it was with a sigh of relief that Tharion sighted the tall turrets of the castle of Great Cornadia. His entrance into the city was with much less fanfare as previously greeted him. It was Daniel that provided the motivation to raise a fanfare, with Tharion's new outlook, he was much happier to enter under the cover of darkness in virtual incognito.

The guard at the castle gates was shocked out of his slumber by the knight's arrival. He allowed Tharion unfettered entry into the castle courtyard and hurried to inform Pedric of his arrival.

The Chamberlain arrived quickly from his bed and ushered the knight into the castle.

"Would you like to freshen up first while the king is aroused, or do you wish to wait in the audience chamber?" Pedric asked.

"Let's get this over with," Tharion said, then without further thought handed the small purse containing Kaith's weapons to Pedric. "Give this back to your mage and tell him they work perfectly, but I have no further use of them."

Pedric took the bag and looked at it inquisitively for a moment before rushing off. Tharion entered the audience chamber and placed the chalice on a small table before the throne. He walked to the window, drew back the drapes and stared out at the quiet dark city.

After several minutes of dreaming about farmlands and what his eventual wife would look like, the chamber doors unlatched with a resounding *clack* and squeaked open on their huge iron hinges.

"Tharion, my boy, welcome back, welcome back," said King Edmund as he stepped into the chamber. He has eschewed any formal attire, instead simply throwing a silk robe over his bedclothes. He walked towards the knight and threw his arms wide, embracing Tharion as if he were a long-lost son.

"I'm so glad you returned safely," he said, hugging the knight to him. The king released him and turned, spying the golden goblet sitting ten yards away.

"Is that it?" he said, walking over the chalice and picking it up. As he examined it, he let out several murmurs and joyous remarks. With a beaming smile, he set the cup down and turned back to Tharion.

"You must tell me all about the quest," he said, "The journey?"

"Long, tiring and arduous," said Tharion without further detail.

"The dragon?" asked the king, his eyes growing wide.

"Fearsome and terrible."

"Dead?"

Tharion nodded. "Yes." He drew out the dagger.

"No thanks to this pig-sticker. Only because of your mage. His little baubles proved to be the beast's downfall."

The king beamed and clapped his hands together. "Wonderful, wonderful. You appear to be in full health, good, good."

Tharion laughed out loud, though not in mirth.

"I am far from that," he said. He sheathed the dagger and unclasped the fake hand, letting it fall to the floor with a resounding *clang*.

Pedric and the king gasped at the sight of Tharion's stump.

"I am no longer a warrior. That was taken from me by Galeru's breath. My squire, just a boy of thirteen, is no more, killed by Galeru's guardians," he said. He stepped towards the throne and picked up the chalice.

"I'm not even sure this is as magical as you say," he said, holding up his stump. "I used it to restore health to my withered hand, but nothing happened. I was forced to have the dead claw removed and replaced by that lump of metal."

He placed the chalice down.

"If you tried simple water then you were never going to succeed," said Pedric. "The legends say that you must use the waters that spring from the source of the river Askerion, deep in the jungle of Feltaran. Only that water is pure enough. It must also be mixed with the venom of the snake that lives beneath the volcano of Xantalos."

Tharion peered across at the Chamberlain, a disgusted look crossed his face. "What idiocy is that? You would need an army to even attempt to enter those places. No offence to your majesty, but the cost in lives alone would far outweigh the cost of the king's life."

"No offence taken, good knight, but we have no want to send an army. One man should be enough," he said.

"What man?" asked Tharion.

The king smiled. "Why you, of course."

"Me," Tharion blurted out, his face a mask of dismay. He held up his stump. "My warrior days are over. I cannot attempt another quest; I would be dead within moments of setting foot within either place."

"Ah, but you made a pact," said the king.

Tharion's anger bristled. He pointed at the chalice. "I have fulfilled my duty to you, your grace. I am forever changed because of it and cannot countenance that I could owe any more," he said.

The king stepped towards the hero, his face lost its joy and turned serious.

"That may well be, good knight, but you made a promise to serve me in any way I required." He picked up the Chalice and held it up to Tharion's face. "On this quest, you have only fulfilled a part of your duties. This cup is useless to me without the ingredients. You have been tasked to gain them. You will accept your duty, or you will die, and your name will be besmirched across all the lands as a thief and a liar."

Tharion's rage fountained out of him. He knocked the chalice from the king's hand. It bounced and *clanged* across the cold stone floor, coming to rest against the bottom step of the throne's dais.

"This is ridiculous. You would send an injured and disabled man to his death. Is that your idea of duty, of honour? I undertook this quest in good faith and you, Sir, have broken your own word to me. I will do no further for you," he said, his voice rising to a shout.

The king moved closer and stared deep into Tharion's eyes.

"Pedric, fetch the guards," he said.

The chamberlain started towards the door.

Suddenly, the king cried out in pain. Tharion pushed him backwards, and he slid off the diamond dagger, his hands grabbing at the tiny hole in his chest. Blood cascaded through his fingers, ran down his belly, and fell to the floor.

Pedric gasped and stepped towards his master.

The king staggered back several steps and dropped

to his knees, his head bent down in pain.

A series of coughs filtered out from the monarch. Tharion's anger subsided a little as he watched the last moments of the king. His mind raced. He needed an escape plan, or he needed to accept his fate.

It was then he realised that the coughs were anything but. The king raised his face and stared up at the knight. A broad smile played out on his lips, his blood-smeared teeth showing through. The king chuckled.

"Excellent. Excellent. That is exactly what I wanted, and needed," he said. The king's eyes rolled back in his head and he fell forward in a heap, his face making a sickening noise as it smacked into the stone tiles.

Tharion's mind exploded in confusion. He peered around, ready to fight the guards or run to the nearest exit.

Pedric stepped up to the scene. A serene expression on his face.

"Do not worry, dear knight. This was the plan all along. Your quest was a simple test of your faith, diligence and perseverance," he said.

He moved over, picked up the chalice and smiled at it.

"This is just a cup. It has no magic. It has no real

value. The previous owner was a coward. He taunted the great Galeru, who killed him and stole this trinket. I read about it in some ancient tomes and decided to use it for your test."

He placed the chalice on the table and stepped up to the king. He knelt down and felt the king's mouth for breath before nodding to himself. He closed Edmund's eyes, removed his crown, and stood.

He stepped up to Tharion and held the crown out to him.

"This is now yours," he said. "The king was dying. There is magic in this kingdom. It is small, but it centres around the health of the king. As long as the monarch lives and is strong, the kingdom lives and is strong. It was Edmund's plan to replace himself, in much the same way as he deposed his predecessor. One day you will need to do the same, but I believe that is many years from now."

"What if I refuse?" Tharion asked.

"Then you will die. You will be hunted for ever and a day. By right of trial you are the king. Something every foot soldier would kill for. Unless you are here, within this castle as the ruler, then they are duty bound to protect you."

Pedric smiled.

"Personally, I would accept."

Tharion thought for a moment before taking the crown and placing it on his head.

"Good, good," said Pedric. "You have the same qualities as Edmund, and you will reign benevolently for many years to come."

Re-invigorated by whatever magic possessed the crown, Tharion picked up his fake hand, reattached it, and walked over to the throne. He sat down, peered across the audience chamber, then out the window. The sun was just peeking over the far horizon.

Pedric kneeled before him.

"Your majesty, what is your first command?" he asked.

Tharion turned his head back towards the Chamberlain, smiled and said, "Breakfast would be nice."

STEPHEN HERCZEG is an IT Geek, writer, actor, film maker and Taekwondo Black Belt based in Canberra Australia. He has been writing for over twenty years and has completed a couple of dodgy novels, sixteen screenplays and dozens of short stories and scripts. He has had over fifty short stories and seventy drabbles accepted for publication.

Bibliography

Sproutlings, Hunter Anthologies

Hells Bells, Australasian Horror Writers Association

Anemone Enemy; Petrified Punks and *The Body Horror book,* Oscillate Wildly Press

Below the Stairs; Behind the Mask; Beyond the Infinite; Beside the Seaside; Tricksters Treats #1, #2 & #3; Shades of Santa; Guilty Pleasures and other Dark Delights, Things In the Well

Beginnings; Journeys; Capricorn; Aquarius; Pisces; Aries; Taurus; Gemini, Dead Set Press

Sea of Secrets; Coffins and Dragons; Organic Ink Vol 2, Dragon Soul Press

Demonic Carnival, Battle Goddess Productions

Deep Space; What If?; Eerie Christmas; Pride; Lust; Jibbernocky; Bad Romance; Storming Area 51; Worlds; Angels; Monsters; Beyond; Unravel; Apocalypse; Hate; Love; Oceans; Year One, Black Hare Press

Curses and Cauldrons; Forest of Fear, Blood Song Books

Sherlock Holmes through Belanger Books and MX Publishing:

In the Realms of H.G. Wells; Beyond the Canon; In the Realms of Steampunk; The Early Adventures; The Great Detectives; The MX Book of New Stories - Vol XI; XIV; XVII, XIX and XX; The new adventures of Solar Pons; The Necronomicon of Solar Pons; A Tribute to H.G. Wells.

Connect

Amazon: amazon.com/-/e/B07916SQQS

Goodreads: goodreads.com/author/show/17100782.Stephen_Herczeg

Facebook: @stephenherczegauthor

ACKNOWLEDGEMENTS

When we embarked on our Black Hare Press journey back in late 2018, we never envisioned the huge support we'd get from the writing community. We have been truly humbled by the number of submissions we've received (around 3,000 over eight publications!) and have loved reading every single one.

So, thank you to everyone who crafted tales just for us—from the tiny tales in our Dark Drabbles series to these magical beauties you have read here in Key to the Kingdom—we thank you from the bottom of our hearts.

To our families and friends, collaborators, random strangers who took pity on us, and everyone who has helped us on the way: we couldn't have done it without you.

And to you, our discerning reader, we and these fifteen talented writers did it all for you. We hope you enjoyed these magical tales of quests and conquerors. If you did, don't forget to leave a review.

Thank you all, and see you next time.

Love & kisses
Ben Thomas & Dean Kershaw

www.blackharepress.com